KV-372-333

To R
you know who you are

Before you think I'm going to continue rambling in this irrelevant way, don't worry, I'm not, and anyway these rambles are not irrelevant, otherwise they wouldn't be here, would they? I'm just trying to tell you that the last two or three years of my life have been hard – very hard. I'm only just beginning to realise what stress I've been under. And before you think this is just a diatribe from a moaning old git, I have to tell you that there are other people involved, people I love who have suffered more than I have.

But that's all by the by. This is a story after all, and you are a reader and there are certain expectations, certain rules that have to be obeyed if our relationship is going to have any sort of validity. I'm telling you a story so I have to obey the rules of story-telling, otherwise you'll get bored or frustrated or just plain pissed-off and I know how bad that can be, so I'm with you there.

So, this story has to have a beginning, middle and end. Fine, I can go along with that, especially now the beginning's done, well, it's begun anyway. The middle? Not too difficult – just throw up a few obstacles, write around them or through them or over them and, and well it sounds easy doesn't it? It probably is easy, relatively easy; when compared to what I've been through over the past two or three years.

Normally I'm a man who can handle everything; it's a curious mixture of Eastern mysticism and Western machismo. Come on you bastards, throw it at me. I can take it. I can take the deadliest disease in your power and absorb its evil energy. I can use my intelligence and charm to avoid the maddest madman. I can sit and smile with equanimity while discussing the utter meaninglessness of existence and the complete irrelevance of the whole of human history in the scheme of things, while blissfully tuning into the absolute oneness of so-called love that is so-called God. But these last two or three years have been a mare, a fucking nightmare.

OK, enough digression for now. I'd better get the beginning of the story started before you piss off and re-read Jane Eyre or something else, equally mind-numbingly mainstream. Mainstream, mainstream, bollocks.

The Three Bears

DEREC JONES

OPENING
CHAPTER

First published in Great Britain in 2006 by:
Opening Chapter, 171 Kings Road, Cardiff, CF11 9DE

International Edition 2008

www.openingchapter.com

The right of Derec Jones to be identified
as the author of this work has been asserted
in accordance with the Copyright,
Designs and Patents Act 1988

A catalogue record for this book is available
from the British Library

ISBN 10: 1-904958-06-0
ISBN 13: 978-1-904958-06-2

Cover design by Andrew at WMD: www.walesmediadesign.com

o n e

It's over. Her face sinks slowly into the black pool. It's the end.

But where did it all begin?

~

I look at her and wonder what it is that has kept us together all this time. I wonder whether she thinks the same way.

"Is everything all right?" I ask.

"How do you mean?"

"You know, we haven't had much chance to talk lately, what with your work taking it out of you, and most nights you're too tired to talk and the television is on all the bloody time, and on the weekends I'm pretty useless."

"Well, I'm here now, I'm talking now. What do you want to say?"

"I thought you said you wanted to talk to me?"

"OK then, tell me about Annie."

"Annie's dead," I say.

"Yeah, but what about when she was alive? You haven't been the same since she died. Was there more to your relationship?"

"What?"

"You and Annie, was there more to it?" There is a distant chill in her voice

"Well no, not really, not at all." I feel myself flushing red. I look at her and I think: Who is this woman?

She looks determined; as passive as a statue, yet as unchallengeable as an angry gorilla. I stand up, it's a natural reaction to threat I suppose, I'm bigger than her, taller and fatter and heavier and I'm a man for fuck's sake.

"Sit." She says.

I sit.

"It's obvious there was something going on – obvious."

"She was just a friend, just another fucked-up human being who I met along the way, someone to share a coffee with now and again, that's all."

"I don't believe you."

"I never did anything, we were just friends."

"You've always been the same, looking for someone else; I've never been enough for you."

"What's going on? Are you all right?"

"Never been better. All these years I've looked after us; looked after you, and now I realise you're not worth it. You've never been worth it. I've given up my life for you. The things I've done for you, don't you see? Can't you see?"

"I don't know what you're talking about."

"It's too late anyway. Too late."

~

Or did it begin here?

Cardiff, 1971. Somewhere in Canton, a side street off Cathedral Road. I'm not sure who's living with me, not sure if I pay the rent. There's something about Hendrix's death, or an anniversary of Hendrix's death. It could be 1970; I'll have to work it out one day.

I'm 18, sharing a house with a few others. There's one or two Cardiff boys and one or two Llanelli boys. Perhaps I'm crashing on the floor in Mike's room.

Been here for a while, a few weeks at least, because I know I'm claiming the dole, ambling down to somewhere near Westgate Street once a week or whatever frequency it is now, popping into the chemist on the way back for cough medicine, or nicking a pint of milk off a doorstep.

Living on chips and cornflakes; chips, cornflakes, cough medicine and stolen milk.

~

Tenby - 1971. I'm sleeping on the beach in a beach hut that isn't mine, or in a tent with Bill. Good old Bill. Trawling the streets at dawn, stealing milk from doorsteps, peaches from outside Woolworth's. Begging when the tourists wake up. Begging with Jimmy, a scally from Birmingham.

~

Leaving Bill behind, going to Torquay, the same year, soon after. Sleeping on top of a shed, eating chips for breakfast with Jimmy. In a café, paying with the cash earned from half a night of peeling/picking/stabbing the eyes out of potatoes.

~

Glastonbury 1971. Definitely 71. Acid-Freaked. Seeking Release. "Fuck off," they say. "We're having a good trip." It isn't a bad trip, just intense, spiritual, deeply mythic. Spiked with acid. A lost tribe. Coming together – smiling. Not hallucinating, apart from the bus coming over the hedge, and Melanie singing. Free food and camp-fires, a glimpse – that's all.

~

1961; a recurring dream. The Three Bears playing touch, Big Daddy Bear's teeth. Panting for breath. Release. "There's no release in this game boy." He says, Big Daddy Bear says, biting a chunk out of my arm, and I wake up with a pain in the right place.

~

2002. A new world all right – a global village on the Internet. Two black cats in the kitchen. Bed Time. Must go to bed. 1:08 am. 1:20 am – up again. Things to do. Things to think about. Cardiff – Tenby – Torquay – Llangennech. Mostly Llangennech.

~

Cardiff 1972, 1973. I'm in a small house in Butetown – Pomeroy Street. Old Sea Captains used to live here, they say. We're sharing a house with a woman called Delilah and her children – Bilbo and Janet. Her boyfriend Ali Baba (his choice) – an Arab Prince out of place. We use a pressure cooker a lot and make lentil and vegetable soup.

It's later – a few months and we're in Canton again. Conway Road, a leafy street, a nice garden, but too many mice.

Riverside – a smelly flat and more mice – even more – mice, and prostitutes living upstairs and drunks trying to break the door down and useless one-eyed cats and working in the steelworks, buying small tomatoes and wheeling them home in a pram.

~

1974. Manchester. 2 large semi-detached houses on 3 floors with attics and basements. This is the place. The Holy Place. 27 adults and 17 children.

~

And some other time. That's when I noticed it first. I'm sure it had been going on for years before that, like the way your gut gradually grows as you get older. Not my gut, maybe not even your gut, you specific reader, but you know, most people's gut, some at least. But you know what I mean. Something insidious and slimy has got into your life and you don't notice it, you don't see it coming. One day it's just there like a boil that erupts on your face overnight. Not my face, maybe not even yours either but you know what I mean.

He was like that; like that insidious boil, and he needed lancing. Should have done it straight away I suppose, you know, I should have recognised the inevitability of it then, but I didn't. I'm not saying I thought he was OK or anything, oh no, I knew straight away he was a bad one, I just didn't realise how dangerous he was, and he had charm.

Have you ever been asked that question? The one about if you knew Hitler when he was a child and you knew what he was going to do, would you have killed him? Slit his throat with a scalpel or pushed him under a bus? Thing is, science fiction apart, there is no way to travel back in time, you just have to accept what is.

One thing you can influence though, without any danger of fucking up the time-space continuum, is the future. It's easy to influence the future, putting aside all that stuff about fate. But then I didn't act and now I'm sorry. What I should have done is to walk away from him then, when he was relatively harmless. I should have picked a fight or something, created an argument, then he'd never have been my friend.

What is this? What story am I telling? It's beginning to sound like Frankenstein, but it's not like that, I didn't create my monster, not consciously anyway.

My monster came disguised as a well-off businessman, an old friend; the owner of a small but very successful car hire and taxi firm, and a night club and other shady businesses. He was a bit flash, a bit crude, a bit misogynist; he always was, but he was easy enough to get on with, a laugh.

He, let's call him by his real name – Bastard – no, that's not it, it's Ken. The bastard was called Ken.

I had a successful business as well. I wouldn't go so far as to say very successful, but successful enough.

He came into my office one day, the bastard, and he said:

"Do you want to make a lot of money . . ." He paused, smiling, waiting for my reaction. I just lifted my eyebrows. "Legitimately?"

~

Place: Llangennech. We've all done that haven't we. Haven't we? When we were young. On the inside cover of a school exercise book or a perforation-marked form in a comic. Name _____ Address _____. Name is simple enough but the longer and more unique the better. The address is another matter, 42 Something Road, Somewhere, Llanelli, Carmarthenshire, Wales, United Kingdom of Great Britain, Europe, the Earth, The Solar System, The Milky Way, The Universe.

The exact place, the uniqueness of your identity and the fixing of your non-uniqueness in one. Position yourself in the universe. Here I am. I was here. I belong yet I am more than this, more than mere belonging. And the time? It is now 4:24:07 in the afternoon of Thursday June 6 in the year 2002 AD. (that's the number of years since a man called Jesus was born – on the planet earth in the solar system etc . . .)

It's not 4:24:07 of course, because now it's 4:26:14, or at least it was when I looked at the clock on my computer 25 seconds ago.

Fix me. Fix me in space and time, and out of the infinite number of other actualities in space and time there are (Were? Will be?) I am here, look I'm here, I'm now. I'm the one that's waving this fucking flag at you. Place: Llangennech. It's already late. There's no more to say, except, except . . .

~

This is my reality. July 13, 2002. This is my reality.

This is my reality. I don't know if I like it; it's got something to do with confidence, ego if you like. And why not? Ego, I mean. Why not ego? This is what I mean, about not knowing if I like it or not. But there's more than that to it. There are moods; deep blue moods, aggressive red moods, incandescently brilliant white moods and occasionally dark black moods. There I go again. I want to talk about the light so I will:

~

"I've got to put some form on this, some shape that can be identified, otherwise it would never sell, never pay the rent."

"But it's beautiful as it is," I said, "maybe a coat of varnish will finish it off."

So banal, these conversations with artists. How many is it now? 45? 50? Over 4 years at least once a month. Perhaps I'll publish them all in a book one day, some of them at least.

Artist number one did all right for herself. Suppose I did all right out of her as well. It was that interview that made my name (for what it's worth), made her name. Then she was some nutter of some interest in North London. Now she's loved and despised, always in the tabloids. She does sculptures – men's cocks mostly. They're not rude though, not erotic either. They're just good. One day they'll be the definitive artistic definition of penises.

When I first met her she was into very beautiful busts – busts of famous people, people in the media, people who had or seemed to have power, like the Prime Minister or the head of MI5, even the editor of the Daily Mirror for fuck's sake.

I visited her in her studio.

(This is hard, this kind of writing. I can do it but it's hard. Is that right? Should it be hard? Might as well work in the computer business. Who cares anyway. In a hundred years we'll all be dust. Mind you I suppose her cocks will live on for a few hundred, a few thousand years even – so what.)

She said: "My heads will live on after I'm dead."

I think she meant her busts, but then she moved on to the other kinds of heads, and she was right – her heads will live on – both types probably, but the first type will only live because of the second type.

What happened to my mortality?

What's happening to yours?

~

"It's a bit like a jigsaw puzzle." She said. "As if, all you've got to do is find out where the relevant bits should go and voila you've got three or four, at least, separate objects."

"Sort of," I said, "but saying it's like a jigsaw puzzle implies that it was once a whole and was then deliberately split apart in order to confuse and pose a challenge. What I think is that it was never a whole, there's no point looking for that sort of pattern in it. I think it was a deliberately random outflow of creativity, albeit confined to a particular point on the continuum between the birth and the death of the artist."

"Now you really are taking the piss."

"No, I'm not, I read it over there, on that panel to the left."

She laughed. It was nice to see her happy in my company, it was nice just being with her. Isn't this what the middle-class aspire to? A debt-free, stress-free, life of Marks and Spencer comfort with enough left over every month to add a few quid to the retirement fund in the building society. God, I wish I wasn't so cynical. It's not easy being a cynic you know, you have to work hard at it, or else you simply get branded as an embittered old twat, poisoned by your failures.

"It was a nice thought," she said, "coming here today. I know it's pretentious but it makes a change, and some of the stuff is OK."

"Let's go and have that coffee." I said.

We walked through the town away from the exhibition and looked for a coffee shop. The one we chose had a narrow windy stairs that led to a cosy, private landing with a few empty tables.

"This is lovely coffee," she said, smiling as she sipped.

At last, I thought, at last we had our lives under control, at last we could enjoy each other's company. This could be the start of a period of . . . .

~

Well you know what happens next; this idyll is shattered by the arrival of a force so strong that it blows the life of our hero apart like so many bubbles in a bubble bath.

Truth is, I don't even know if I want to reach that plateau of comfort and stability. Pass me my pipe and slippers for fuck's sake.

t w o

Cardiff 1971. He came back one night with a stolen car. I can't even remember his name – Alex? Fred? Dennis? What's a good name for 1971? Something weird, something a bit hippy. Probably a nickname then. Because if he was of that sort of age in 1971 he must have been born 1951, 1952 something like that. That would make him a David, always a favourite, or a Paul, or maybe even an Eric or a Kevin. Let's call him Gammy, Gammy will do, not that he had a gammy leg or anything, not that I can remember anyway.

Gammy came in pissed, he always was, he was one of the local Cardiff boys, thought they were a bit hard, coming from the city and all that, but then the Llanelli boys had a reputation as well. That's why it was OK for us to live together, couldn't imagine Cardiff boys living with Swansea boys – even then.

"Who wants to go for a spin? Come on boys."

"Fuck off. You're pissed."

Gammy sighed and dropped into the empty armchair, wood shavings spilling out like a soldier's guts. "Got any shit?" He asked.

Mike chucked the end of a joint at him and turned up the volume on the stereo. Graham Nash – Songs for Beginners. *'We once had a saviour, but by our behaviour he's gone.''* Something like that. Gammy puked over the side of the armchair. I nearly slipped in it on my way to bed. Bed? Floor? I can't remember that much detail.

He came to visit me there, that fucker, that bastard Ken. Stayed one or two nights and then left with a smile. I remember it because he took me and Mike out for a curry, a very rare luxury for two unemployed drug addicts. That's not really fair, I was never a drug addict. But I think Mike got close with the cough medicine. I remember once, the parents of another of the Llanelli boys came to visit and they brought some bin bags. They cleared the kitchen: four or five bags of empty cough medicine bottles, another couple full of empty milk bottles, and a few bags of scummy mess from the cupboards – mostly almost empty cornflakes packets.

The curry was gorgeous, they'd done something with the cubes of meat, it was as if they'd injected a series of unique spicy flavours directly into the cubes, flavours that did something to the pleasure centres of your brain – a memorable meal indeed. Ken was on form, he was a together sort of guy, always a pocketful of fivers and a newish car to boot. He made you feel special, a special friend.

Gammy woke me up. When he eventually persuaded us to go outside, we saw it.

"Shit Gammy," Mike said.

"Fucking wanker," I said.

The car Gammy stole, it was Ken's. Ken's father's to be precise. But it was done, so we went for a spin, but Mike drove, he wasn't pissed and well on his way down from the cough medicine.

Ken knew about the car, he brought it up during the curry that night. He wasn't pissed off at all, he laughed about it. Fucking smug bastard.

Come to think of it, Gammy wasn't from Cardiff at all. He was from the Valleys, Ystrad something-or-other. Don't think I ever got to know any genuine Cardiff boys – not then anyway.

~

Tenby 1971. Her name is Greta and we're sharing an omelette on the beach. She's brought me a cold cheese omelette and some half-warm chips. She's a nice girl but I'm not really interested, got to get on with my own life, I know it's out there waiting for me – there's something important I have to do – but I don't know what.

Jimmy's good at begging, he's exactly the right distance between pathetic and threatening so that the punters play safe and lob him some decent denomination coins. I'm not so good, but I try and that's all it takes, we are a mini-communist state, we share the pot, we do our best, at least that's the principle, but I'm sure he slips a few silver shillings into his back pocket now and again, how else would he always find the cash for fags, drugs or chips when we should be broke? Or is it my maths?

This is how you beg.

You hang about in a place where there's a good steady flow of people, not the same people going back and fore, that way you'll exhaust the position very quickly. No, you have to be cleverer than that. Outside a railway station's good, if you're in a city that is, it's not so good in a small town like Tenby, where the trains, even in the busiest season, only come every couple of hours. In a city, near a train station, travellers equal money. You can't travel without money and everyone takes a bit spare.

You find somewhere where you can stand back occasionally and sit on a bench or lean on a low wall, somewhere to retreat to, and somewhere to launch your attack from. You wait for a fresh face to pass by, avoiding the hard looking men and the obvious grumpy old gits of course. With a bit of luck they haven't spotted you before you move into position. When you do you have to be polite; say something like: "Excuse me." For fuck's sake don't say "Excuse me sir." or "Excuse me madam." That's much too sycophantic, nobody likes a sycophant, especially a sycophantic beggar.

Don't bother with long explanations or sob stories, they don't want to know, just cut to the chase. People appreciate directness, besides they want to keep the exchange as short as possible, they're on holiday for fuck's sake, or travelling, or going to meet a loved one, or even rushing back to their poxy offices. "Can you spare some change for a cup of tea?" I know it's a cliché, but who's kidding who? They know you don't just want the price of a cup of tea and you know they know and they know that you know that they know. So keep it simple. Simple and quick. Don't give them time to think. "Excuse me. Can you spare some change?" See, you don't even need the "for a cup of tea." explanation. The hit rate isn't brilliant, but it's good enough to eat well and have a few bob left over for a couple of beers, if anyone will serve you that is, otherwise it's the off-licence.

Jimmy's all right, although he's a bit scary, unpredictable, but in a conventional sort of way. To him, everything is fair game; he's like a clever kid scrumping for apples; he waits for the fruit to ripen and just when it's at its peak he moves in. Like the time he nicked a handbag left in a pram when the parents were perusing some holiday crap in a tacky shop.

"Stupid fuckers, they're lucky I didn't take the baby as well," was how he justified himself.

There's two of these valleys boys here, in Tenby, amongst the motley crew of dossers and seasonal workers, Serge, and somebody? Can't remember the somebody's name now, but he's tall, long dark hair and long dark coat, the type that Mike used to nick from charity shops. Or is it a military uniform? It's too hazy from this distance.

Now they are real nutters, don't give a fuck about anything. One day we sat on some rocks overlooked by groups of tourists and we ripped live flatfish apart and ate them raw, all the time grunting and spitting to freak the onlookers out. Serge and the dark one light barbeque fires on the beach and cook stolen potatoes and sausages. And then there are the drugs.

Greta comes to see me again, but it's too late, she doesn't know it yet, neither do I.

~

My mother-in-law likes structure, she likes to know what she's supposed to be doing and where she's supposed to be going at all times. She hates waste, that's why she freezes empty margarine wrappers, the foil kind that cover blocks of margarine for cooking. She uses them to grease cake tins and tart dishes; handy I suppose, not just thrifty. It's got something to do with growing up during the Second World War.

My mother grew up during the war as well, though she is younger than my mother-in-law and lived in a different environment – a poor working class area of Llanelli called Seaside. Sounds nice doesn't it. My father came from another poor working class area called the Morfa; it means something like Marshland, a soggy place.

July 29th, 2002, around midnight. I'm 50 now.

Place – Llangennech. Nowhere. This is what I was meant to do. This is what I was meant to do? I don't know, but this is where I am and this is what I'm doing. Bastard Ken. Bastard Ken.

"Legitimately?" I repeated as a question.

He winked. To be fair Ken had never really done anything that could be classed as evil, not that I knew of then anyway. When we were teenagers he led me into multifarious petty-criminal escapades; the worse was when we broke into a cockle factory and robbed the safe. We got less than two quid out of it but it was a hell of a buzz.

He must have thought all those years that I was like him, just like I thought he was like me. But he wasn't. He is an evil bastard and I'm not. I know it's no big deal, the world is populated by human beings whose ethics and morals range across the whole continuum from absolute evil to absolute saintliness, and I'm just one small creature scrabbling for survival just like the rest of them.

I mean, coming across an evil bastard like Ken is fuck all in the scheme of things, when you compare it to the vileness of war for example. I could have killed Ken after that, but before then I still thought of him as a friend – dodgy but still a friend.

~

Friday January 11, 2002. Do you know? Describe the place where you live.

I live in a village. It's called Llangennech. The name probably comes from Llan, i.e., the church of, and Cennech or something, meaning Saint Cennech. So it's the church of Saint Cennech. Anyway, that's all been done in a book called "The History of Llangennech" so I won't bother with all that.

What I will do is to tell you what Llangennech is like now. It's a bit of a sprawling village with over four thousand inhabitants. There's a co-op mini-market, a family bakers, a newsagent, a petrol station, a Chinese and an Indian takeaway, not to mention the bookies, the garage, the pubs, the chapels and the church, the post office and the rugby club. There's loads of other stuff going on of course, down alleys, up side streets, at the back of houses and so on, but it's all too much and too complicated to go into here.

But I will mention the schools and the nursery and the park and the train station and the old Royal Naval Establishment warehouses now filled with paperwork and caravans.

As far as I can tell most of the people of working age and ability leave the village each day to earn their living. Apart from those and the rugby and cricket types and the townies and the alternatives and the nerds and the petty gangsters (we had a murder recently), there is a massive contingent of old people – mostly old women.

If you drive into the village from the east you'll probably leave the M4 motorway at junction 48 and head towards Llanelli. Turn left at the lights and you're in the village. At that point, by the traffic lights, on the hill, after climbing up from the motorway for about half a mile, you can see most of the village as you look down into the river valley on the left. The river Loughor is a tidal river that separates the village from parts of Swansea on the other side, but the river is too wide for that to matter.

It's actually a very nice welcoming view over the soggy marshland and onto the grass-encrusted mud banks that make up what is known as "The Tide".

You can see a similar view as you roll over the hill from the south-west on the old road from Llanelli.

Llangennech is like the bit that's left after you've removed a scoop of ice-cream from a tub of Neapolitan, but mostly brown with green instead of pink.

Enough bollocks about Llangennech.

~

I've been trying to write a poem about Christmas for years. I've finally come up with the first line, it's:
Christmas glows in the dark.

~

There's something about the smell of a city; not the fresh coffee, like fragrant earth, curling into the nostril, inviting indulgence and satisfaction. Not the sweet antiseptic of expensive perfume in the city centre department stores; not even the accumulated newness of plastic and metal, freshly machined and polished and hung like Aunty Betty's curtains against the grime of visceral life in the computer games' shops.

The smell of the city, the real smell of the real city, hovers like mist on a windless day on the paving slabs, the door handles and the goods in the corner shop. It lives in the long terraced side streets and the twee green avenues of the inner suburbs. It smells like bad breath, like blood congealing on a butcher's slab, like fear, like stale adrenalin sweat. It smells like birth and death; most of all it smells of raw, exciting, energy-charged life.

~

About 5 to 9.

Things to do/get with a hundred quid. That's what's available to me after the debacle of my birthday and the trip to London that never happened because of sickness. One hundred pounds equals ten times ten pounds equals one hundred times one pound equals two hundred times fifty pence.

Could buy loads of paints and canvases? Or buy plain canvas and make my own? Or frames? Or? Let's think . . . . (still thinking, just can't be bothered with the dots) One hundred pounds? In some ways it's a lot of money. I could get 5 of the radios that she bought me for Christmas. (I found the receipt so I know it cost £19.99) In some ways it's very little money. I could get 0.5 – 1 per cent of the cost of a new moderately priced car. Twenty odd packets of tobacco or packs of fags. A couple of ounces of hash. Nearly an ounce of skunk. One week and a bit's worth of Tesco shopping. A couple of nights on the piss for a piss-artist. Two or three Playstation 2 games. A goodish second hand camera or a mountain bike. Membership of a gym for a couple of months. A bloody big box of Lego.

5 past 9. So – what do I want?

Paints and canvas? A foray into oil painting. The start of a savings account towards openingchapter.com? A Zip drive and a Webcam? One hundred things from the pound shop? Drawing pens?

11:37 pm – no closer to deciding how to spend my hundred

pounds.

~

A Week in Bed. Friday night. Indian takeaway. A week in bed, puking and aching. It wasn't the food. Some bug. Some stomach bug. What a bug. What a week. Lentils and spinach like mud splashed on a tyre, lining the ceramic. A week ago, I was a man. Not old. Not young. Healthy. Stable. Comfortable. Naïve. Cocky.

Old women, shattered and bitter. Small hurt voices, looking for affirmation. I think they know what I know, feel what I feel, see what I see; but they don't. They don't see, feel, think; they just hurt and they don't know why. Puzzled and wounded, falling over like dying primroses, wanting spring, getting only cold winter. It hurts too much to pretend any more.

At first it's just unpleasant. Someone has poured castor oil down your throat while you were sleeping. Then you wake up, clutching, rubbing your stomach, moaning – no one's listening. It's 4 o'clock in the morning; they're all asleep.

Puke – cold, sweaty, bitty sleep. More moaning and clutching and rubbing, then puking again and again and again until it's only bile and an intestine like a grammar school science specimen.

This goes on for days and it hurts and aches in the joints and the small of the back and the muscles in the legs and all she wants to do is talk about the garden and what annuals we're going to sow this year and whether we'll get a new cooker or a new back door first.

Until she goes down with the same thing two days later, and that shuts her up and I've got to get out of bed, or off the settee and deliver cool crystal water and hot lemon drugs because the worse is already over for me.

She makes a big deal out of it and hates it when she can't go to work, because then she's stuck at home with me and I feel fat and useless and she's crying and talking about divorce.

A walk to the Co-op to top up the paracetemol stocks, and I see old men, wiry old men, late developers, smoking, walking dogs, crying with pain because they don't see or feel or think either. And I know I'm going to die, I'm an old man already and without memory, I would be nothing.

That's what stopped me going to London for my birthday.

~

The things you try to avoid: reminders of your mortality, dog shit, and Songs of Praise. Why?

"Why?"

"Why what?"

"Why do old women try to push in front of you in queues?"

"They don't."

"Ha, ha, you haven't shopped in Marks and Spencers."

"Shut up."

"Ha, ha."

"OK, what succeeds?"

"Me."

"No, a gummy budgie."

"Ha, ha. I am going to succeed though, you know that, don't you."

"I know that if anyone will, you will Ken."

"I will. I've been thinking a lot lately and I've decided that this world is a pile of dog shit, I'm not going to be the one to step in it. I'm going to be like one of those Lotus flowers you always go on about – floating above the world, sitting pretty on top of the stinking pond."

"I don't think you're supposed to take it like that."

"That's what you said didn't you? That you had to be in the world, but you don't have to be above the world."

"Shut up Ken, if you weren't stoned I'd fucking clatch you."
"You won't be doing any of that."
"I was only joking." His mood had taken a turn for the worse, I told him not to touch those pills. Graham, Ken's cousin, a boy I hadn't met before spoke up.
"I believe that life is like a railway track. You can see the path clearly, disappearing into the distance. The only thing you've got to do is follow it. It's easy."
"Shut up Graham," Ken said, "you're a boring bastard."
"But I only want the same things as you."
"Take it easy boys." I said. "Lighten up, for fuck's sake. We're wasting good grass. This stuff wasn't cheap."
"Who cares," Ken said, "who cares about money, except the poor. I'm not going to be poor."
"Nor me." Graham said.
"But why do old women push in front of you in queues?" Ken said.
We all laughed.

~

We all laughed.
This was a rare treat, being in the pub with her and some good company. It takes two to tango, and I suppose it takes some effort to make and keep friends. I've never been very good at it. I'm too intolerant of other people's foibles and bad manners, and if I'm honest, I'm a bit embarrassed about being a bit scruffy and overweight. I should be more like Johnny Vegas, he obviously doesn't give a fuck, but he's still got friends, at least in the TV programme 'Happiness', which is what I'm going to watch later on tonight.
But, hang on, I can't, I'm in the pub, and it's not tonight, this was last week, last Saturday night in fact. I think the difference is

that there were more of us than usual. We were in a group of eight. There was me and her, then there were two other couples, couples from the village, couples we'd known on and off for years but had never thought of socialising with before; and then there were two of the regulars from the pub, again we had seen them about, especially on our occasional visits on a weekend, when we invariably ended up bored and going home after two or three pints, stuffing ourselves with Chinese chips on the way.

Tonight was different; tonight we had friends.

She was enjoying herself, on her fourth or fifth glass of red wine, and showering her charm over five-eighths of the group. I was chatting to Frank, a man in his forties and someone who I'd always admired in a reluctant sort of way because of his ability to hold a good job down, and dutifully report to some manky establishment, five days a week for most of his useable life.

"I don't know how you do it," I said.

"What?"

"You know, go to work every day, slave away at some boring desk so that you can bring a good standard of living in for your family."

"My job isn't boring, we have a good laugh in work, and there's always some scam going. Last Christmas, me and the two guys who work for me did a roaring trade in copied CDs and men's underwear that we got from the warehouse. You wouldn't believe how many boxer shorts went through those factory gates."

I was surprised. "I thought you worked in an office."

"I do," Frank said, "but the office is attached to a factory full of women who haven't got time to go out and do Christmas shopping because they're in work; and of course, because they're in work they've also got money burning holes in their overalls."

"But that's only Christmas," I said, what about the rest of the year?"

"I enjoy my work, it's what I do."

"Don't you mind the driving?" I asked.

"You get used to it, it's only thirty-odd miles, I can do it in less than half an hour on a good day, as long as I get a clear road to the motorway and then past Port Talbot. It's all about timing."

I'm afraid to say that the novelty soon wore off and after another hour of listening to him droning on about work, boxer pants and the dismal performance of the Welsh rugby team I was nearly ready to take an overdose of heroin.

On the way home with her, I said: "Boring lot, weren't they?"

"Oh no, I had a good time, it's interesting to see how other people live don't you think?"

"I suppose so." I said. "Do you want a bag of chips?"

Who needs friends.

three

So where are we?

Cardiff 1971: Gammy, Mike, Ken.
Tenby 1971: Jimmy, Greta, Bill.
Torquay: Jimmy, potatoes.
Glastonbury 1971: Release, Melanie, a bus coming over the hedge.
1961 or earlier: The Three Bears.
2002: Cats, Internet, Llangennech.
Cardiff 1972: Bilbo, Janet, Delilah, Ali Baba, one-eyed cats, mice.
1974 Manchester: 27, 17, Holy.
NOW: Nightmares and Jane Eyre, Ken, Bastard. (mentions for Hitler and Frankenstein)
   Llangennech: Here and now. This is my reality. The first artist. Cocks. Some places, some people, sometimes, but only a tiny bit of one man's life. It starts to get very fucking complicated when you start to analyse it. Take what you want, spin out a particular thread, follow one path. I promise you it will all make sense in the end.
   Ken of course is the villain (at least for the time being). I'm the hero. We, that's the hero and the villain, are surrounded by lesser forces – this is my reality after all, I'm allowed to take centre stage.

~

The next passage is optional, (but it will give you an insight into the mind of the hero), you can SKIP it if you like.

START SKIPPING NOW

The World is Mad. A quick stroll around the town and I came to the conclusion that the world is mad. This is serious stuff; this world, that is the world that we people who live in the affluent west as it is known, live in, is completely and unashamedly off its trolley. We like to think that society is an ordered, cohesive whole, but in fact it's completely cracked. People are utterly lost and alone, without hope, blindfolded, buffered, sheltered, or simply hiding from the truth. This isn't real life, any more than the false glitter of Hollywood is; this is just another part of the same thing. The Neanderthal from the rugby club getting pissed on a Saturday night and puking up his Chicken Korma against the chemist's wall is very closely allied to the fat producer in his open topped Corniche and the gorgeous-bodied starlet whose picture is pinned to the office wall of the manager of the motorway services near London.

This town that I'm in is mad anyway, even if the rest of the world isn't. I'll give you an example: here we have a chip shop; it's a very famous chip shop, in this town at least. This is the type of chip shop that serves very traditional fare. This is the type of establishment that is looked back on with sentimentality by fat middle-aged men who used to pay frequent visits there in their youth. The chip shop has been there a long time, ever since I can remember and I'm a fat middle-aged man myself. The service is fast, faster than any of your new-fangled fast-food hamburger joints. The main item on the menu is of course chips, oblong chunks of potato fried in what I assume is cheap vegetable oil. This is a perfectly acceptable food in this part of the world. A steady stream of people leave the chip shop holding yellow polystyrene cartons containing soggy, fatty, oblong lumps of potato sprinkled with salt and sprayed with acetic acid or non-brewed condiment as it is politely called. The more affluent in the community don't just stop at a packet of chips, they proceed to add even more exotic delicacies to their cartons.

How about Gravy & Chips, Peas & Chips, Turkey Burger, Meat pie, Pastie or *Battered Mushrooms*?

OK I think I wrote that last Saturday. It's now Tuesday June 18, 1997 3:20 pm. I think it's me that's mad after all not the rest of the world. For example I dialled a number in the Midlands and I dialled it wrong 3 times. That doesn't happen to me usually.

Now it's Saturday September 27, 1997 – 12:40 am, in other words it's actually Sunday morning.

The world is still mad. I'm a part of it of course, part of this world and I suppose I must be mad too. The point is that it doesn't matter that I am mad or that the world is mad, as long as we can keep it just within the bounds of normality and don't let ourselves or the world slip into chaos. That is if we have any control at all, perhaps this is actually chaos and being conscious beings we have to make sense of the chaos in order to survive.

So what is it all about? Alcohol, sex, drugs, rock and roll, and death. There are so many ways of coping with life. Some of us need, or think we need alcohol to survive, or drugs, illegal ones like cannabis and speed and heroin, and legal ones like prozac and valium and god knows what else. Some of us are do-gooders or entrepreneurs or fire fighters or policemen or gangsters. Some of us bury ourselves before we've left our teenage years and emerge with a pension at sixty-five. Some of us end up sleeping and dying under motorway bridges or getting blown to bits by a terrorist bomb. Some men shag women, some shag other men, some women shag other women.

What motivates us? Is it our genes as some claim? Are we are merely hosts for the genes that influence all our actions? These genes drive us; they are the real masters of the universe. Genes have an overriding priority to procreate and then to protect the results of that procreation. Thus we find a genetically suitable mate and then have children and then nurture those children merely to ensure the survival of those genes. If we're lucky our children have children of their own and we can then help another generation of genes to survive and continue the race to eternity. But what of the disabled, the mutations; the weak genes you could say. No these genes are not weak; even our genes must change in order to survive, therefore anomalies only serve to strengthen the gene pool. If I thought that scientists would eventually achieve the supposed goal of stamping out all illness and disease then I would believe that the end of the human race is in sight. But I do not believe this. Our genes are stronger and more cunning than we think. There will always be these outsiders, the freaks, the mutants, the rebels, it's what keeps the human race alive. OK, like the dinosaurs, one day humans will face extinction but what then? How will the all powerful genes survive. Some say that the dinosaurs evolved into birds or reptiles. Will human genes take on a different guise? What will it be? We can only speculate.

One thing is sure – whatever I do now during my life, whatever Shakespeare did or Da Vinci, or whatever the combined genius of all of mankind over all of its past and future history does, then one day it will all be only so much dust.

These then are my pathetic scratches in the sands of eternity. There is however one tiny glimmer of hope, that is that whatever else has happened or whatever else will happen we have the now. In the end it's all that means anything. I'm writing this now, you're reading this now. Be happy, be here now.

One o'clock in the morning – twenty minutes later.

~

Sunday September 28,1997 – 8:27 am

Before I start to play any games I must write. Let's put some words into the mouths of characters. What do I want to say? How about the ridiculousness of life, but the sense also of keeping a routine. Having a set of values and mores versus exposing the hypocrisy. What wins in the end is art. A way of expressing these ultimate 'truths' or questions in a beautiful and challenging way, the skill of the artist. Artist = one who paints a picture using paint and canvas, music, words, sculpture or any other medium. Without art (in this sense) life is a meaningless pile of rotting material. Another question that could be asked, though with very little chance of being answered, is – is religion a form of art in this sense?

All this has to be set against a background that the reader has to be able to understand. The reader must also get some kind of understanding and joy from reading the piece or watching any subsequent play or whatever that is developed from the writing. The piece must operate at several levels and across a wide field. It must be deep and wide. These should be the underlying principles when writing the piece. What comes out is unknown at the beginning but by always keeping these principles in mind then there must be some of these truths in the finished piece.

So now the practicalities – who, what, when, where, how etc. The story. The characters the plot etc.

Perhaps a discussion of a piece of modern art a la Damien Hurst or whatever his name is. That adds another dimension – discussing a piece of art that already exists to illustrate these deeper points of what art is.

Clues – leave clues planted in the text to point to the real meaning of it.

Exciting – it has to be exciting and dramatic.

Characters – the characters have to be interesting.

Situation – the situation has to be familiar.

Humour – there has to be a strand of humour.

Satisfaction – the reader must feel satisfied at the conclusion.

~

Now it's Sunday September 28, 1997 – 11:30 pm

Let's change the script –

Time to

A: *(Rhetorically)* I don't want to smoke any more. I don't want to eat, I don't want to drink, in fact I don't want to do anything any more. I don't want to live any more.

B: *(Absent-mindedly)* That's a bit harsh, isn't it?

(C Enters)

A: *(Addressing C)* Hello.

C: *(sniffs as if offended and ignores A)* Did it come? *(Addressing B)*

A: What?

C: *(Again)* Did it come?

B: Ssh!

(Doorbell rings – C dashes to the door opens it and takes a parcel off someone)

C: Thanks. *(Closes the door)* It's here. It's bigger than I remember. *(Struggles with the parcel – puts it across the coffee table and unwraps it – a large painting emerges)*

(A, B, and C gather around the painting laying on the coffee table – it consists of several deep-coloured squares, the paint thick and textured)

B: It's a bit abstract isn't it?

A: It's meant to be. It's supposed to represent the harmonisation and the clash of sentient beings. It's an expression of human consciousness. It's actually quite beautiful. See the way the colours overlap and yet maintain their integrity.

B: It's beyond me. Give me a portrait any day. Take Van Gogh's 'The potato eaters', now that's a good painting. It means something. It's not afraid to come right out there and shove it in your face.

A: That painting sends shivers down my spine, it's so dark. It's

Llyfrgell Ganolog Caerdydd
Cardiff Central Library
02920382116

Customer name:
FORD, Jeffrey (Mr)
Customer ID: ****8165

**Items that you have
borrowed**

Title: The three bears
ID: 02966618
Due: 23 April 2019 23:59

Total items: 1
Account balance: £0.00
02 April 2019
Borrowed: 1
Overdue: 0
Hold requests: 1
Ready for collection: 0

Thank you for using the 3M™
SelfCheck System.

not a celebration of life, it's more like having your head pushed down a toilet. That's the sort of painting that would really make me tired of living.

C: *(Nods, but will not look directly at A)*

B: Isn't it about time you two stopped this nonsense? For god's sake it was only a joint, it's not like it was food or something.

C: *(Sniffs)*

A: I'm sorry OK? Next time, I'll make sure you get double shares.

STOP SKIPPING NOW

~

I've got to keep Ken going until the end of the story, otherwise what would be the point? I have right on my side and I will eventually triumph over that evil bastard Ken. I need to get to know him a bit better, find his weak points, push and prod him until he disintegrates like an old wasps' nest.

Oh, what's the point in fucking about, Ken is already beaten, he's history, I sorted it out, I killed the cunting fucker. There, I've done it now, I've confessed. I did it. I fucking did it. It wasn't hard, the murder I mean. The killing itself wasn't hard, but afterwards, it's been a fucking nightmare. Take my advice, don't do it. It's not fucking worth it. Change your identity, move to Iceland, just don't kill, there's always a better way.

~

I remember once, when I was about seventeen or eighteen, I took some speed; they were probably tablets that one of my mates used to nick off his mother, who was a big fat woman with a penchant for swearing at children. Anyway, I took some speed and went home. It was probably about eleven o'clock or something, because it would have been difficult to justify getting in any later on a weeknight, since nothing went on after half past ten in the town anyway.

So, I went home and my parents were just going to bed; probably waited up for me to come in, since my father had to get up for work in the morning and my mother always got up early anyway to tend to my younger brother. I managed to hold it together until they went to bed by pretending to have a headache. I said I'd have a cup of tea and would go up to my own bed soon.

After they went to bed I was downstairs, in the living room, on my own, in the quietness of the night. I wanted something from the top drawer of the sideboard. I can't remember what it was now, a pen or something, so I opened a drawer and started rummaging. Seven hours later, my father got up for work and I was still rummaging, or rather rearranging. I'd gotten so engrossed with the task of sorting the mess in the drawer out that I'd forgotten to go to bed, I wasn't tired anyway.

When my father saw me, he tutted a bit before taking advantage and sending me to the newsagents for a packet of fags and a newspaper, while he made his breakfast. By the time I got back, the comedown had started and I went straight to my room pretending to be tired. I cried for most of the day, ostensibly about the girl who had dumped me a few weeks earlier.

That's why the work of John Treorchy interested me so much. When I first saw it it invoked a sense of loss and pointlessness that at first made me want to run straight back out of his studio in Morriston, Swansea. But I didn't run out, I stuck it out, and I'm glad I did, because this artist is extraordinary. He's extraordinary in the way he uses everyday objects to make 'moments of frozen time' as he puts it. for example the work that provoked those reactions in me was based on a drawerful of objects almost exactly

like the drawer I had so meticulously tidied up thirty years earlier.
"All my pieces seem to do things like that to someone or other,"
he explained, "and I don't know why. It doesn't seem to matter
what I do, sooner or later someone comes along and tells me a
story like the one you've just told me. I like to think that I've
somehow tapped into some universal truths and can create works
that somehow channel that truth directly into the soul of the
viewer. You can have it if you like."

"Oh no," I said, perhaps a bit too abruptly. I didn't know how
many useless pieces of art I'd had thrust on me during my time as
an art critic for the Internet site but I knew I didn't have any more
room for them, besides I didn't really like the piece personally and
the negative feelings it evoked.

What he'd done was to take an ordinary drawer from an
ordinary house, that was full of a jumble of ordinary objects and
pieces of detritus, like hairpins or staples or half-chewed biros or
half-dead hairbrushes, complete with wisps of hair, and he'd
encased the lot in thick clear plastic. It looked simple enough but it
must have taken an age to tease the molten plastic into the correct
nooks and crannies to avoid destroying the obviously meticulously
planned composition. The objects were so common and so
unreachable at the same time, the plastic was so transparent and so
unbreachable that the conflict caused in the mind of the viewer was
enough to call his creations works of art.

four

There's a reason for every molecule of ink on this page, or every pixel of light on this screen, or whatever. So there must be a reason for everything. So, nothing is pointless, *nothing* is pointless.

~

OK, I did it. I had to fucking do it. The bastard had been shafting me all my life and for the first few decades I didn't even know it. What would you do? He had to go. Now that's a funny thing about killing someone. Sure, you've taken their life, extinguished their consciousness, but that's only part of them. Mostly, these people, the people that you hate, or love – live in your head – and you can't kill them – the bits of reality in your head – you can't kill them.

Maybe if I'd done it twenty years earlier, maybe then, I'd have got over it in time to have some sort of life. But I didn't and I suspect that if I had it wouldn't have made a difference. I'd just have had twenty more years of this shit. Anyway, I didn't know then and I'm glad, because at least I had a life. Now what have I got? How the fuck am I going to sort this out?

~

London – another perspective. An August Saturday in 2002. I gave the beggar-woman on the millennium footbridge two pounds and lost a twenty-pound note while having a sneaky one-skinner under the bridge, staring down at the Thames. A boat passed in the middle of the river, a sort of barge – but wide, with its cargo covered in green tarpaulin. It went quite fast and left a brown lapping on the rubble.

The power, the privilege, the clichés of the British era. One day, social historians will discuss the dark days of London at the beginning of the twenty-first century. London, it's a big word, two big bass notes – Lon-Don, that boom with power and privilege. The way the Lunnoners say it, it loses its power and becomes instead a dirty, hard and noisy city, filled with poverty and stress, holding itself together by tiny fragments of the adhesive that makes everything move and keeps the status quo at the same time – money, the key to survival.

I came here with Ken once. (once with Ken that is). It was the Pink Floyd concert in Hyde Park at the end of the sixties I think. We scored some grass off a Spanish guy under the trees and lay back on our elbows to stare at a distant stage with sound coming from speakers behind our heads somewhere. I was not impressed; London has never impressed me.

That was the year Phil died, near enough. He was the first. He had a habit of driving his car too fast and too recklessly and flew over a hedge on the road to Llandeilo (he was going to score some acid). Hit a tractor thing and died in a coma two days later. His brakes were fucked, apparently.

~

August 2002. How fucking weird is that. I bumped into Phil's mother today. She looks just the same as she did then only more wrinkled. She recognised me straight away and she said the same things she said about Phil she's been saying for the last thirty odd years. We went for a coffee; it was strange, drinking coffee with an old woman, reminiscing about her long dead son.

But Phil was something special, the kind of guy you only meet once in a lifetime. Well, not a kind of guy, you couldn't say Phil was a kind. He was unique, a one-off . . . what the fuck am I going on about, he was hardly more than a kid when he died, a couple of years older than me, but just about still a teenager, I think.

She can't accept that Phil died because he was a complete head-case. She's convinced that he was murdered. She's blaming the police. Fuck that shit, you don't want to go round calling the police murderers, they've got the power.

I promised I'd call in to see her sometime; she still lived in the same small house just outside town.

~

I'm on the train to London, minding my own business, trying to melt into the back of the seat and giving off a "don't fuck with me" vibe when a man comes in and sits in the seat across the aisle but facing me, if you know what I mean. He's staring straight ahead, upright, full of paranoia and tension. He's in his fifties, but straight looking, straight casual though with blue jeans and an expensive white sports top.

I'm doing a good job of avoiding eye contact but it's tiring and I wish he'd go to sleep or at least sit back and relax with a fucking book or something. Then, thank fuck, a younger man sits opposite him and they talk shit all the way to Paddington. I'm obviously listening but not listening obviously if you know what I mean.

These fuckers! They've got no more to say. Everything they're saying has already been said. There's nothing new for them to talk about. What they're really doing is playing games of the 'my cock is bigger than yours' variety. The first guy was born in 1946, (do the maths yourself) and the other one is round about twenty-one because he's in a drama school in North London and he talks about his parents a lot.

"I'm bigger/wiser/more knowledgeable than you."

"My choices in life are well chosen."

So there's fuck all to say.

There's a 21 year old moaning that young people today are only interested in pop music and it's a shame that they're not into Brahms or someone.

For fuck's sake, make your own culture.

But I get to London unscathed and settle down with my lovely 30-year-old son, in his flat in South-East London, with a spliff, a vegetable biryani and Cool FM playing Jungle on the radio.

How lucky am I.

The next day I get up early and sneak into London while he's sleeping.

~

London, Saturday Morning

I had a piss in the Tate Modern and gave the £2 "suggested" donation to a beggar on the millennium footbridge because she deserved it more. Saint Paul's Cathedral was underwhelming and the bobbies looked like characters out of Fireman Sam.

London – towering buildings – modern art – small Asian men selling Guardians and phone cards. Sometimes I feel like a vaguely interested alien. The big city institutions, the monuments to tradition, the exploding sheds and large pieces of coloured paper – homeless beggars and the old River Thames – so what?

I had a thought about the beggars; this particular one, a grimy woman in her thirties, smiled with a light when I gave her the two quid.

I said: "Better you have it than that lot in there," pointing at the Tate Modern.

She smiled the light again but I'm not sure if she understood the gesture, or even if she heard the words, perhaps the two pounds represented 29 squillion litres of cheap cider or something, but there you go.

The thought I had was:- We (that's you and me, you know, the sort of people who go to the Tate Modern and read books like this). (I'd better repeat that because the brackets went on too long). The thought I had was: - we, feel sorry for the homeless beggars, or we feel pity, I suppose some of us feel disgust, anyway we generally feel something.

What do I say? I say, stop. Stop feeling sorry for them, or pity, and especially stop feeling disgust. Why? (Oh, by the way, I don't mean stop giving them money). Why? It's all about the light. I saw it twice today – once when I gave the beggar the money and once when I spoke to her directly afterwards.

And that's what it's all about. These people's homelessness and poverty is a metaphor for their inner homelessness and poverty – it's all about their need for light. Say, for every one thousand people that walk by a beggar, 999 of them do not react, or pretend not to have a reaction – well it's still worth it to them (the beggars) because that one in a thousand delivers the light. And the thing about light is that it gets reflected straight back at you; it's like instant good karma. We supply the beggars need for light and they supply ours, it's a symbiotic relationship. And it's not only about giving and receiving money, sometimes a guilty glance is enough. They're laughing inside, these beggars, living off the light. Light bombs planted on the street waiting for your detonator.

And then there's the Tate Modern – a groovy collection of the best of what's known as 'modern art' in an even groovier building in a groovy groovy part of one of the grooviest cities on Earth – London. What could be groovier? Huge entrance hall of cathedrally majestic proportions. Me – unimpressed (I've worked in more impressive car factories). Hours long queues to buy tickets to see Matisse's and Picasso's work (of which I am a huge fan) – fuck that. Poncey café, half-baked exhibition pieces, two pound suggested donation – fuck that too.

I'll tell you what's groovier – it's the light – the light – there is nothing else.

In the afternoon. Three women on the bus – figures like fifteen-year-olds, faces as old as their privilege. Hawk-eyed, high-voiced – pampered. Five hundred dollar jeans, two thousand dollar jackets (dollars sounds nicer than pounds – more international and sexy. Don't you think?). From the trendy outskirts of Brixton to posh Dulwich, some drinkies, some posing, some men, maybe even some sex. They have the hunter's look, alert to their own safety, focused on their prey, oblivious to extraneous distractions. I don't register in their vision

"Skunk weed."

"White."

The dealers emerge from the mass of excited bodies on the streets of Brixton in South East London. Why me? Why are they targeting me so vehemently? Do I look like a drugs tourist or something? I wouldn't mind but I'll never buy dope off someone on the street, a complete random like that. I'm afraid I'll get ripped off, a couple of grams of oregano or a lump of henna for twenty quid or so. Anyway, I don't need any skunk, I've got my own, grown organically on a sheep farm in Wales (so they told me), and I wouldn't touch the white shit, I'm too old to get into that now.

We sit in the gardens outside the Bug Bar and smoke a joint. The dealers leave us alone. We talk about London and free parties and Jungle music and jobs and art and I tell him about the shit in the Tate Modern. I don't tell him about Ken, I've never told anyone about Ken, even her. They don't need to share in that fucked-up shit. But Ken is on my mind, he always is.

~

Beetle stained custard. Chemically enhanced nutrition. Unnatural colours. Food that isn't food. Food that is plastic. Consistency. Hills infested with fluorescent flora and dripping with blood. Baby food. Immaterial material. Artifaction. Acid dreams becoming reality. A manufactured world. A thin world. A light even in these darkest days.

These are just some of the themes running through Steven J Powell's work. He was brought up on a dairy farm just outside Llandeilo and he noticed when he sat down to eat one day, that the food he was served by his adoring mother was not the same as the food that his father grew and produced. He noticed the difference between the sanitised sludge of the child's dinner table and the congealing bloodiness of the cowsheds and the milking parlour where he helped his dad harvest the products of the animals that they nurtured from bloody afterbirth to bloody steak.

So, Steven J Powell started to create representations of the feelings he experienced, brought on by the juxtaposition of raw life and death with the homogenised, pasteurised, sterilised bottles of cows' milk that appeared on everyone's doorsteps every morning. As he grew up he experimented with different forms. He started by drawing farmyard scenes with wax crayons, using the most brilliant colours in the packet and ignoring what we would call the actual colours that we perceive.

This, in itself, was a great achievement for a ten year old, for that is the age at which he had this first epiphany, but his work even then, goes much deeper than that. He moved quickly on to attempting to make representations using the actual foodstuffs themselves so that by the time he was sixteen his mother nearly lost her mind looking in the cupboards for the custard powders and sugars, the colourings and fats of her farmer's wife's trade – the items he stole from the kitchen to use in one of the run-down outhouses that surrounded the farmhouse.

He soon came to realise that he was never going to be able to construct anything that lasted very long with the perishable goods he had chosen as his medium so he started to experiment with harder materials, like bits of wood and old milk churns, bits of electric fencing and corroded rubber teats. Some of his earlier works in these materials are now on show in the parlours of rich and slightly off-key farmers, but it is his more recent work that is receiving the most critical acclaim.

Now, nearly three decades after his attempts at permanence with food colourings, flour and milk, his work has evolved, so that it bears the assured sharpness of vision associated with a master of his medium. Now, he makes sensual sculptures out of plastics and paints, using the most fluorescent and brightest pigments he can muster. His latest award-wining piece is a triangular structure of three spheres that have the texture and colour of the bright green, pink and yellow custards and blancmanges you see at the best children's parties.

~

Phil wanted to come to the Pink Floyd concert in Hyde Park but he never got it together. In the end me and Ken hitchhiked; good thing we went three days early, because it took us nearly that long to get there. The night before we left we were in the pub, that's me, Phil, and Ken.

Phil and Ken didn't really get on so I was surprised to find them sitting next to each other in the modernised upstairs of the pub. The landlord and his partner had made some concessions to the drug-induced unconventionality hard won in the sixties and had furnished and decorated the upstairs with more than a nod in that direction. I suppose that the main contributors to the room's ambience were the lighting and the up-to-date stereo system. The lighting created a dim atmosphere that was nevertheless very colourful, with greens and reds and blues, yellows and whites; with flickers and starbursts, glows and sparkles. The music was well-chosen with Crosby, Stills, Nash and Young, Jefferson Airplane and of course Pink Floyd among the offerings.

Phil said something to me as I sat down and he pulled himself away from Ken's ear, they were both laughing, but I couldn't hear him because the music was too loud. I stood up again, went over to the unattended bar and turned it down. There was no one else in the room.

I sat down again. "Can I have a sip?" I asked, pointing at Phil's glass of coke.

He shrugged. "I was just telling Ken now," he said, "I might be able to come with you after all. I might even be able to bring my car. But I would need you to chip in for petrol."

"And I told him it would take more than petrol money to get that heap of his to London." Said Ken.

I shrugged. There was no way I could afford to chip in for anything, let alone petrol to London. All I had was thirty bob and no prospect of getting any more. The concert was free and hitchhiking was free, so what did I want with a poxy car anyway.

Ken noticed my mood. When Phil went to the toilet he said to me. "Don't worry about the money. I'll lend you some."

My mood lifted, even thought I had often 'borrowed' money off Ken there was never any pressure to give it back and it didn't bother me. Phil took a while in the toilet and then we saw him, silhouetted in the doorway, whispering to someone. When he came back his mood had dropped to a point well below where mine had been earlier.

"What's up?" I asked him.

"I can't fucking go." He said.

"Why?"

"It's my fucking brother."

"Paul?" Ken said.

"Yes, that wanker."

"But you said Paul was cool."

"Well, it's not really his fault, it's my mother."

"What's wrong with your mother?" I asked.

"She's freaking out, Paul says she's going mad worrying about me. He came down specially to talk to me. She's convinced something bad is going to happen to me."

"Fuck her." I said.

"I've tried to ignore her, but Paul came looking for me. It's that fucking gypsy's fault."

"You don't have to listen." I said.

"You don't understand," he said, "she lost my twin brother at birth, she's never got over it. I'll never be able to get out of this poxy town. Not until she's dead anyway."

"Oh!"

"Listen," Phil said, "I'm going to have to get home. You two enjoy yourselves."

After Phil left Ken went downstairs and bought me and him a pint of bitter each.

"Would have been a nightmare if he'd have come anyway," he said, "can you imagine three of us hitchhiking, not to mention the broken down wreck of a car of his." Ken laughed and took a big swig of the beer.

I walked home on my own to save the bus fare; I'd deliberately missed the last bus anyway. I enjoyed the half hour walk back from town to the estate, especially after pub closing time. It was even better after the discos closed down late on Friday night. Then you got to chat to all the random semi-drunk, semi-strangers; you got to know things about people you'd never have got to know otherwise. There's something about a walk through quiet streets, along deserted main roads that brings out the confessional in people.

I got talking to a bloke who I think was known as Ferret, because of his white hair and skinny pink body.

"Where you been?" He asked as I drew alongside him.

"Just out." I said.

"I've been walking my girlfriend home. She's forty tomorrow.

I'm only twenty-nine."

"Oh yeah." I said, slowing my pace, deciding it would be a reasonable way to spend the time during the walk home – he lived somewhere on the estate, I wasn't sure where and normally I'd have avoided him, he was a lot older than me and a bit rough if you know what I mean, but he came across as harmless enough, at least he was in a harmless mood, so I decided to risk it.

"Where's she live?" I asked, trying to be friendly.

"I saw you in the pub earlier," he said, "in Station Road."

"Yeah, I was there."

"Saw that kid too, the one with the smart mother."

"Phil?" I said.

"No, not Phil."

Ken then?"

"Might be. Anyway I've always felt sorry for him I have."

"Oh, why?"

"Well, his mother isn't it."

"How do you mean?"

"She's on the fucking game isn't she."

"Nah," I said, "you must have got it wrong. She's posh, could never imagine her on the game."

"Who the fuck do you think you are?"

When he turned and snarled at me I could see another reason why they called him ferret – the sharp white teeth that bared themselves against his pink gums. I decided to get the hell out of there and immediately started running. He tried to keep up with me for a few yards but soon gave up cussing and swearing. I reckoned he'd forget about it all after he'd slept off the alcohol so I wasn't too worried.

f i v e

1971: Serge and the other one. Faces from the tribe. An ancient gathering, the light forces and the dark. Our collective power, harnessed, we are warriors of the light.

"Where am I?"

"Who the fuck are you?"

Now, they're gone, merged back into the Maya, perhaps they're on the other side – the dark side. Fucking hell, it must be the acid; didn't I hear John Peel's voice warning about the bad acid? Or was that Woodstock? The bastards have spiked me – free food by fuck. There's no such thing as a free lunch – "there's no release in this game boy." Help, I need help, I've heard that a couple of handfuls of sugar, or, failing that, as many fresh oranges as you can cram, will bring you down.

I know, I'll go to the Release tent, maybe they'll give me some Valium.

There's a couple of freaks sitting on the floor inside the tent.

"I'm having a bad trip," I say.

"Well fuck off, we're having a good one."

I fuck off, back into the battle; are they on the other side too? Or is it just a test?

It all started about three hours ago, I must have been coming up on the acid. Ken freaked me out. Nothing he did specifically; just something about the way he looked, the way he is. I think he thought it was a bit of a laugh, a joke – filling my head with his inane, insane face. I freaked and stumbled off and ever since I've been cutting criss-crosses across these fields.

Where am I? Glastonbury. Some farm in Somerset. Last night, was it only last night? Last night, Ken grabbed me outside the pub and stared into my eyes, a hypnotic stare. He showed me a magazine cutting about some free festival in Glastonbury. There was some buzz in the air, (do buzzes live in the air?) so we came. A magical start, a magical arrival (but that's another story) – and now, this nightmare.

Hold on, get a grip, it's just the drugs, this will pass, everything passes.

A holy voice like a sheet of fire splays over our heads like a giant golden discus, is it John Peel again? No, it's a different kind of voice, it's more of an inner voice. It's probably the acid again.

A double-decker bus comes flying without wings over a hedge and Melanie's on the stage, her voice like a sweet execution. Things are cooling down. I can almost breathe again. I'll go down closer to the stage. Ouch – what's that? It's like a force field, an invisible electric fence. I can't go that way. Ouch! Or that one, or there, or there. I have to climb the hill again, the forces have to be aligned correctly to kill the darkness.

The campfires are lit – time passes, hours, days, millennia, I can't work it out. Arthur Brown is on stage – he's the devil, he's the one we have to vanquish.

The sun rises, it's midsummer's day and we did it, we did it again. We always do. Now we must reconvene in another hundred life times (it takes that long to recover).

I'm back in the tent with Ken. Now it's only cannabis and deciding when to go home. Nothing else is mentioned.

~

The Three Bears. I painted a picture once, when I was less than seven years old. I know because it was in the infants' school and you have to leave there to go to the big school when you're seven. I painted a picture of the Three Bears in their living room with wallpaper and everything. I won a prize with it. It got hung up in Park Howard or somewhere.

I didn't paint anything else except for doodles until about four years ago after I started interviewing artists for the Internet magazine.

~

The last artist I interviewed worked with straw. There are so many artists out there, even in a small country like Wales, so many that each one has to have some sort of gimmick. This guy is very clever. He can take a bale of ordinary straw and turn it into something that reminds you that you're alive. On the surface they're just randomly shaped balls of straw, painted in bright, almost fluorescent colours and hung from another piece of treated straw; like heavy mobiles.

You want to watch out for this guy. At the moment you can pick up his balls of straw for about thirty quid each in craft shops. But they're not craftworks, they're true works of art. His name is Dai Jones.

Dai likes to talk, to philosophise about his art, unlike many of the artists I've interviewed who just point at the art and shrug when you ask awkward questions. That art, their creation is what they want to say and how they want to say it. This is an excerpt from that article about Dai Jones but if the link is still working you can find the full article at www.openingchapter.com/daijones.

"Creativity is the first step to decomposition. The moment you create something it begins to fall back to the pool of molecules. Like gravity, it is an irresistible force. You lob your art in the air like a cricket ball; it falls back giving up its energy. Perhaps the reader *(he called people who appreciate art – readers)* gets the benefit of some of that energy and with it catches a tiny flash of truth that enriches their existence on many levels: mentally, emotionally and spiritually."

Dai writes poems as well, they're not as good as his coloured straw balls, here's an excerpt from a poem of his that tries to describe his ideas about art as a giver of energy:

The Mona Lisa as a Raindrop
a bubble of precious water
like a river of love
rushing through the centuries
sustaining life
as it goes.

~

I forgot one place, one relevant place. London, 1969. A 17-year-old lugging speakers and drum kits up wavy stairs and along thin corridors. Working in a photography studio in the days, mixing with the peripheries of the late 1960s scene in London in the nights. A pub, round the corner from the flat, filled with transvestites. We think we invented this twenty-first century world in the twenty-first century, but let me tell you, WE invented it in the sixties, we planted the seeds.

Then – two lovers, a young Welsh man, eighteen or nineteen, with a roadie in his late twenties. Mike was with me there, (a different Mike); then it was only Mexican grass bought in Carnaby Street or off some famous rock musician, (I can't remember that much detail and I'm not going to make it up.) We set up in the Marquee Club and devised a system for beating the traffic lights in central London by driving at a constant speed on the way to the studio. I made the coffee and went out for food and beer.

We had a thing going; I was Derek from the Humble Pie, Mike (the other Mike) was George Harrison and a guy whose name I forget (Alan?) imitated Jimmy Saville poor sod. George Harrison was the best. He waved at John Lennon once, in Soho – poor John looked confused. That's the legend anyway.

The things I've lost – the people I've lost, we've lost.

~

NOW! I'm standing at the kitchen sink washing dishes and she's next to me peeling potatoes. This *'I'm'* shit isn't a literary device by the way, nor is it fiction. I really am standing at the kitchen sink and she really is next to me peeling potatoes. What it is, is that I'm testing out a new top-secret product from one of those mega-rich multinational computer companies that started life in a garage in California or somewhere.

This device/product/gadget allows me to get my thoughts typed directly on to the PC in the other room via my super-duper, plastic-fantastic new wireless network system. The beta version that I'm testing has a large battery/interface attached to my waist that doubles up as a muscle-toning machine.

That's why this is a bit of a ramble, but it's still edited and sifted consciously by me before I think the command "SEND", so bear with me.

Anyway, back to the dish-washing, potato-peeling, silent, contactless intimacy of this August (august?) evening in 2002. Washing dishes is a chore in the "why the fuck do I have to do this shit now when I'd rather be prostrate on the settee with a long spliff and a bottle of red" sort of way. Peeling potatoes is a chore but in the "this is a bit of a pain but it has to be done if I want to eat" sort of way.

The thing though, about standing here, with her, doing these banal tasks is that it's not about the potatoes or the dishes, or even the expectation of a good meal. It's about just being here, with her. There's something about being a human being that makes you feel special. Part of it is the feeling that you can do anything, you know, given this and that and if this or that happened then you could go to the moon or sail round the world, or win the Nobel prize for literature (like fuck). You could be a lawyer or a teacher or a doctor.

I could easily have been a doctor. I'm not going to be now of course because I'm too old to start the training process and I can't afford to pay for the years of learning. What it is is that I've suddenly come to a complete understanding of the human body. Obviously I don't know all the details, and I don't even want to know and I'm sure that some people or even the majority of people would look at me and say "so what?" if I explained my new understanding to them.

They'd say "so what, that's obvious isn't it?" and maybe they'd add "are you thick or something?". But I'm not thick, and yeah, maybe I did understand the obvious before but now I've reached a much deeper understanding; it's either that or I've finally flipped and gone mad.

Thing is, we're independent creatures, we're not directly attached to anything we can see, or hear, smell, touch or taste. We move through the universe in our curious animalistic way and experience it through our senses; the physical connections between out there and in here.

So, the body is a vehicle that needs fuel and maintenance, and doctors, are just the mechanics, the people who unblock a pipe here or weld a fuel tank there. That's all there is to it really, the rest is just knowledge, and knowledge you can acquire easily through the aforementioned five senses. It's just a matter of life, and death really.

So, here I am, washing dishes at the kitchen sink while she peels the potatoes. Don't know if I like this Mentally Activated Device, So Hot It's Terrifying (yes M.A.D. S.H.I.T – don't blame me it's those fucking weirdoes from Silicon Valley). Don't think I like it at all because no matter how hard you try to control it, it still picks up thoughts you'd never really commit to paper normally, thus exposing the thin hold you have on sanity as a human being.

Fuck – all this is being recorded on the PC and because it's a Beta version and because I signed a consent form, it's being internetted straight to the corporate headquarters in the USA and published simultaneously on secret web sites where the covens of million-dollar executives can probe it and analyse it and sell it to advertising agencies. But it pays well. I don't have to work for a couple of years unless I tear this fucking contraption off my precious human body and throw it in the Salvation Army clothes recycling collection point in the supermarket car park, thus breaking my contract.

One good thing, I'm allowed 5 twenty-minute breaks a day and it switches itself off automatically when I go to sleep – that's a godsend, I've never slept so much in my life. I'm switching off now – OFF – NOW.

"You OK?" She asks. "You're very quiet."

"Yeah, just thinking that's all."

"What about?"

"Oh, not much, you know, the usual stuff, you know, money, work, the kids."

"It'll be all right you know, we'll get through this, I heard Roy Noble on the radio saying there's no hole so deep you can't climb out of it."

I make a suitable appreciative sound, almost a laugh. Why is that funny? Except death, I think. That's the trouble with truisms, they're not true.

She doesn't know everything about Ken. Well she knows he bankrupted me and nearly got me sent to prison. She doesn't know I killed the fucker, or many of the details of our relationship – mine and Ken's I mean.

Nobody else knows this shit, and I mean nobody, just me, me and you now.

"Think I'll start a diet tomorrow," I say "'bout time I think."

"Yeah – could do a bit of exercise as well – get your

metabolism up – I heard on the radio that once you've got it going it keeps on for a bit, it's not just for the time you're exercising."

"I know what you mean," I say, "after you exercise it's like you glow for a bit, I suppose that glow is the heat produced by the energy you're burning up."

"What do you want with the potatoes?" She asks.

"Don't know, how about some Linda McCartney sausages, some frozen peas and an onion gravy?"

"Do we really need the gravy? And wouldn't you rather have some fresh veg – I don't mind cooking"

"We'll cook a proper meal tomorrow. Come on, how about it? You've done the hard work already, peeling the spuds."

"Oh all right."

I make the gravy anyway:- a whole onion, very finely sliced, I like the long strands cooked slowly in a bit of sunflower oil. Two large cloves of garlic chopped and crushed, flour of course, a dash of tamari, a couple of twists of black pepper and a teaspoon of marmite – lovely, but I made too much as usual. I ate it all though.

"I'll start the diet tomorrow, promise." I say as we're washing the dishes again (together this time).

She tuts.

"It's just been hard lately, that's all, I can't quite get it together, nearly there though. I can feel it."

"Yeah," she says, "I know, don't worry about it. It'll be all right, you'll get over it."

"Yeah, I feel a lot better actually, it's just habits that's all."

"I've noticed you're looking better, just keep busy – don't dwell on things."

It's the truth; I am feeling better, ever since I killed that cunt (I don't say this).

~

Do you find it funny that whatever you say, whichever way you explain something, the other person, or persons, you know, the ones on the other side of the explanation, never get it right? No matter how close you are to someone, no matter how long you've known each other, no matter how many secrets you've shared, they still don't get it. In the end you usually just give up, not in a nasty or spiteful way, you've got it out of your system, you've had your say, now it's up to them.

I've been having a bit of trouble communicating lately. Perhaps it's me? Losing it? Lost it? I don't know.

I suppose it's my fault. What it is, is that I never seem to be able to give something one hundred percent. Don't get me wrong; I can work hard when I want to, bloody hard, but it's like I always hold something back; keep something in reserve. No one else can ever really know you, can they?

She's looking at me as if I'm mad.

"Stop looking at me as if I'm mad." I say.

"You are."

"I'm not."

"I don't mean mad mad, I mean you come up with some crazy ideas."

"Life is complex, and nobody really knows what's true and what's not, nobody really knows, with any certainty, that something is totally right or totally wrong."

"But what you're talking about is dangerous. Imagine living without law. I don't think so."

"It's not about laws, I never said that it was about laws. It's about respect. No, what am I doing getting dragged down to this level. What I'm talking about is what society, not just this society, but any society, even a chimp society has arbitrary rules, and that it's OK to break them if you know what you're doing."

"So who decides where the boundaries are? Who decides that one person can break a rule and another one can't? Is that you? Is it?"

"No need to get like that, I was only talking theoretically. Anyway, there are people who make decisions like that, they call them judges and politicians."

"But they only operate within a system. They still have to obey the rules themselves."

"OK, it's like this, suppose it's illegal to piss in the street, well suppose it's only you in the street, what's the problem? I mean, who do they think they are, as if they own the streets. If I want a piss, I'll have a piss"

"Grow up."

~

Now look, I don't want you to think that this is a literary novel, literary in the sense that it is obviously based on a classical education and a penchant for the author to read copious amounts of other author's books. It's not about that. Nor is it literary in the sense that it makes clever intertextual references to other media products, whether they be old books or Hollywood films.

I want you to forget everything you've read before. Please don't compare this to some other work, don't say things like: "Well, I thought the style was a bit like Neville Shute.", or "it's like an extended short story of Italo Calvano." Don't even try to stuff it into a genre like 'Thriller' or 'Mystery' or 'Epic', because it's none of the above.

This is the truth, the truth as it happened, and told with whatever skills the writer's (that's me) acquired in his life. I'm telling it because I've got to tell it, it's as simple as that.

~

I get the feeling I've left something behind, or missed something back there in my past – something important, something crucial, to me and to this story. So, me, like a twat, goes looking for it – whatever it is.

I get a job for two weeks as an extra in a television series about a probation officer. The star of the show is Keith Allen, who used to be a good friend of my brother. (That's not the reason I got the job by the way – it's only when I arrive on set that I realise he is the man.)

So, the set is in Cardiff Bay; they've converted part of the old Coal Exchange into a suite of offices and this is where they'll shoot most of the internal scenes for the series. I'm one of the office staff, meandering about in the background on instructions from the assistant directors.

You'd think it'd be interesting, what with famous faces like Andrew Sachs (Manuel from Fawlty Towers) sipping tea and eating cheese rolls across the table in what passes for a Green Room, but it's not, it's the most boring work I've ever done (including the time I fell asleep three times during an induction at GKN in Cardiff). Basically, you're told nothing about what's going on, you never see a script, unless you pinch one of the copies the actors and crew sometimes leave lying around. You have no idea of the story, the scenes you're supposed to be in or whatever. You're just told to go and wait somewhere until you're needed; when you are you're wheeled out like a prop, positioned and then shooed off set. You're told to wait until the actors and crew have finished getting their food before you approach the catering truck and then it's usually just the leftovers.

I stick it out for the required two weeks even though the pay is pretty shit, around seventy quid a day before substantial deductions, and anyway I won't see the cash for a good couple of months. So, I'm broke and I'm mixing, (on the periphery), with a bunch of overpaid lunatics (actors, directors, etc.) and one of the days' filming goes on too late and there is an early start the next morning, and I've got no money anyway, so I phone my beautiful, intelligent daughter. (Who happens to be living in Cardiff, doing a journalism course.)

She buys me a curry and lets me crash for the night.

I arrive on set at seven the next morning and do absolutely fuck all until 4 o'clock in the afternoon. Whatever I'm looking for, it isn't here.

~

There are bits of me in every part of this world. In fact, I'm only borrowing the materials that constitute my physical existence. Every molecule has to be returned one day; but like Julius Caesar's dying breath they'll last forever in one form or another.

The truth is not out there.

s i x

Now.

Let me tell you about Phil. I'm thinking about Phil because I'm on my way to see his mother. I don't like doing this, it was such a long time ago, I would have thought she'd be dead by now. How old is she? Let me think. If Phil was nearly twenty when he died in nineteen sixty eight or sixty nine say? When the fuck was that Pink Floyd free concert in Hyde Park? I'll have to look it up one day. So, say he was twenty in nineteen sixty eight (worst case scenario), she must have been at least say, twenty years older than him, making her about forty, but she looked older than that then, or perhaps it was the clothes she wore and the greying permed hair?

Hang on, I'm sure Phil had an older brother, quite a bit older, if I remember about seven or eight years older. So that makes her closer to fifty in nineteen sixty eight, say forty eight, forty eight in nineteen sixty eight equals forty eight plus thirty four (the number of years since nineteen sixty eight) equals eighty two, around about eighty anyway. I suppose that's not so unusual these days. My mother is seventy one and my mother-in-law is seventy eight and they're both as sharp as acetate. So eighty two isn't that old, for a surviving woman in 2002.

There's a lot of them about, I should know, I live in Llangennech. Old women that is, if that's an appropriate word – old – it carries so many negative connotations:- worn-out, weak, ill, useless, past-its-sell-by-date. Old should mean wise and kind, experienced, empathetic, useful and beautiful.

But they're not are they? Old people are not wise and kind, they're stupid and selfish. They're not useful and beautiful, they're pathetic and twisted, just like everyone else in fact, except that because they've lived longer they've had more time to absorb the blows that this shitty world delivers to them. They're full up with blows, full up and bloated with whingeing cynicism. Thank God for death.

All that is a disgustingly blatant generalisation of course but you get my drift. There are some nice old people, perhaps Phil's mother is one of them. Perhaps she'll turn out to be an earthly Obi-Wan-Kenobi or like the guy in the Kung Fu series who called David Carradine *Grasshopper*, or like Gandhi, or like Mother Teresa (but I'm not sure about her).

~

"OK, it may be art, but he's not the artist." Another artist.

"Opera, lovely in its place," his eyes sparkled, "but those opera singers. Even if they're as personable as our Bryn Terfel, are just vehicles to deliver the composer's and/or the librettist's work."

I scribbled it down. Mostly I just take notes and cobble an article together a few days later; sometimes, when someone makes a bit of sense I write it down as near to verbatim as I can manage. It's rare to get a quote as definite as that.

This is part of the article. There was that quote above then this:

His work sparkles like his eyes, he is an old man now and happy with it. This is an artist who has achieved his vision and a fine sight it is too. He paints his pictures with a clear, certain stroke, like an athlete at the peak of his career in beautiful slow motion.

"Art," he says, "is the only evidence we have to prove we are human."

There is a spiritual quality in his voice and you still believe him when he tells you he's an atheist.

"We don't need a god," he says, "being a human being is enough."

I believe that too.

~

Phil could have been an artist, I'm sure of it, but his mother wanted him to go and work in the car factory like his father. He never would have though, there's no way he'd have allowed himself to succumb to that dirty swamp of a hell-hole.

I knock the door, number 63. It takes a while but I hear it opening and there she is. She knows I'm coming. I expect her to be welcoming, fussing, fawning even, but she's not. She's got a severe, morose demeanour and she doesn't say a word.

She acknowledges me with her eyebrows and invites me in with the same gesture. The passage is thin, dark and long and endless in the silence. We arrive in a small, cosy living room with nylon floral seat covers and a large blue radio-cassette dominating a tall round table next to a portable television on a wooden trolley.

There's a man sitting stiffly in one of the small square armchairs. He doesn't get up but acknowledges me with the morose eyebrow gesture he shares with the old woman. He's in his mid to late fifties, almost an old man himself.

It's got to be Phil's brother. What the fuck was his name? I feel awkward, Mrs-whatever-her-name-is delivers us.

"You remember Paul?"

"Yes." I say.

She smiles. It's faint.

"It's been a long time." His voice is not quite right. It's older than I expected and very American.

"Sorry." I say. This gives me a chance to get out of here. "I'll call back another time, it's not a problem." I start to turn back towards the front door.

Paul is on his feet, his hand on my shoulder.

"Please stay."

I shrug. "OK."

I'm sitting in the other armchair, next to the tall round table. There's a shelf underneath with a neat pile of papers and envelopes addressed to Mrs Rita Davies. I'm saved. Rita Davies – Mrs Davies, and Paul – Paul Davies. Now I know who I'm dealing with. This is a bit odd. Mrs Davies sits down on a hard high-backed wooden chair near the gas fire. She looks distracted.

"I'm glad you came today." She says.

Paul shuffles.

"It's Phil," he says through the sighs.

Rita starts crying, dabbing at her eyes with a paper tissue.

I didn't expect this.

~

Gammy died of an overdose. Not a quick overdose, but a long and painful death. He overdosed on alcohol, on speed, on valium, on mogadon, on cough medicine. His life was a perpetual overdose. How do people get so fucked up?

~

What the fuck. Let's get the deaths out of the way. OK: Phil and Gammy, you know a bit about those two, but there were others; Mike, who drowned, Sam fell off a cliff, Kath, who jumped off a road bridge, and of course Ken, who I murdered. (There are a couple of others but they're not relevant yet and you'll only forget if I tell you about them now, it's hard enough remembering the names of the characters that have been mentioned so far. I hate that in a book, you know, right at the beginning lists of characters and places with weird, hard to pronounce and hard to remember names, like Shamrox and Deerbjont and Iksjopetci and suchlike. A couple of pages in and I find myself having to look back at the earlier pages to see whether it's Deerbjont who's the intergalactic pencil sharpener or it's Iksjopetci, or maybe it's the Gery-Bearded Wunderkid I'm thinking about.)

~

September 20th 2002. Yesterday was a weird day because I behaved normally and everything I saw and everyone I encountered seemed weird. For example, a couple of old codgers, and I mean old codgers, hardly able to walk and doing that only by clinging on to each other and baby-stepping along, stopped on the pavement on the other side of the road and stared at my house, peering through their saucer-sized spectacles, nudging each other and pointing at my roof. Then they babystepped a few metres along the pavement, stopped, and turned towards the big house opposite me, and did the same thing.

Now, this is a village full of old codgers, as I've told you before, but these two were strange, not the usual sort. They were both very small, a man and a woman I've never seen before, and they don't hide themselves away as a rule around here, and if they do, they don't pop up after a couple of decades and perform weirdly in my street. The minister (of religion) who lives next door, a sturdy man of eighty-odd, went over to talk to them as if he knew them. After a few words he turned and walked briskly in the other direction towards the top of the road and the Co-op shop. He's never done that before.

There were other things, other events associated and not associated with the codgers but their exact particulars are not all that relevant, well they are relevant but you'll have to take my word on that because I don't want to repeat the same sort of stories and I'm sure you've got my drift (about the weirdness) by now, and in any case I don't want to bore you.

Today has been weird too. Not because everyone and everything has been strange, but because today everything has been normal and everyone has been normal too. It's me that's been weird. I've done strange things, behaved in a not normal manner. For example, and it's only an example, I bought a car. It only cost me £225 plus another £147 for insurance and it's a bit of an old banger, though not quite as much of an old banger as those two were old codgers yesterday, it doesn't move in baby steps for example – it zooms along. It's not every day I buy a car, even a cheap car, but there you go. I bought it trade.

That's an idea, I could buy cars like that trade, do them up a bit, then double the money by selling them – it's worth four hundred and fifty quid at least, well maybe three hundred and fifty because of the high mileage, and the crappy paintwork, and the rusty wheelarch, and the fucked-up headlight and . . . we'll call it three hundred then, still a tidy profit, that's like a thirty three per cent mark up or a twenty five percent gross profit, before the cost of cleaning materials and the odd headlamp bulb.

Some cars can take it, the high mileage, and some can't. Some quite new cars fuck up even, and they cost a lot to look after, never mind the depreciation, and if you buy them on credit you can pay a hell of a lot more than two hundred and twenty five pounds a month, every month, anyway. So, I'm quids in aren't I?

Aren't I?

~

I was there. I was there the day Sam met Kath, or Kath met Sam if you like, except that Sam was my friend, he was the one I knew first. When I say I knew him first I mean I got to know him as a friend even though I actually knew of Kath before I got to know Sam. That's the sort of thing they do to your head; they fuck it up. That's Sam and Kath all over - fuck-ups, it must be the acid.

What happened was that we, me and Sam, were in the bowling alley drinking coke in between nipping into the toilet to pop some pills. I can't remember what the pills were now, probably something stupid like codeine tablets. We thought the combination of codeine and coke did something, anyway they were cheaper than dope or speed or acid or whatever and easier to get, you could buy them in any chemist's shop for example.

Anyway that was then and this is now – August 1975, or thereabouts. I'm in Sam's mother's house attending his funeral. She, his mother, kicked his useless father out a few years ago and she won't even let him in for the funeral of their son, so he (the father) is hanging about outside, sitting on the wall by the gate, smoking those big fat roll-ups of his. Kath is walking up the path from the house towards him with a plate of sandwiches and a cup of tea. I'm standing in the front room with Ken, looking out at the scene through the dirty net curtains.

Ken sighs: "Look at her," he says, "she's off her head on something."

"Well you can't blame her, her husband has just been cremated." Ken is annoying me, all he's going on about is Kath. Never mind Sam, our dead friend. Maybe he has got a point, life is for the living after all, but he isn't half getting on my wick.

"Yeah, I suppose," he says, "but she looks as if she's trying to avoid facing up to the truth. She's got a life to lead, she's still very young. How old is she? Do you know?"

"No," I reply, "I've never thought about it. Younger than you and me I think. Anyway, I could do with a smoke. Have you got anything?"

"Wish I had but you know I haven't smoked for a couple of years, not since I got the job in the bank."

How the hell Ken ended up working in a bank I'll never know. I shake my head in disbelief: "The bank."

"It's not as bad as you think, and I've learned a hell of a lot."

"What? How to count other people's money, how to make tea for the manager."

"You'd be surprised," he says, "there's money in some very strange places, people you wouldn't imagine."

"Like who?"

"Oh, I can't give any specific details, it's all very confidential you know. But I reckon that if you know where the money is then that's half the battle. All you've got to do is find a way of getting your share. Look, she's coming back."

Ken goes out of the room and opens the front door for Kath. I watch as he puts his arm around her and leads her back into the house. She gives me a weak smile as they pass.

Sam's brother is here, an angry man in his late twenties. I'm a little afraid of him. When me and Sam were younger he tried his best to spoil our friendship. I don't think he likes me very much – thinks I'm a bad influence or something. Me? A bad influence. If only he knew. He comes into the room before I can get out.

"Hello." I say timidly.

He grunts.

"Fell off a cliff by fuck." He says.

"What?"

"There's more to this than a cliff."

"How do you mean?" I ask.

~

Now Gammy was, as his name suggests, well gammy, meaning he was sort of dirty and sort of sticky, he lived in a style that was just a bit out of sync with the rest of the world. Now I know we're all a little bit askew but Gammy was extraordinary, I don't even know if he was conscious of the same common realities we all share, like it's stupid to cross the road when there's a car coming. He seemed to live according to stimuli from another dimension. Most of the time his reaction to the other dimensional aspects of his life coincided with what his reaction would have been had he been reacting to aspects of ours, but often enough they didn't. Therefore it was inevitable that he should end up screwing it up and dying, as he did from an overdose of something he probably had no concept of.

I remember about a week before he died I'd gone home to my parents' house in Llanelli. I'd only intended to stay for a couple of days but ended up staying the whole week. In fact, I might have never bothered going back to Cardiff if it wasn't for the funeral. His father, a small, dark, worried man, appeared from somewhere and buried him in a nice plot in Cathays cemetery. The man wasn't happy.

"I've been told you lived in the same house as my son." He said, his expression as fixed and as solemn as he could make it, although you could tell he wasn't in the habit of communicating seriously with younger people, or indeed any other category of people other than the barmen of the local pubs. I felt sorry for him; he looked very small and helpless, as if he was now in total acceptance that his life was a piece of shit.

"Um, yes," I said, "you're his father aren't you?"

"It wasn't his fault."

"I know. He was a good bloke he was."

""Did he talk to you?"

"A bit. Like you do." I didn't want to give anything away yet, if at all, so I deliberately answered vaguely. He sensed this and turned away.

"Well. Never mind."

"Sorry, yes, he talked to me, he talked to me enough for me to know he was a good bloke – sound."

The man hesitated, a tiny spark of life appeared in his eyes: "Did he ever talk to you about his troubles? You know?" He asked.

"Well," I hesitated, "the drugs you mean?"

"Yes, and the other stuff."

"The other stuff?"

"Yes, there was someone."

"Oh. I didn't know."

"No, not someone like that."

"What do you mean?"

"Oh it doesn't matter. It doesn't matter." The spark died and he turned and walked away.

Ken and Mike arrived then, together – late. I tried to ignore them but they caught up with me walking back through the graveyard on the way back to the house in Canton.

"Hold on." Ken said.

I stopped and waited.

"What was it like?" Ken asked.

"What happened? You're too late. The least you could do was show. . . . ."

"Hold on," Ken said, "My car was fucked, all right? If it wasn't for Mike here I'd never have made it, at least I came, and it's not as if Gammy was my best friend in the world, is it?"

"I've just been talking to his father, he's in a bit of a state."

"Stupid old git never bothered with Gammy before. Anyway, he's a fucking alcy."

I left them there, pissed off with Ken's attitude, wondering whether he was the man, and the friend, I thought he was.

s e v e n

Writing I will do.

Life is a mystery that can never be solved; it is, and if it is, it always will be and always has been. This is, for me, now; this is, for you, now. We perceive our nows to be different, but they're not, there is only one now. Fucking hell, I'm freaking myself out now. Better stop all this philosophising crap and get on with it.

So what was it? The thing I'm supposed to get on with. What was it now? Where am I? Ah, hang on, yeah I remember now. I'm sitting in the kitchen at Llwyncelyn writing this. But wait a second, when am I? In other words, what is now?

It's all in place now. I can recall it faster than I can speak and a hell of a lot faster than I can write. I'm in the kitchen at home in Llangennech (if that sounds like a nostalgic reference to this pit of a village, it's not. Though scarily, I'm actually starting to understand what people see in the place). It's eleven-thirty in the night of August 20th, 2002 and I've got Chris Needs on Radio Wales on in the background. It's all very normal.

I can't let it be normal, not after what's happened; how can anything ever be normal again? That smug bastard on the radio (sorry Chris, nothing personal, you just happen to be in the way), people just getting on with their lives, grazing at their putrid junk-shit food like cows in a byre, not knowing who they are and worse, not caring.

But I've still got to get on with it, otherwise I'll atrophy and that wouldn't be good until I do what I've got to do, must do.

Sorry, went off again then; got distracted then forgot what I was doing, it could be something to with the spliff I had earlier on, short term memory loss and all that. I can't continue writing at the moment because I'm too stoned and all my insecurities and issues are bubbling up in my head.

She says: "What are you doing?"

I say: "What does it look like?"

She says: "Are you writing again?"

I say: "It's what I do."

She says: "You're never going to get any of that crap published."

I say: "But I've made a contract."

She says: "A contract?"

I say: "Yeah, I've made a contract – with them." I'm pointing at the writing pad.

She says: "Are you losing it?"

I say: "Aren't we all?"

She says: "It's late."

She sighs.

I say: "I'll be up soon."

She says: "Good night."

See, she doesn't get it, she can't understand that I am actually talking to you now. But you know I'm not losing it, don't you? You know I'm not mad. I mean, I really am talking to you aren't I? Otherwise how the hell are you reading this? How the hell are you listening to what I'm saying?

Look, I'm not going to pretend. I'm not going to kid you into thinking that I'm perfect, or brilliant, or perhaps a better word would be flawless. I'm not going to pretend that this story is flawless. It's full of fucking flaws, just like everything else, every other person, every other writer – Shakespeare even. (hushed silence (what the fuck does that mean? – hushed silence – huh!)). Where's the line between amateur and professional? Between beginner and genius? Between sanity and madness? Between lies and truth?

Where is that line? Where are those lines? Only thing I can tell you for sure is that this is the truth, believe me, this is the truth.

Now, let's get back to it. The story continues.

~

"It's not exactly the biggest tragedy in the world is it?" She says. "It's just some man getting into financial difficulties. You've got to get over it and get on with your life."

"You don't know what it's like." I say. Then I start to cry again. She puts her arm around me and pulls me to her.

"Sorry." I say quietly into her ear, my tears cooling on her cheeks.

"Look, it's not exactly Othello is it? That's a tragedy, or Hamlet, that's a tragedy. Or is it? Oh, never mind, just snap out of it."

I can't help it, I have to get out of the way – there is too much tension between the story I'm telling and the reality of what's happened. How can she know? I'll have to make more of an effort.

I say: "I'll have to make more of an effort."

She says: "It's not all your fault. It's that Ken. I told you he was bad news. He encouraged you to overstretch yourself."

Ken made me do it. Ken made me do it. Ken made me do it. Isn't that what I've always been saying? Ken made me do it. Yeah, that's a point, whenever I've been in any sort of trouble, or through any sort of pain he's been there for me. There for me? There with me. Always there, in the background, or in my face, cajoling, sniping, controlling. He's a bastard. But not a bad bastard, just a hard bastard. (Note, this is before I found out just how much of an evil bastard he was. i.e. sometime in 1999, the year I went bankrupt)

So, Ken, my oldest friend, the one who would have been the best man at my wedding. if I'd had a best man. Wait a minute, wasn't my brother my best man? Who cares, it's just a detail. Isn't it funny, I can't remember if I had a best man. It's not funny really, it's obvious, because we didn't have any photos in our wedding. My in-laws, who organised it all must have deliberately avoided photographs, because they hoped it would all be over and forgotten within a few months. How they must have hated me.

Look, I know, I should have sorted it out. I should have organised some photos, but it was all done very discretely, out of the public eye, almost out of my own eye, and anyway I was a bit of a stupid fuckhead then.

So, I can't remember if I had a best man at my wedding because there were no photographs. That's sad. Does that mean we need photographic reminders to tell us who we are? I bet if the marriage hadn't lasted I'd forget I was married too. But fuck them, we've been married over thirty years, fuck them all.

Ken would have, should have, been the best man at my wedding because he was, is, my best and oldest friend, but for some reason we'd lost touch for a year or two at that time. I can't remember why, it was probably something to do with the religious cult we joined when we sidestepped, more than dropped out of society, normal life etc for a few years. Come to think of it, those years were fantastic, clean and free, blissful and timeless.

He came back though, he came back when we left the ashram and rejoined the shitfaced rat-race because we thought our kids needed stability; and they did, and we did come to that. He came to visit us in our council house in Pembrey, a place where on a good day you could smell the sea and on a bad one you gagged at the stench from the chicken processing factory up the road.

He hung around for a few years, then he got married and went to live in Australia. That wasn't long before our luck changed and we bought a house in the village. It wasn't long after Mike was drowned either.

Mike could have been my best friend but he was too unreliable, too hung up on pills and cough medicine.

I decide to go and confront Ken.

He's in the club as usual. (What a cliché that is, but it's true). Despite everything he's managed to keep it going. I know he's hurting, almost as much as me, but he reckons he's got a business partner, as far as the club goes, and all he's really doing is managing it for a favour and getting paid a pittance. He's always been a bit secretive about his businesses, usually doesn't get involved with friends he says, well he fucking did this time didn't he.

When he sees me his expression is warm and welcoming.

The Ken Story.

I am suspicious. She has planted doubts in my mind by being so nice, so caring, so loving even.

"What's happening?" I ask.

"Not a lot. I'm still trying to sort it out but I'm not getting very far."

"It's too late for me anyway," I say.

"Just because you're bankrupt doesn't mean you can't start again. You've still got it in you."

"I don't know. I'm not sure."

"Look, I promise you'll get some of your money back – even if I have to pay it myself, it might take a while that's all."

"But I still don't get it. Why did it all go so wrong, so quickly?"

"It's just business, you win some, you lose some."

"What about the investors? They lost a lot of money."

"There's nothing you or I can do. Serves them right anyway, expecting to get something for nothing."

"I don't know Ken, I don't know. I'm still confused. And I'm broke."

"Ah! Is that what's bothering you? Look, I shouldn't do it, but there's some latitude you know, when you run a club. There's always a way. I've got a bit stashed. It's only a couple of hundred.

Hang on . . ."

Before I can react he's gone, as he passes the bar he whispers to the bar man. A few seconds later I'm drinking a pint of draught Caffreys.

I look around the club, it's still early. A few of the seats around the dance floor are occupied. There's a group of young women having a hell of a laugh around one circular table. They look like students on a night out. I feel old.

At another table there's a group of older women, in their thirties say, they've tried to glam themselves up but they're mostly too fat to pull it off. They're having a great time though.

At this time the music is still quiet, a few chilled-out CDs on a loop because the DJs haven't arrived yet. I'm getting bored waiting for Ken. One of the young girls comes to the bar; she sees me and comes over. It's Lucy, Ken's daughter. She's tipsy.

"Oh hi." She says with a smile. She's always got a smile for me, we've always got on, ever since she was a toddler, ever since she came back from Australia with Ken. You had to admire him for that, keeping it together all those years as a single father, except for his string of girlfriends that is.

"Let me get you a drink." I say. I feel in my pocket, there's a fiver there and a few coins. I hope it's enough for two drinks in this place, I need another, one is never enough.

The bar man refuses to take any money off me, thank god.

I say: "How's college going?"

"It's gone," she says, "I've just finished my final year."

"Oh yes," I say, "I remember your father telling me. So, you're going to be a lawyer then."

"No, I'm going to be a social worker."

"I thought you did a law degree."

She laughs: "Yes. I did, but I know what I want to do now."

Ken comes back. Lucy gives him a strange look, it's as if she's frightened of him. She knocks the rest of the vodka back and goes towards the other end of the bar.

"See you." She says. She's smiling again.

"Lovely girl." I say.

He looks at me with a cold stare, it only lasts a millisecond before he pulls his face into a smile.

"Here." He says, handing me a brown envelope. (Yes – I know but it's true, that's how it's done.)

The envelope feels firm yet it gives like skin, a very sensual experience – fondling a bundle of money.

"There's five hundred quid there," he winks, "did a good deal the other night. I said I'd look after you, what's mine is yours and all that."

"Why didn't you go bankrupt?" I ask a bit too abruptly.

He doesn't seem pleased. "I didn't have to, you didn't have to, but I understand why you did."

"The hearing is tomorrow." I say.

"Why didn't you tell me sooner?"

"Why? It's not your problem is it? I'm the one who's bankrupt. I'm the one with no equity left in the house.

By now, I'm draining the dregs of my third pint. Another one appears.

"I'm in the same boat," he says, "and I haven't even got a house of my own. I'm lucky I've got Sandra, she looks after me."

"I still don't get it."

"You're worried about tomorrow that's all." He says, handing me a double whisky chaser.

I'm pissed, it's just after midnight and I'm still on the street outside the club. I can't resist it, I push through the cluster of clubbers queuing to go in, and into the Chinese takeaway. Despite the queue outside it's not busy. I order two large chips, two poppodums and a carton of curry sauce.

While I'm waiting I phone a taxi.

The young Chinese girl hands me the white plastic bag with a smile. I wonder if it's genuine. I'm sure it is, perhaps she finds a pissed forty-odd year old amusing. Perhaps she's one of those genuinely nice people like Ken's daughter Lucy; perhaps she's naïve.

She'll learn.

I know the taxi driver; well I used to know him. We used to hang around together in the primary school. A lot of the people I used to hang around with are taxi drivers now. Perhaps that's my destiny too. I give him a twenty-pound note and tell him to keep the change. He's chuffed. Maybe it's because I'm drunk but that makes me feel so good about myself I almost cry.

She's still up, reading a book by Anne Tyler, it's supposed to be good. She's nearly finished, just half a centimetre of unread pages left.

She puts the book down on the coffee table.

I slump in the chair. Now I have to clamber upstairs to the toilet.

Now I come down and the chips are piled up in a big bamboo bowl and the curry sauce is open beside it. She's also made me a cup of strong black coffee. My head's still wobbling, but now after the coffee and half of the chips I'm feeling more grounded, if more grotty as well.

"My mother phoned when you were out." She says.

"Oh yeah, any news? What's the latest on the hatches, matches and despatches front? Especially the despatches, she loves them."

"No, it wasn't anything like that. It's Lizzie, her friend – she's been questioned by the police."

"The police?"

"They wanted to talk to her about your friend Ken."

"Ken?"

"Apparently she invested in that scheme of his."

"But I've been with him tonight, I don't understand."

"Now I know why you're so pissed, you always overdo it when

you're with him."

"I'm just worried about tomorrow." I say.

"Well you shouldn't be, you've done nothing wrong. It's just business. In America you're very employable if you go bankrupt. There's no shame in it."

"I haven't told you everything." I say, throwing the remains of the five hundred quid on the coffee table.

~

I've been to so many so-called art exhibitions, (it's the art that is so-called, not the exhibitions, they are exhibitions all right, exhibitions of mediocrity) where all that is on show is walls full of pasty, insipid watercolour paintings of flowers and meadows. Yuck. So, when I went to interview Sarah Dwrlliw, I'd already decided that it would be a test of endurance rather than an experience to be cherished.

When I got there, however, I was delighted, not only by the watercolour paintings but by the artist herself. I always say it takes a special kind of person to be a good artist, to be any kind of artist at all in fact. Don't try and tell me that just because someone's been to art school they understand what art is, and just because somebody's read books and attended life classes for forty years they are dedicated artists. Fuck no. These bastards are ciphers, pale facsimiles. How can you understand art if you don't understand life?

Anyway, as I have already intimated, Sarah Dwrlliw is an artist, not only that, she is a great artist. What I mean is that not only does she have the insight and the sensitivity and the understanding, she also has the skill and the perseverance to create real works of art. Never mind David Hockney's recent foray into watercolours, this is the real thing.

As usual, you've got to see them yourself to appreciate them properly, but, I know that there are so many people who only read the reviews and have no intention of going to see the works under discussion, (not that I think that's a bad thing) so I'll have a go at describing Sarah's paintings anyway.

First of all, Sarah is beautiful, in every physical sense. She's also erudite and full of life, but I have to admit that she is weird, not the sort of woman you'd want to spend a weekend in a log cabin with, she'd drive you bonkers.

One of her paintings, a clover field reminiscent of Monet's Water Lilies except it was an unfocussed close-up . . . (no, stop, I mustn't say it was reminiscent of anything, I've promised myself I wouldn't do that. Forget it will you, forget that I said that – please!) Anyway, it changed my view of the potential of watercolours forever. The colours in it were so unlike anything I'd imagined could be achieved using the medium that I couldn't believe she really had used them.

"I do have a few trade secrets," she said, "but I don't mind sharing them. Sometimes I mix my own blood into the paint. It doesn't keep very well, so I also add in household bleach and sometimes, random bits of ground up anything I happen to find, like the shells of dead sea-creatures or the chopped-up hairs of cats. I never know what's going to come out when I start mixing."

Sarah isn't doing very well, so I bought a small painting of a bee on a dahlia for twenty quid from her. I would have liked to give her more, but as usual, I was nearly broke. She was chuffed though.

"Remember," she said to me as I was leaving, "life, like art, is what you make of it. It's not reality, only raw material for you to construct your own reality from."

eight

Progress report: Saturday August 23, 2002, 6:41 pm.

This is chapter 8 of the novel "This is my Reality" (Note: Before the title change) written by Wynford Brennan (Note: Before the name change). At the moment I am writing these in sequence, i.e. chapter eight (this chapter) is being written after chapter seven was written. Only thing is I haven't finished typing up chapter seven yet and I'm typing this straight into the computer. (Pentium three PC and Word 2000, seeing as you asked). Anyway, bugger it, there are no rules really.

Anyway, I thought I'd let you know how it's going. It's not fair is it? That I get all the pleasure of picking the ripe pods of my experiences, cobbling some words around them and sticking them under your nose all mushy and processed. It's not fair that I get to choose and you just have to take the filtered, edited, subjectified shit without complaint. I've told you enough times that I'm telling the truth. How many more times eh? How much proof do you need? Look, if I was the kind of guy to lie about something as important as that then I wouldn't be writing this would I? Because unlike other novelists I'm not pretending that you don't know that what you're reading is just a construction of words designed to enable you to pretend that you've entered some special strange world where it is absolutely forbidden for you to acknowledge that what you're reading is something that has been written by a writer who has at some time sat in front of a computer screen just like I'm doing now and paused and edited and thought until he or she came up with a sentence designed to convey his or her very subjectified version of a very small subset of his or her experiences that isn't even reality.

How about that then eh? Good isn't it eh?

The thing is I can't imagine what it's like not to have something huge in your life. The hugeness I'm talking about is hard to pin down, part of it is ambition, but that's only a part. It's also about immortality (not in the vampirical sort of way), and there's a fair bit of altruism in there as well. But it goes much deeper than that, there is a desperate need to communicate, to have an effect, to tell the fuckers that you were here.

So, how's it going? Well, I'm enjoying writing it, though the Ken bits are quite hard and I'm aware of you all the time, you fucker. But apart from that it's going good. The way I'm defining good, by the way, is simply that if I like what I've written, it stays in, if I don't it goes out. It's going so well though that I've got to say that I've chucked nothing I've written away yet and I haven't edited it much at all from the moment it left the end of the biro until it got typed in here, firm as stone, apart from a few typos and the odd comma.

So yeah, it's going great thank you. I've already written about (hang on I'll just check) about fourteen thousand words, that's a fifth of a small but respectably-sized novel. But we've got a long way to go with this story so we'd better get on with it.

~

I got past it, past the bankruptcy, past that shithead Ken, and now I'm all right. I've got a new career as a lecturer in FE (Further Education). I teach Media Studies and Scriptwriting. I also do a bit of freelance writing work, like that gig I've got with the web-site. It's taking over in fact, the other stuff. The teaching stuff is only part time and I don't do it for the money any more. It's just to keep in touch, to ground myself.

~

London 69. There's not a hell of a lot to say about this really, it didn't last very long, less than three months. Fucking hell, I've spent longer than that waiting for a sub-plot on Brookside to develop. Why has it become so important in my life then? Eh? I know I'll go back to 1969 and see how it goes. September 1969, somewhere around then.

~

I'm 17 and I normally live at home with my parents and my brothers. I started an apprenticeship a year ago, in the car factory where my father works. It was the worst year of my life, for two reasons. First, the place is a fucking Nazi concentration camp with two Birmingham born fascists fucking around with your head. I'll come back to that. Then there's her. That is such a small word isn't it? Her. Just three letters, one of the smallest words you can get. But boy did she have a big impact.

There was Before Her and then there was After Her. Before her I was a nice normal intelligent lad who had only been done for shoplifting, oh and breaking into a cricket club, after her I have become an angry fucked up dope-smoking fuckhead. We only went out for two weeks; I think she ran away because I got too serious.

Only thing is, I was fucked up in the car factory BH. I hated the shithole from day one. Can you believe what they had us doing? There we were, twenty odd 16 year olds, fresh out of school, innocent as fuck (in relative terms), and the fascists give us a lump of metal each and a file. They made us stand at a bench, clamp the metal in a vice and file it until it became 'square'. It took two fucking weeks and they loved every minute of it, the fascist cunts.

(Future Note: So basically, if I'm honest, I just used H as an excuse, she was fuck all really, what really fucked it all up was this fucking ridiculous world we find ourselves born into, and it can't be anything else really, can it? When you think about it I mean, it's a ridiculous situation and we only accept it 'cos we're used to it and 'cos we're fucking stupid, as fucking daft as a fucking dog who's smelt a bitch on heat – get fucking real.)

So it's AH now (After Her, remember!) and I'm 17 years old, in a flat in Paddington, London, England. Oxford and Cambridge Mansions it's called, sounds posh doesn't it, and I suppose it is quite posh. The flat is on the something floor of a tall old building. There is one of those lifts where you slide the concertinaed metal grid doors open and shut, very old-fashioned (even now). There's a big living room at the front of the building and a long corridor that leads to the kitchen. On either side of the corridors are rooms. There's a bathroom and four bedrooms. I'm crashing on the floor of one of the bedrooms, working in a photographic studio off Baker Street and lugging speakers and drum kits around the country as a kind of roadie's assistant (not all at the same time obviously).

My mother thinks I'm going to be the next David Bailey. Who the fuck is he when he's at home eh? Some photographer who's been on the news a bit because he hangs out with some so-called beautiful women – so what.

It's later, I'm 17 and I'm angry because this fat fuck who lives in one of the rooms and is the roadie for some obscure band tried to chat me up. I wouldn't mind but he smells and I'm not homosexual. The other day he brought a boy back with him, someone he'd picked up in Soho or somewhere.

The people in the shop around the corner can't understand my accent so I have to modify it when I go there to buy fags or whatever. I'm lying on the mattress that is on the floor of the room I'm staying in and listening to Led Zeppelin – "Whole Lotta Love." As the chorus is repeating "Whole Lotta Love" I'm getting up there in a kind of cosmic force field sort of way. You'll just have to smoke a lot of Mexican Grass and lie on a mattress while listening to the record if you really want to know what I mean.

I'm in the kitchen opening the fridge.

No I'm not, I'm in the bedroom listening to the record.

No I'm not, I'm in the living room talking to a Bunny Girl, somebody one of the roadies is going out with at the moment.

No I'm not, I'm in the bathroom cleaning the scum ring from the bath after the fat fuck has sluiced his smelly body again.

No I'm not, I'm in the shop asking for twenty Embassy but they keep looking at me as if I'm dying.

I'm in the kitchen again.

Fuck, this is strong grass, I wonder if it's been laced with opium or something?

This music is tripping me out.

Is time a triangle?

~

When I was seventeen I went to live in London. A friend of mine, who was a roadie with a soul band (Jimmy James and the Vagabonds if you must know) let me stay on the floor of his room in a flat in Paddington. There were a few other roadies living there. I couldn't drive so I got a job in a photographic studio off Baker Street. At first I made the coffee, got the sandwiches from the sandwich bar and ran back and fore to Selfridges to buy props and equipment. Then they put me onto processing the big colour transparencies they used in their work for a large catalogue company.

They offered me a chance to get to know the photographic equipment and they even suggested that I could use the studio for my own work outside normal hours. I had a thought that I could use my connections with the bands and do some photography for their album covers but a batch of Mexican grass fucked me up, so when I came home for Christmas I never went back.

~

It's time for another artist, but this one is a relevant one. That's the title I used for the interview I did with him and published on the website www.openingchapter.com/relevant - *A Relevant Artist.* Not that there was anything in the interview that referred to the fact that he was a relevant artist, it was just my little joke, my own little piece of planted sub-text if you like.

When you plant something you hope it will grow but you generally have to nurture it especially if it's a man-made hybrid specifically designed to create a particular effect at a particular time. (This was after I got to know just how much of a bastard Ken was but before I killed him.)

I'd set up the interview a few months before, when I was still just about friends with Ken. He got me in with the artist. It's not easy getting artists to open up to a hack from a second-rate internet e-zine, especially when they've got a bit of a name like he has / did (he died a few months later of alcohol related thingies). Thing is I didn't like him at all and by the time I got round to interviewing him I didn't like Ken either.

The reason Ken was able to help me to make the contact with the great artist was that he was screwing his wife; I didn't know that at the time of first contact but I did by the time I got to interview the bastard. I was glad he was a bastard because I'd already decided to fuck them all up, that's the Great One, Ken and the Great One's missus. When the time came I didn't feel at all comfortable or sure that I could pull it off.

The Great One was in his studio, his wife showed me through (couldn't see what Ken saw in her myself – a raggedy old bag if ever I saw one). *His paintings are bright swathes of cobalt blue and cadmium yellow splayed across backgrounds of orange suggesting the fire and the ice in the heart of the mountain people of Wales* (my arse!). That's what I wrote in my review anyway and it's a fair enough description in its way but this man is a swaggering old git who smokes seven inch cigars and tries to make you feel like a turd. He's the sort of bloke who believes it is his duty to employ artisans to do the menial tasks in support of his pathetic life and thinks he's doing them a favour with his patronage. Still his paintings sell well (even better now that he's dead), and he's achieved his immortality.

I planted my seeds during the gaps in the interview when I usually put my pen down and just chat about politics or the weather or something. I'm afraid that I ranted on a bit about Ken though he claimed he'd never met the bastard. I wanted to undermine Ken in every aspect of his life, I wanted to see him broken and rejected by the same pretentious pratts he aspired to be like. I questioned what sort of person would be a friend of a villain like Ken knowing that he would think of his wife who he knew associated with him. I told him I felt his paintings operated on two distinct levels: they displayed the landscape of Wales as a place full of wild sexual, almost animalistic energy and they betrayed the hidden landscapes of doubt and jealousy inside the artist who painted them. When he asked me to explain I mumbled something about his landscapes mirroring the curves of a mature yet voluptuous woman's body and that secretly he felt betrayed both by his country and by women in general.

I also planted seeds in the review that was published on the internet a week later, pretending to see in his paintings the *anger of a man betrayed by his beloved country* knowing that he would interpret this as a reference to his wife. He split from his wife immediately after that, I didn't know at the time but apparently she used to be a famous actress; it was all over the Welsh news for a few days; he had become a national institution, but they didn't mention Ken by name so it didn't touch him, the bastard.

~

I'm getting to a point now where I can't distinguish the memories of yesterday from the memories of decades ago (or decades hence?). It's like, there I am, in my bedroom or the kitchen or whatever, and it's even worse when I'm somewhere neutral, like a field, or a country road, and I'm remembering something, but I forget where I am now. The memory is good, I'm sure of that, but I don't know where the memory is in relation to where I am now.

I mean, am I a middle-aged man? Am I a ten-year old boy? Am I a twenty-something father of three children? Then, just before the loony wardens turn up to lock me up, it comes back to me, or rather, I come back to it. It's usually to do with someone else.

"Hey, wake up," she says, "wake up, food is ready."

It's 1986 of course. Here I am, and she's here, she's always been here. Then there's the children. They're definitely here.

"I love you," I say.

"Come on, food's ready, you were snoring."

"I was dreaming."

"Anything interesting?"

"Depends what you mean, it's hard to describe, hard to remember. Something about the three bears, I used to dream it a lot when I was a kid."

"I know, you told me about it, but I thought you hadn't had it for years."

"No, I haven't, but it wasn't that dream. It was a much more complicated one, and it seemed to last a lifetime, it's like I dreamt a whole life, yet I know I've only been asleep for an hour."

"More like two. Now, come on, get up, it's time for Coronation Street."

~

Coronation Street, a constant throughout most of my life. My old Gran used to shuffle out of the parlour promptly, the only time of the week when she joined the rest of the family in the living room. I think she liked to let us get on with it.

I wonder if it will ever end? (Coronation Street, I mean.)

n i n e

You should see a difference in my writing from now on. What it is, is that we've had, sorry, I've had, a lot of debt for a long time now. You know all those clichés about a cloud hanging over your head and like when it goes it's like a weight being lifted off your shoulder? Well I've got to say that the cloud is not as fluffy as it sounds; in fact, it's not really a cloud at all, because even a dark cloud is still a cloud and wispy and light with it. It's more like a heavy coat with poacher's pockets full of lead. I knew a gypsy once, called Wisdom, who used to buy lead from boys from the estates and me and a few mates got locked up in the police cells on suspicion of nicking the stuff – but we didn't. Some halfwit had given our names when he got caught on a factory roof pinching lead to sell to Wisdom. He was too scared to give the names of the boys he was with – they were harder than us. We got off, but that's another story.

When you take the coat off it's like losing two stone in weight (you'll only appreciate how that feels if you're fat like me). It's like suddenly discovering you're not as old as you thought, you've got a future again. This debt that I've had hanging over me like the sword of Damocles (there I go again) is finally going away, thanks to a rise in the value of the house and we're doing the windows and the kitchen as well.

So, with a bit of luck, and if I haven't been permanently tainted with the valium of debt, you'll be noticing a lighter, happier kind of writing from now on.

~

Hello, I'm ten years old and I live on a council estate in Llanelli.

It's nice living here most of the time but I am afraid of some of the bigger boys from the top and bottom sites. I'm quite happy. I go to a primary school that's about two minutes walk from the bottom of my garden. I go down a couple of alleys and across a couple of roads and into the school gates, except when the school is closed for holidays. I like school; I didn't used to but that was when I was in the Bs and Cs; now I'm in the As and I get top marks for everything I'm happy. I've got certificates for being top of the class and even for full attendance.

I've told my parents I want to be a vet when I grow up but I'm not really sure myself. I like writing but I don't know if it will be any use to anyone. I play with my friends in the alleys around our house and in our gardens and sometimes we go across the road to a grassy bit next to the private houses and play touch or something, I can see it from my bedroom window. I say I'm happy but I do have these nightmares – nightmares and thoughts.

One nightmare I've had a few times is the one about the Three Bears. There's Daddy Bear, Mammy Bear and Baby Bear and they're my friends. We go across to the grassy bit and play touch. So there I am playing touch with the three bears and according to the rules of the game if you get tired you are allowed to stop and say 'Release'. The other players have to let you rest for say ten seconds; then you're fair game again. When you're playing the game if the one who's 'on it' touches you, you become the one who's 'on it'

So, I stop and say 'Release', and I'm laughing and out of breath. And I think they're laughing too. Then Daddy Bear comes up to me and I hold my hand out to him and say 'Release' again; I'm still laughing. He isn't smiling; he's got these huge sharp teeth and his eyes are narrow and mean. He says 'There's no release in this game boy.' Then he bites a huge chunk out of my arm. That's when I wake up and my arm is aching but there's no bite out of it.

Another nightmare I have is that I go to school without any trousers or pants on and everyone's staring at me but not saying anything. I have that one a lot, it's quite common, apparently.

~

Sometimes I feel like a computer. Someone has programmed me to help figure out some universal truth. The thoughts come and settle for a while just as if I am being fed data to work on. I process the thoughts and usually come to some conclusion. Sometimes I cannot come to a conclusion and so I bury the thoughts deep in my storage systems or try and get rid of them altogether by an effort of will or by concentrating on something banal. You know how they tell you to think of beautiful things or places when you're freaking out or having negative thoughts and emotions? Well it doesn't work for me. If I try to think of something nice it soon gets nasty, like a lovely puppy dog getting splatted by a car. I concentrate on banal things instead, like politics or better still some form of academic study, that's a hell of a distraction, it gives you the illusion that you are doing something challenging and worthwhile.

I have been told that physical exercise helps a lot, and meditation, that's a good one and it works, I should know.

~

The Holy Place. I know it's there, this divine experience. It's somewhere just behind my eyes, just inside my ears, just on the tip of my tongue and just under my breath. I know it's there, just out of reach, but it's fun trying to get there. We sit around in the evenings and chat about holiness; it's Satsang, speaking truth or something like that. In the day we go about our work, happy in the knowledge we're doing Service. And whenever we can we sit down and engage in Meditation. It's OK, it's really not like a cult or anything, we get a lot out of it, a lot of Bliss.

It's 1974 and I'm twenty-two years old. I've got two young kids and I live in a big house in Manchester with a total of twenty-seven adults and seventeen children. The community is based on the principles of Satsang, Service and Meditation; it's like an ashram for families. To be honest most of the people here piss me off. Don't take that the wrong way, it's not bad or anything, it's just an observation. Because of the way we live we are free from the concerns of this material world, this Maya. That's the theory anyway. We don't drink 'gross' tea or coffee, we don't smoke anything or drink alcohol, we don't have any money of our own and we don't have to worry about bills or anything. Everything's taken care of.

Who am I kidding?

The sooner we get out of this shithole the better. It's a difficult environment, especially when there's kids involved. The underlying principles are still good but the practice is a bit dodgy. The people here carry too many bags of shit in their heads and they're not afraid to splash them over everyone else. It's like living in an institution. Hang on, what am I talking about? It's not like living in an institution – it is living in an institution. It's time to move on.

~

Memory is a funny thing, but it's all we've got. Imagine I can't remember what I'm doing, can't remember what a computer keyboard is, can't remember the English alphabet, can't remember: how to think, how to talk, how to write, how to breathe. Imagine that. As the thing you're remembering fades back in time it becomes less clear, gaps appear in the memory, it starts to get dilapidated and yet you have fill the gaps somehow, to make it all make sense. That's why I'm writing this now, in real time, or as close to real time as I can. So that what you're reading is closer to the truth, closer to reality.

But why do I think that would be important to you? This is a novel isn't it? You read novels to escape from reality; you want them to be fiction, entirely made up, yet entirely plausible. That's the key isn't it? You want to believe in this reality but you know it's completely untrue. That's because there's more truth in this reality than in reality itself. It's a funny thing, a novel, but then one meaning is that it's *novel*, i.e. *new*. So that's what you're getting isn't it? This is an innovative novel. (Is that a double positive?)

After I got back from the club that night with the five hundred quid I bottled it. I didn't tell her the complete truth. I just told her that I'd been doing some secret work on a computer program to record the chargeable work done by Ken's accountant, and that I'd done it to give her a surprise. I couldn't tell her the truth could I?

"That's the truth." I said.

"Very sneaky of you," she laughed, thank God, "it should be enough for a new cooker."

"Well, maybe," I said, "but we'll have to be very careful because we've got so many things to sort out."

"At least the big debts are gone. Come on let's go to bed. You've got to be fresh for the hearing tomorrow."

I didn't go to the hearing; I couldn't face it. I persuaded her not to come with me even though she'd taken the day off work. I said I needed to face it myself but really I was afraid of what would come out.

I sat on a bench outside the courts in Swansea and phoned them on my mobile to say I was ill. They didn't seem to care. That's when I met Annie.

She reminded me of a girl I used to know, an Irish girl with a spark like a Van de Graf generator and an appetite for drugs as big as her moon-shaped face. I don't usually like to use that generic term drugs. It's a nonsense term. What do they mean by drugs?

Coffee, beer, tamazepams, cannabis, heroin or what? But that girl really did like her drugs. Anything would do – uppers and downers and rounding and rounders – anything. She must have been full of shit as well as full of sparks. Anyway she died a long time ago. This girl, this Annie was almost a reincarnation of the original but not so fucked up and a lot older than the Irish girl was when I knew her. Annie sat down next to me on the bench.

"What are you up for?" She asked.

"Um, er. . . "

She laughed: "It's all right, I know the look. The hunched shoulders the fag butts on the ground around your feet, the constant glancing over your shoulder at the court."

I laughed. She made me laugh. I decided to trust her for a while. I wouldn't give her too much personal information though, just in case.

"Bankrupt." I said.

"Bugger all then." She laughed again. "Have you got a fag."

I handed her the tobacco and papers.

"Roll-ups, I hate them, but they'll have to do."

"What are you up for then?" I asked.

"Me? Not up for anything. Anyway, this place is all about debt and broken marriages and children and stuff. This is where normal people come to have their lives sorted out when they go a bit wrong. I'm more of a criminal court sort of girl. Stealing and fighting and pissing in alleys and getting too drunk, that's me."

I made a noise like a wild pig grunting. Maybe I'd be better off making a run for it, I thought. She sounded too dangerous.

She laughed: "You think that's bad? I've just done five years for manslaughter."

There was a silence.

~

Now. I've given up smoking. Less than sixty seconds ago I stopped. Only I know it, only me, and you now, but I knew first. This time I really am not going to smoke cigarettes again, not one more. And while we're at it I'm going to go on a diet as well; this human life deserves more respect and so does my ego. I'm fed up of being a fat tobacco-addicted fifty year old. I've wasted twenty-five years of my life being fat and the smoking became serious about the same time. But now it's changed.

We didn't buy the cooker then, the five hundred was hardly enough to pay the telephone bill and do some decent shopping. Do you know what it's like to be broke, so broke that you can't fish a fifty pence piece out of your pocket to buy a newspaper? It's not a matter of choice; you just can't do it. How do you think it feels? You've got no power, no control, no effect, no value. At the same time you're angry and you still feel as if you do have these things, these powers, controls, effects and values. You've still got them but the other bastards can't see it because they're so up their own smug arses they don't even see the suffering on their own streets; what chance has the elimination of world poverty got?

~

Same day but 23 minutes past 23 hours. I'm down, I'm blue, I'm sad, I'm unhappy, I'm a miserable old git and you don't want to hear any more of this depressing shit. I'd better stop because otherwise you're going to get fed up and go and watch Brookside, or a repeat of The Sweeney on some satellite channel. Talking about the Sweeney, there was something on the news today about a memorial service for John Thaw who used to be in the Sweeney, then, later, his widow, Sheila Hancock, was on in a programme called Bedtime. Bedtime is like a soap opera except the writing is good and the actors are good and the photography is good, but really it's just a posh soap opera. It goes something like this.

"I'm a really interesting character."

"I'm sure you are dear."

"No, I really am a really interesting character."

"Is it because you're old?"

"You'll never understand me."

"I know."

"I'm not interesting because I'm old, but because I'm old and I don't give a fuck."

Or.

"I've got a troubled relationship with you my son."

"You're fucked up in the head dad."

"I know you don't mean that son."

"Fuck off with the *son*."

"There's no need for that. What's really troubling you my so. . ."

"I accidentally killed my pet mouse when I moved the sideboard this afternoon."

"Oh. Fancy a brew?"

See what I mean? Anyway I'm pissed off. Pissed off? That's much too simple a term to describe how I'm feeling, but it's the closest I can get without inventing new words. Words like bluuuuuhhh and well, bluuuuuhhh, that's the only one word way I can describe how I'm feeling tonight. Maybe it's because, as I told you last night, I'm giving up smoking? But it's not that because I haven't stopped smoking, I lasted about five minutes longer this morning before I started smoking but that's when I started to feel bluuuuuhhh so I thought I might as well carry on smoking for the time being; smoking and eating.

Another thing that pisses me off is psychobabbling acquaintances, and I've come across a few of them today. (I wish I could get out of here.) Do you get them? Or are you one of them? Are you a psychobabbler or are you a psychobabbler's listener? With psychobabblers it's all in the subtext, there's no overt meaning to their words and actions. Have you noticed that? They tell you about their lives; all the little dramas, the same sort of little dramas that they and everyone else including you, the listener, experience and never get a chance to relate. What do they think? That they're the only ones with anything interesting to say? Or do they think that you're so dull that they have to drench you in psychobabble to shut you up?

What else is pissing me off? Other stuff too boring, complicated or sensitive to go into here but it's all pretty much in the same vein, hewn from the same tree so to speak. The psychobabblers are much more interesting. Here's two people talking, see if you can guess which one is the psychobabbler's listener and which one is the psychobabbler, it's not hard.

"How you doing?"

"All right."

"How's the kids?

"Well, you know how I told you about Graham's knee operation?"

"Oh yeah."

"He doesn't have to have it now, because . . ."

"I'm sorry I was in a shit mood yesterday."

"Never mind. Graham said. . . ."

"I'm just pissed off that's all and angry that twat in the pub he really wound me up he always does it and I drunk too much because I was waiting for him for so long and I can't help it but pricks like that wind me up and there they sit on their fat arses in their fat chairs and fuck around on the internet all day and every month they go to the fucking cashpoint that's a joke cash point what's that suppose to mean eh what's that supposed to mean it's not as if I'm lazy or anything but I work bloody hard I do and I go to the bank every month and practically have to beg to extend my overdraft even though I work twice as hard as pricks like him but I'm sorting it out I really am sorting it out I mean because I know

I'm better than them just because they shag the right people and . .
."

"I've . . ."

"and then when the bloke from the burger van came in for a piss I thought . . . ."

"I've got . . . ."

"he was trying it on and so I had to have a go at him because that's how I am I'm like that I like to be . . . ."

"I've got to . . . ."

"straight with people I tell them like it is I do and don't take any bullshit and I'm. . ."

"go"

"never the one who gives up trying I practically run the fucking place single handed none of the other fuckers know how to flush the toilet for themselves. . . ."

"I've got to go."

"What?"

"Sorry, I've got to go, I'm tired."

"Yeah, I was tired last night after the pub and I nearly couldn't handle those . . . . . ."

And so it goes on, and all the twat really wants is to remind the pyschobabbler's listener that he still owes a fiver for his half of the takeaway that he didn't even want on the way home from the pub last night. Why doesn't he just come out with it for fuck's sake?

~

The bankruptcy hearing, I need to tell you more about the bankruptcy hearing but I'm not in the mood at the moment. I'll come back to it, I promise. There's other stuff first.

~

Poor old girl. Poor old girls. Poor young girls. Poor girl. Poor boy. You get the drift. Ken stitched them all up, he didn't care whether they were girls or boys or whether they were young or old or whether they were poor or rich. Ken stitched them all up.

First of all he got them to sign up for some sort of home maintenance package, then he swamped them with top professional workmen and fixed all sorts of problems, problems that had been niggling them, so they were grateful. Then he offered them an enhanced service and they gladly signed because they thought that they would continue to get the same sort of treatment.

Bit stupid really though, it doesn't take much of a mathematician to realise that the sums just didn't add up, but there you go. Anyway, it was the next bit that was the cleverest. He offered his victims (although he preferred to call them his clients) a stake in the business. He invented some kind of pyramid scheme where if they got so many people to sign up they would get an exponential return on the stake money they paid to him up front, that made even less sense mathematically.

If I'd had half as much cheek as Ken, I'd be a millionaire by now. Instead I'm just a sad, broke, middle-aged man. Hang on, no I'm not, I'm a dynamic, intelligent man of around thirty who knows how to use the world's resources and has a great future ahead of him. No I'm not, I'm a speck of consciousness that exists in some unknowable void with memories of things that may or may not have happened a nanosecond or a million years ago.

I am.

t e n

And so it goes on, day after day, death after death, life after life, life after death even. It goes on and I'm still here and you're still in your 'here' and so it will always be. So, get happy. The bankruptcy is still with me even though it's been three years and I'm now relishing the esteemed status of being a discharged bankrupt. The lovely financial establishment has deemed that I can now start operating as a normal person again and borrow money off them and buy goods I can't afford and pay half as much again in interest so they can sit on their fat arses in their leather executive chairs bought from a mail order stationery company out of the profits they make from the interest mugs like me and probably you allow them to take from our pay packets every week or month or whatever.

And so it goes on. Except it isn't going on for that scrap of consciousness that inhabited Ken's stinking body for nearly fifty years.

~

Annie was a godsend, an angel sent from God, a positive goddess with powers that us mortals have no explanation for.

"Manslaughter?" We were still outside the courts in Swansea, me and Annie.

"Yep." She said proudly. "I killed the bastard, except it wasn't manslaughter, it was murder. I did it deliberately, I wanted him dead and I killed him. Life has been sweet ever since."

"Your husband?" I still feel safe even though I'm sitting with a murderess.

"No, I'm a lesbian. It was my boss. My employer."

"What do you do?"

"I'm on one of those crappy government training courses, getting IT literate to provide me with the best chance of employment. Except I'm not on it. I'm supposed to be there now but I couldn't stand it any more so I walked out."

"Oh."

"They were taking the piss. Just give me the fucking money, I'm never going to work again, not for a proper employer anyway. They won't let me and I don't want to. I'm done with this world."

I knew she didn't mean she was going to kill herself but the sadness in her voice under the bravado got to me and I blurted out.

"You're not going to do anything stupid are you?"

"I hope so." She laughed. "But no, never, life is too good."

"Oh. What did you do before, you know, when . . ."

"I was a solicitor."

"A solicitor?"

"Do I look stupid then?"

"No, of course not, it's just you don't look like a solicitor."

"What do you mean? Do I look like a toilet attendant then?"

"No, you look too, too . ."

"Too ugly?"

"God no." What was I getting myself into?

"Too fat. Huh? Too big-headed? Huh? Huh?"

This was getting a bit scary. "Too cool," I said, "yes, too cool, you look too cool to be a solicitor."

Annie laughed. "Got you."

She sprang up from the seat and started dancing around the flower beds and patches of brown and green, clapping her hands above her head and singing: "I'm too cool, I'm too cool . . .", in a soft high voice that haunted like an Indian wedding.

I looked around embarrassed but no one else was paying attention.

"Look at you," she said, sitting down breathing with great

gulps. "Isn't life amazing."

I shrugged.

"Ligthen up man, for fuck's sake, here."

She pulled a spliff from somewhere in her clothes.

"I can't," I said, waving it away, "not here, not now."

"Come on then."

She stood up and held out her hand. Instinctively I put my hand out and with a gentle tug she lifted me off the bench. We continued to hold hands as we walked away through the market and over the footbridge towards the leisure centre and the marina. I kept looking around paranoid but not wanting to lose contact with her soft skin. It was a sensual hand and I was ashamed of myself for thinking the things I thought then. I couldn't remember holding another woman's hand since I met my wife. The intimacy of it surprised me; and it thrilled me.

We passed the marina with its oil-slicked water and its white swans gobbling puffs of white bread and sat on a bench that overlooked the bay. She insisted that I spark up the spliff.

"Tastes nice," I said, "is it strong?"

"Moroccan pollen. Yeah it is strong, very good, but it's not too heavy."

I took three long drags and kept the smoke in my lungs between each one. Annie smoked most of the rest before handing me a small roach.

"Sorry." She said. "Got carried away."

The cannabis enveloped my anxiety and hid it inside a buzz of warm numbness. I relaxed, deciding to enjoy the moment for what it was worth.

"I've got more," she said. "Back at the flat."

"I'm fine," I said, "anyway I've got to drive home later."

"Where do you live then?" She asked.

"A village, Llangennech."

"Llangennith? On the Gower?"

"No, Llangennech, near Llanelli. Do you know it."

"No. Is it a nice village? I used to live in a village. I grew up in a village. Well I say I grew up in a village but really I didn't grow up until I left the village and went to art school."

"I thought you were a solicitor."

"You didn't believe any of that stuff, did you?"

"Um, well."

She laughed.

"So, you're not a solicitor and you didn't really kill anyone. Did you?" I wondered if she really was a lesbian as well.

~

"I met Annie outside the court in Swansea not long after I went bankrupt."

"Oh, bankrupt?"

"Yes, bankrupt, I was made bankrupt."

"Why was that if you don't mind me asking."

What choice did I have? Of course I minded him asking. I didn't want all that stuff about Ken and the business picked over by his magpie detective mind, picking over the bland twigs and rotting leaves; looking, always looking for the gold and the gems. I couldn't let him find my gems.

"It wasn't my fault, just one of those things. I made sure that no one local suffered."

"When was this exactly?"

"Just over three years ago. 1999."

"So, how well did you know her?"

"Um . . . um . . ." I fumbled over my words, not because I felt any guilt, but because I still hadn't got my head around referring to Annie in the past tense. Fucking hell, she was dead. My number was one of those in her mobile phone. This was just a routine enquiry, that's all. It had nothing to do with me and Ken. This copper didn't know anything.

I continued: "Well enough, she was a good friend."

"When did you last see her?"

"A good few months ago. I was in Swansea, so I give her a call, we met for coffee in the Dylan Thomas Centre. Ty Llen."

"What about phone calls, text messages or whatever?"

I had to think for a second. "Yes I suppose so. She rang me a few days ago, but I missed the call, never got around to phoning her back. She did send me a text as well, a day or so after that."

"What did it say?"

"I can't remember. Hang on, it's probably still on my phone."

The detective waited and watched as I retrieved my phone from the kitchen windowsill and pressed the appropriate buttons. It was still there. I read it out

"Need talk meet soon, miss you. Take care. LAX"

"What does LAX mean?"

"Oh that's just the way she finishes all her text messages and e-mails, it means something like Love Annie and a kiss, you know an X."

"E-mails? Have you still got them?"

"Not sure, I tend to delete all my e-mails as soon as I've read them, unless there's some information in them I want to keep, like an address or a telephone number, or a link to a website that I might want to read when I've got the time and the inclination. They might still be in the deleted items folder though, I don't empty that much. Do you use the internet much?" God, I was babbling. What did it look like.

"The e-mails?"

"Oh, yes, hang on, I'll have to switch the computer on."

We were in the middle room of my house, the room where I spend most of my time, working away at my computer, wasting the potential of a human being on some business's website or on a computer program to analyse the amount of material they need over the next month to make another batch of useless widgets to keep the world supply of wongols or whatever topped up to critical mass. I switched the computer on.

There were three or four e-mails from Annie still in the 'kept' folder. Information about artistic events in South Wales including one about a literary debate on the parlous state of Anglo-Welsh writing at Ty Llen that hadn't taken place then. There were another three or four in the 'Deleted' folder, including one about a "Stop the War" march in London. I was glad I had deleted that, wouldn't want the police to think I was some kind of left wing revolutionary, not after all these years of keeping my head down and my nose clean.

The policeman stood up.

"I'm just going to make a phone call," he said. "Please don't touch the phone or the computer. We're going to have to take them away for examination, but we'll bring them back as soon as we can."

When I caught my breath, I started to protest. "How can you take my phone? My computer?"

"Sorry sir, but a woman has been found dead, probably murdered, you understand."

Murdered. It hit me then, of course she'd been murdered.

"Don't worry sir, we just have to eliminate everything, that's all"

"Of course, of course . . ."

~

There are outsiders even among outsiders; there is a camaraderie there too, a feeling of being part of something yet still being allowed to be yourself. But, don't kid yourself, there is just as much shit going on in a colony of so called 'alternatives' as there is in Dallas (the Soap Opera, not the city, or then again, maybe the city as well?), but Sam and Kath were different. You just had to love them.

Kath looked at me through those big dark eyes as if to say, 'look, here I am, a fellow being, another scrap of consciousness, wanting you to acknowledge my existence.'. I didn't like it, but I had no defence.

"OK." I said.

"Come on then."

She grabbed my arm and tugged me on to the bus.

"Sam will love it." She said, her mood a bit too childlike to be healthy.

"Yes, I'm sure he will."

When we got to the Loughor river we got off the bus and walked under the road bridge to where she had hidden the stuff. What a weird girl, I thought, sweet, but weird. It's as if whatever she was before had disappeared, and now she only lived as a part of the Sam and Kath phenomenon, and that was just how she wanted it.

Sam was the same, he was literally her other half. Between them they didn't make one sane person, but when you added them together a new kind of energy was created, a unique energy, the Sam and Kath energy. That's why it was so unusual for me to be alone with her. Sam worked in the mornings and Kath usually slept in until he got home and then he went to bed while she got up and prepared one of her incredibly complex, usually weird-tasting, meals. Then, in the evening they usually listened to records and got stoned.

"Here it is," she said, pulling a bundle of hessian from a dark corner above the normal tide line.

We crawled back to the beach and sat down. She opened the parcel carefully, throwing the damp pieces of material haphazardly all around her.

"Good," she said, "no one's touched them. That's how it should be. Now do you still want to help me?"

I looked at the objects. Maybe I wasn't so sure any more.

"Why aren't you answering?" She asked. "They're perfectly OK. They're not dark or anything. I followed the rituals very carefully. First I had to make them out of new wood, then I had to clean them in sea water and hide them in total darkness for 28 days. Now they're ready for use. See how they glow."

She was right, they did glow.

"Magic." I said.

"That's right – magic"

Away from the beach, on the way back to town on the bus, I watched Kath enraptured by the roughly fashioned wood. I concluded that the objects themselves didn't glow, it was the light from her face that shone on them and made them appear to glow.

"What do they mean?" I asked, more because I was scared for her sanity than out of interest.

"I told you." She said, not taking her eyes off them.

"I know that they're for the secret binding ceremony that you are planning for Sam, but I don't know the details."

"Well, it's a secret ceremony that only a few of the women in my family know about, so I can't give away too much, but this one here, the bear, he's the protector, he symbolises masculine energy, and warmth. He's powerful, but he's a gentle giant."

I couldn't make out which one she meant, they all looked the same to me. I pointed at one I was sure it wasn't and asked: "What about that one?"

"That's both forces, the masculine and the feminine, that's how they come together at the end. Don't you think it's the only one that looks complete. They're all mixed up but between them they can overcome everything. That's what's so beautiful about it."

"Oh," I said.

I think she needed more practice with the penknife.

~

Here's a secret. I wasn't going to tell you this; and as I write, I'm still not sure whether I will - but here goes. I'd better make sure that I keep this secret safe. I mean, if she found out about this secret then things would be different - worse. It would probably mean the end of things.

Thing is, I haven't been completely honest about me and Annie. Thing is, I think I fell in love with her; I mean, what else can it be? I longed for our meetings, pined for her company, gasped when I saw her name in my e-mail inbox and thought about her most of the time. It baffled me and it scared me, and I tried to deny it.

Maybe I haven't made it obvious enough, but her death has left me completely fucked - fucked up inside. There is no reality for me any more; I am an automaton . . . I am an automaton . . . I am an automaton.

I feel better now - more real, just a bit more, but enough to kickstart my return to sanity; perhaps all I needed was to write it down, tell somebody, if only an imaginary reader.

I hope she doesn't read this.

e l e v e n

I'll get back to the stuff about Phil and his mother, and his brother, in a while but at the moment I need to tell you about some other stuff about the background to it all. It's important that you know about the background because then you'll appreciate the story more. Don't ask me why, but somehow, human beings, or more specifically, readers of literature or watchers of films or theatregoers or students of the visual arts or even cricket fans like to know the back story; you know, where the characters come from, what influenced them, that sort of thing. Getting back to the cricket fans for a minute; there's something I've noticed about cricket and its enjoyment thereof. What it is, is that I've noticed that cricket is a fucking boring game, come on, you've got to admit it, it's a fucking boring game – on the surface that is.

On the surface cricket is like this: 23 people (usually men) stand around on a nice piece of grass all afternoon (hopefully in the sun) and chuck a small hard ball around, occasionally hitting it with a piece of specially fashioned wood and even less frequently running back and fore between some strategically placed sticks of some other wood. Afterwards they have tea and once a year or so they all get together and give each other prizes. Isn't that fucking boring?

But cricket isn't really like that, not at its core. Its true meaning is much more prehistoric, more tribal, more clever, more brutal even. What the players really want to do is to clout each other around the head with the bats and throw the ball so hard it breaks the batsman's face into a thousand and one shards of red blood and white bone. I've seen it happening but of course, in true cricket style it was put down as an accident. So if the true nature of humankind (albeit in this example we could call it mankind as opposed to womankind) is to cripple and destroy members of other tribes then what hope is there? What is the fucking point of all this shit we call life?

If that was all it was then yeah, it'd be a complete waste of fucking time pretending to be civilised (whatever that's supposed to mean), but it's not – there's more again. Ok, so playing cricket at a reasonable high level are perhaps a few hundred human beings, not much more than the combined casts of all the soap operas we allow into our homes on a daily basis. Right, so only a few hundred permanently active participants then, but what about the millions who follow the game, the fans? There must be millions right, otherwise how would you explain the extensive coverage the stupid fucking game gets in the media, you know, the newspapers and the television. So these millions of people follow the game and they get to know all about the players, they get to know them as individuals, their batting averages, how good they are at catching balls or throwing them and so on. The cricket fans know a lot more about the players as well, things about their personal life, their families, who they played for when, how much they get paid, how likely they are to lose their temper or to cheat etc.

So cricket, along with many other mainstream sporting activities, is like reality TV, reality TV before reality TV was invented. People, e.g. fans or reality TV watchers, feed off other people's emotions, their weaknesses (did you see Uri Geller eating maggots in the jungle? Idiot!) and they respect other people's strength (as long as they're remote enough – you don't get that kind of respect if you're too close to people). It's like as well as a planet full of food for the physical being there is a parallel world of emotional feeding going and it's a fucking sight to behold if you open your eyes now and again. It's all in the fucking subtext.

~

Phil and his mother and his brother are all in this room. Yes, even though Phil's dead he's still here. He'd still be here even if he wasn't in the tired eyes of his mother, even if he wasn't still in the timid demeanour of his brother. He'd still be here even if there wasn't a photograph of him as a fifteen year old on the mantelpiece, smiling at the camera as if he expected a long life full of love and family and achievement, poor sod. He's in the pauses between the words, this time he's in the words themselves.

"Oh yeah." I say, waiting for Mrs Rita Davies to continue.

"It's Phil," she repeats. "Philip, my Philip." The emotion inside her overloads and has to find a way out; she starts sobbing. There's something about seeing an old woman cry like that, something so sad that you have to think about something else, you have to refocus your attention onto something more banal. I think about whether I'll stop off and pick up a bag of chips on the way home afterwards. I wonder how the chips are in The Savoy since they reopened it after the fire. Savoy chips, if not the best, used to be the most consistent chips in town; you could always depend on Savoy chips.

"We think he was murdered." Paul stands up and puts his arm around his mother. He looks at me with eyes that are helpless and resigned.

"Oh." I say and try to look shocked. Truth is I expected this, well I didn't expect this specifically but I expected something along these lines, I always expect to hear things like this, it protects me from the trauma of shock. It's a useful skill to have because then whatever happens you can always say you're not surprised. The downside is that it's hard to enjoy yourself, to let go, to relax; and everyone thinks you're either a clever bastard or a miserable bastard or both. But fuck them.

"We found some old papers of his. Well we always knew they were there, but Mam only just got to read them. She was clearing out the back room, you know it used to be his bedroom and . . . he used to write you know."

Paul's arm slips from his mother's shoulders like a snake dropping from a tree and he sits down with a sigh. He leans over the side of the armchair and slides a cardboard box out into the belly of the room. I'm not sure what to do but I go over and pick it up, it's heavy, and sit back down with it on my lap. It's full of notebooks and papers covered in what I assume to be Phil's handwriting.

"Have a look," says Paul. "See that big brown envelope – that's it."

Hey, some of this stuff is quite good. I say quite because I'm too afraid to say it's brilliant (which it is by the way) because that means I'd be putting myself up to ridicule if it's not (I am a writer after all). I don't actually say it in the sense of vocalising but I certainly think it. It's fucking brilliant. There's me thinking all these years that I was the talented one in our group, talented in literary terms that is (I couldn't play a guitar for example, my fingers are too short), and all along there was Phil with these jewels tucked away under his bed.

"Well? Well . . . .? Well?"

"Yes," I say, "yes."

"What do you think? Do you agree with us?"

"There's so much stuff, I don't know. I don't know. Most of it looks like fiction, like stories that he made up."

"It's not just stories."

"I don't know."

Paul stands up. "Please do me, us, a favour. Please take them away and look through them. Come back as soon as you can."

I nod. This needs time. Yes, it's a good idea; give myself more time.

"Don't lose them, it's all we've got."

I reassure the old woman and leave with a black bin bag, containing a box full of 30-year-old scribbles.

~

What the fuck was happening to me? I was surrounded by weirdness. Annie, Annie, how long had I known her? Not long enough. I was stunned. I could hardly write. What the fuck was going on?

The house seemed more alien than usual without the constant whirr of the computer fan, and my mobile phone had gone too. I wished I'd protested more but I gave them up too easily. I didn't even ask for a warrant. What would that have looked like?

When she came home I was hiding in the toilet. She shouted up the stairs. I grunted back through the locked door. Eventually I found the courage to go downstairs.

"Do you want a cuppa? Where's the computer gone? Has it broken down?"

"Cup of tea please." I sat down in one of the surviving hard kitchen chairs we'd bought in a junk shop ten years earlier, two of the four had already fallen apart. Buy cheap buy twice.

"Well?"

I went for it: "The police took it."

"What?"

"Don't worry, it's routine. It's Annie."

"What do you mean? Annie? Annie who?"

"Remember that woman Annie that I met in Swansea that day."

"Oh, her."

"Yes."

"Well?"

"She's dead."

"Dead?"

"Yes."

She sat down opposite me. "How?"

"Don't know, they think she was murdered."

"Murdered? What's it got to do with you?"

"They're just checking all her contacts."

"Contacts?"

"Yes, mobile phone records, e-mail records and so on."

"Oh."

"Why did they take your computer?"

"And my mobile phone."

"But you need them for work. How are you going to work?"

"I'll probably have them back tomorrow, it's just a check. They don't mess about with murder."

"What's going on?"

"Nothing."

"Why are you so upset? You didn't know her that well. Anyway, you said she was a nutter. Used to hang around with all sorts of drop-outs and bums. Was it drugs or something?"

"I don't know. I don't know."

"OK, calm down, do you want a spliff instead?"

"As well."

"OK."

~

An installation artist he was. He built/installed a temporary structure by the beach in Llanelli. It was supposed to last a minimum of five years and a maximum of twenty, something about the transient nature of politics, the length of one or of a few parliaments. He said that his art only existed in its time and could never be appreciated afterwards therefore there was no need to make anything permanent. The only permanence that mattered, he said, was the memory. Everything is a memory, he said. He explained it like this: I'm typing these words on a computer keyboard (and I'm not bragging, but I'm pretty quick, a whole word every second or so) and I see my hands moving over the keyboard. But what I'm seeing is only the light reflected off them, however many nano or pica or whatever seconds ago, the event has already happened the moment you sense it in some way.

The installation consisted of the contents of a house, selected at random from all the addresses in Llanelli. The owners were allowed to keep certain personal and sentimental things, which were then substituted by similar items donated by some of the businesses in the town. Of course the owners had to be compensated, everything replaced. They even took the wallpaper and the plaster off the walls, leaving only a shell, but the doors, windows, stairs and roof were still in place. The owners were given a four-week Caribbean cruise while the house was reconstructed.

The artist took all the contents of the house and had them squashed into blocks in a scrapyard, he then poured some sort of weak concrete mix, guaranteed to crumble after a few years (minimum of five, maximum of twenty) and built the blocks into a shapeless mass of about three metres tall overlooking the sea. Then he wound string (perishable especially with all that sea air) around and around until it looked like one of those balls you make with elastic bands when you're bored, only it was a giant ball, more than three metres tall and almost as wide.

I know all this because I saw the video in the visitor centre and because I interviewed the artist for my Internet column.

~

This is me, I can't help it. I'm not going to bother trying to be someone else any more, I'm not who you want me to be, I'm not even who I want me to be, I'm just me and that's that. So how do I make the best of this me that is the real me then? How?

How about if I just carry on being me and doing the things I want when I want. I mean if I fancy a bowl of cornflakes with unrefined sugar and soya milk at midnight then I should just have it, shouldn't I? But what about this other I, the one that doesn't have a death wish, the one who wants to grow old healthily and leave a lasting impression, if only on my family. When I was young I remember thinking that I had things to do, things to say, but that I had time to experiment, to be adventurous, to try different things out. But I know now that that was all a waste of time, because I was me then and I'm still me now. So why bother? I'll tell you why; because if I hadn't bothered I wouldn't have known then would I?

She was like that, Annie I mean. She didn't take any shit off anyone, she was who she was and that was that, except I think that underneath that lunatic exterior she was as sane and straight and bored as the rest of us, but then that was also a part of her so she was still being true to herself so to speak.

I didn't think that she would understand about Annie, how much she meant to me. It wasn't sexual, not overtly anyway. Annie just plugged a gap in the map of my self-actualisation needs. With her around I had no need to question any more, no need to search, no need to pine and moan and grumble and sigh and bury my head in the settee in the middle of the day when I was alone at home. I suppose I must have loved her in some sort of way.

"Probably some smackhead, the investigation is continuing and I'm sure we'll catch the bastard soon, but don't expect too much of a fuss, just one bum gone and one bum going to prison. It happens all the time."

What an insensitive twat, but I just nodded and made a non-committal grunt. The policeman handed me my mobile.

"It's fully charged," he said, "sorry for the inconvenience sir."

~

Phil's papers, where do I start? Some very childish scribbles here, in amongst the brilliance, after all he was only nineteen or twenty when he died, something like that. Here's one:

There's a fire on the hilltop
There's a fire in my heart
And it's always been there
Since the very start

There go by the engines
The engines there go by
But they can't put mine out
So they needn't try

There they go again now
Racing from the hill
They've put out that fire
But mine is burning still

It's signed by Phil and dated 1962, making him twelve or thirteen at the time, so bearing in mind his age it's not too bad. I tip the box on my bed (I'm at home on my own, she's in work and I haven't told her about the papers yet), there's a lot more pieces: poems, mini-bites of philosophy, some half formed stories and some drawings. Phil's work is scrawled on random bits of paper and card, there's a couple written in thick black pen in the margins of old newspapers. He signs and dates everything. As time goes by his writing becomes much harsher, more abstract, almost meaningless ranting in fact. But I'm sure there's something more to all this.

There's a small green-covered hardback notebook, it's sealed with ancient sellotape. The tape crumbles under my scratching fingers. I flick quickly through the book; every page is covered in close neat writing. It fools me at first but when I look closely I can see it's Phil's writing though much more meticulous than the rest and it's written in code. It doesn't take me long to figure out the code either. I'd completely forgotten that we used to share our codes, they weren't very clever but good enough to fool the casual perusal by a parent or more importantly a girlfriend. We used to write notes to each other using the code. As I said it was quite elementary. Here's a section from the notebook followed by a translation.

yadtoziiztwenzotzhtezefcazdnazwaszrehzehszsawzhtiwzmihzniaagzi iztndidzevahbezyrvezllewztubzehzdenethreatzemziizevolzrehziizeta hzmihzenozyadzmizgnigozotzllikzmih

Today I went to the café and saw her. She was with him again. I didn't behave very well but he threatened me. I love her. I hate him. One day I'm going to kill him.

Have you worked it out? It's easy. First you take the last syllable of a word and write it backwards. Then if it's only two syllables you take the first syllable and write that forward hence *today* = *yad* + *to* = *yadto*. For single letter words like I or a, you write them twice as in *ii*. The spaces between the words are *z*'s (you just didn't use words with natural z's in them). No punctuation, no paragraphs except random ones to break up the page but you took no notice of them, it was all in the words. If a word had more than two syllables as in *elementary* you repeated the pattern with the inner syllables so *elementary* becomes *yelerament*. Ok, so it's not perfect, there's a lot of educated guesswork involved but you'd be surprised at how *ylquick* you start to recognise *nomcom* words and mentally turn the *z*'s into spaces.

I have been avoiding opening the envelope that Mrs Davies and

Paul had pointed out to me. It was a large thick brown envelope padded with papers. I think I'll make myself a coffee and a spliff before reading the contents.

~

This is the world I live in. What can I do about it? It's full of idiots. There's an old joke about a boy who on seeing his father marching with a large contingent of other soldiers, proclaims that his father is the only one marching in step. I've always associated that little story with the lesson that if everyone else is doing it one way and you're doing it different then you must be out of step and therefore wrong. I've just had a thought though, what if it's meant to be the other way round, the soldier that's marching differently to the others isn't out of step at all, but he actually is the only one who is in step; in step because the only way to get anything changed is to be different, and if things don't change they will, of course, stagnate and die.

Then there's the angle of the love the boy had for his father, so much so that he was blinded by it, and that's rather cute, isn't it? But, leaving all that aside, the world is full of idiots, don't you think? Fucking idiots, selfish bastards, warmongers and fucking idiots.

Ken is a fucking idiot, that's not to say he's stupid, although he obviously is; he's too dangerous to dismiss with a glib phrase, even if it is true. He keeps going on at me about her, even though they've hardly met. He says it's because I'm obviously unhappy and he thinks that I don't know how lucky I am.

"I know where you're coming from," I said, "and I think that, considering how you became a widower so young, you've coped very well, but it's not about that, me and her are fine. We understand each other. There's no problem, all right."

"You're a bigger fool than me if you think you understand the ladies. They're not there to be understood, you've just got to know how to play their game. It's a simple set of rules really. Now, if I were you . . ."

"Shut up, I told you didn't I."

"OK. Now look at those two over there. A nice pair of uncomplicated girls about town. How about it? You must be tempted."

I looked over. There were two women in their late twenties, too much make-up and too much flesh showing for me, but you get used to that on a weekend night in Ken's club.

"I'll call them over."

Before I could stop him, he gestured with his index finger and the two young women toddled over to the table we were sitting at.

"I only popped in to tell you I can't make next weekend." I said. But I thought, and to see how you measure up for your coffin you twat.

"Aw," he said, "I should have known."

Yes, I thought, you should have known. Over all the years I've known you when was the last time I went on one of your dirty weekends to Amsterdam. Never, that's when. Why the fuck would I want to waste such precious time listening to your bullshit and wanking-off your ego. No fucking thanks.

The girls sat down at the table. Ken waggled his finger again and a barman came over to take an order for drinks.

I didn't want to, but one of the girls was actually quite attractive under all that greasy slap, and I thought, well I'm here now, so I ordered a pint.

Of course, I couldn't enjoy myself because for one thing, I didn't like the company, and for another I didn't like the company. A few more pints would have helped, but I had the car parked a couple of streets away.

"Well, fuck off home then you boring bastard."

I said ta-ra to the girls and ejected myself from the building with a great sense of relief. Not yet. I wasn't ready yet to kill the bastard.

t w e l v e

"Cadw pethau'n taclus yw'r allwedd i lwyddiant" Now my Welsh isn't brilliant but that's the theme of a dream I had last night, it means "Tidiness is the key to success." I would add perseverance and innovation because otherwise you can get obsessed with tidiness per se and live your life as a cleaning machine.

Why do we have to know the reason for everything? Why can't we just meander our way tidily through our existence taking the fruit when it's offered and respect each other and all the other elements of life on this planet? I'll tell you why, it's because there are other forces at work, evil forces. On a philosophical level evil is the tendency for destruction, like the Hindu god Shiva there is a force that's only mission is to bring everything to an end. This is necessary because if nothing ended then nothing could begin; as soon as something is created it must eventually be destroyed. This in itself is not evil; it is our reaction to it that is evil. Evil only exists in the hearts of humankind.

This doesn't mean that you just have to roll over and die at the first sniff of the tiger's fangs. You have to fight it; you have to be a warrior of the light. The problem with humankind is that we are very stupid and tend to translate this inherent need to fight, to survive, into a physical thing bristling with bullets and poisons, but that's just making it evil.

There are people like that, people who are, knowingly or unknowingly, predominantly agents of death and destruction, I've met one or two of them. It doesn't mean they can't change, be redeemed so to speak, and become instead agents of light and life; all it takes is the will. That's why I suppose I tend to ignore the extremes and try to find a path down the middle where I will do least to unbalance the universe that I live in. Notice that I said 'the universe I live in', not the actual universe, not the shared universe we all inhabit, although if I was honest I'd have to admit that even my universe, my personal universe, touches on that great shared universe and all the little lives that inhabit it. So when I say I like to flow down the middle I don't mean the middle in terms of the shared universe, i.e. the norms of whatever society I happen to be living in, in this incarnation, but the norms of the universe as I see it. Saying that, there are certain norms that we all must share otherwise there is only death and destruction and thus no life and thus no universe, shared or otherwise. I'm digging myself in deeper here, aren't I? I'd better stop before you get pissed off and fuck off. Please don't, fuck off I mean, you've come this far, it must be halfway by now. (Though I don't know that for sure because I haven't finished telling you the story and you know how stories are, they can take unexpected twists that drag them on for ages, or they can come to abrupt ends.) Anyway, it's easy for you to check how far into this story you are: all you've got to do is take a peek at the last page in the book without looking at the actual words of course, make a mental note of the last page number and then deduct this page number from it. If the answer is the same as this page number then you're more or less exactly halfway through the story. If the answer is less than this page number then you're over halfway through the story, and if the answer is more than this page number then you're less than halfway through the story. So what have you go to lose, eh?

"I'm half doing it to please myself and half doing it to please other people, more specifically the critics and those people and institutions that pay money for art."

Thus spoke Malcontent Buggeredup (not her real name of course). She lives in a shed in the bottom of her ex-husband's garden in Tenby, while he (her ex) lives a hundred yards away in the house with his second wife and three children, one of whom, a stroppy ginger girl of thirteen, is Malcontent's, or Malbug's for short.

While I was in Tenby I thought of Greta, the girl I begged off all those years ago with Jimmy, the scally from Birmingham. I asked Malbug if she knew anything of her.

"Nah, don't think so. Was she straight?"

"Just about," I said, "but she was quite young, so I don't know how she turned out."

"Did you shag her then?"

I'd gotten used to her directness by then so it didn't faze me: "No, it never came to that. There was only one girl for me that year, that was the year I retired from all that."

"Retired or took a break?"

I blushed; she got me.

This interview took place a couple of weeks after the bankruptcy hearing I didn't go to, the time I met Annie. I hadn't done anything active with Annie by then but the thought must have been there, because I blushed.

"Were you in love with the lovely Greta?" She asked.

"In love, no, of course not."

"Why do you still think of her after all this time then?"

"I don't know. Associations. Tenby. I don't know."

"Oh!"

"You're the interviewee." I said uncomfortably. This one had a knack for peeling onions.

"Don't mind me, it's a habit – and a skill."

"How do you mean?"

"I'm a bit of a witch as well," she said. "White of course. I have a certain knowledge of these things, certain powers."

"A witch?"

She looked at me silently, she was obviously trying to freak me out but not in a nasty way, there was a clean devilment in her eyes.

"A white witch?"

"Of course," she said. "What other colour would I be?"
"I don't know, black?
She laughed. "How could I be a black witch and be this happy?"
I laughed.
"That's the first time you've done that for a while."
"What?"
"Laugh."
I felt my laughter muscles sag.
"It's all right." She said. "People come and go. We all come and go. There is only one truth, one reality. You have to find equilibrium, a path through the Maya. You will. This too must pass."
I nodded.
She reached behind her and retrieved a small painting – a picture of a woman sitting on a bench. I gasped with astonishment. It was Annie, a younger, less troubled Annie and she was sitting on a bench.
"You know her?" The witch asked.
"I'm not sure, it looks like a woman I know."
"Annie." She said.
"How do you know?"
"Annie is a famous character in West Wales. She's travelled these roads for many years. She is a seeker. Sooner or later all true seekers turn up outside my shed. But I sense something is wrong. What is it?"
"Annie's full of life." I said.
Malbug sighed and went quiet.
"Are you all right?" I reached out my hand towards her in a gesture of sympathy. She grabbed it, held it tightly and looked into my eyes.
"Like I said, all things must pass, Annie, you, me, this world even – in time."
She let go of my hand and held the painting out to me.

"Take it." She said. "I can see that Annie means a lot to you. And don't worry. Your troubles will resolve themselves. You have started on the journey back. Don't despair. Remember – this too must pass."

I left the shed in a daze; I don't remember the drive back to Llangennech. There was no one in when I arrived home. She was still in work. I put the painting on the kitchen table, sat opposite it and stared at it for a long time. The painting was in a simple style, no fussy detail, just the necessary coloured marks and scratches that brought the essential energy of the subject clearly in focus. After about an hour of quiet contemplation I hid the picture behind the filing cabinet while I thought about what to do with it.

"What's up?" She said. As soon as she walked through the door she sensed my mood.

"It's been a strange day," I said. "I met a witch."

"Me too." She said. "Maybe I should say I met a bitch."

"The world is full of bitches," I said.

"What do you mean a witch?"

"Just a crazy artist."

"Oh yeah."

"Yes. I think I'll pack it in. It's not worth the effort. I've spent a whole day travelling and interviewing and now I've got to write it up and ftp it up to the website. It's not worth it for a few poxy quid."

"I thought you loved doing it."

"I did, but I'm getting fed up with it all, I need to concentrate on making proper money. It's not fair that you have to work in that place."

"Oh, I'll be all right. Did you make food?"

"Shit – no."

"Never mind. We'll get a Chinese. What do you fancy?"

"Not bothered."

~

Do I know you? Do you want to be in my book? Do you have a choice? Who are you? Are you that person who sometimes avoids looking at your reflection in the mirror so that you don't carry that image that challenges your self-perception around with you? Or are you a blind narcissus who smiles at your own reflection, even though you can't really see it? I suspect that you are a bit of both and, depending on the way your biorhythms or whatever are, you are currently leaning more towards one or the other. Is that the balance Malbug talks about? Is that even valid? Why should balance be the good guy anyway?

~

Right, it's now again. I need to stand back and examine the whole thing so far, even if you don't. This is how it goes.

Like a normal human being of fifty years old I've had a longish life filled with experiences. Some of these experiences are better than others in memory, though looking back, it's sometimes the bad experiences that are the most memorable. Like the time a mate of mine fell out of a tree. He could easily have died but instead I still carry that surreal image of him falling about thirty feet through the branches and landing with a squeal on the bank of the river in Dafen Park.

Thing is, things have happened lately – over the past couple of years – that have changed the way I perceive the other things that have happened during that half a century and all this is just my way of making sense of it all. I don't know but I suspect that this account will become an important historical document one day. It's important that I get it all down now, even in this jumbled up way. I might not get another chance.

So, there's the timeline: Born late nineteen fifty one. It's now late two thousand and two. In between lives have happened. They've begun and they've ended. It's not very long is it? It's doesn't seem to be very important either, does it? But as I've told you before there's other people involved, innocent people if you like, and I owe it to them to tell the truth.

These are the bare facts. Nineteen Sixty One – The Three Bears. Less than ten years later Phil died. Zoom forwards (or should that be Pan?) to now and I killed Ken. In between other things happened and when you come to think about it, it was all inevitable really. I should have seen it then, right at the beginning, perhaps I did but blanked it out, buried it until I could cope with it all – this vast vault of unknowing, this immeasurable space between the back of my eyes and my consciousness.

So, I went bankrupt three and a half years ago, I met Annie about that time. She died. I pandered to Ken's ego for most of that time, and most of my life before that if truth be told. Then about a month ago, I killed him. There are a lot of reasons why I killed him. When I've finished this I'll read it slowly and carefully looking for clues and then perhaps I'll come to a conclusion, but at the moment I'm not sure why I did it. Don't get me wrong; I don't regret it. I know it was the right thing to do – absolutely. Perhaps there's more clues in my past, my history, my story.

~

You know those game shows on television where people win money and the presenters ask them what they're going to do with it? Well, I'm surprised that more of the winners don't say they're going to pay off their debts. Surely that's the first thing you'd do if you got a windfall like that?

Look at me talking. That's not what I did.

I get the money to pay off my debts and a bit extra to do up the house, but it's not really enough so I end up not paying off all the debts, perhaps I've grown attached to the feeling of being in debt, perhaps it keeps me on my toes.

Anyway, the point is that, even though I should feel all relieved, like all my karma's gone and I've reached some sort of debt-free nirvana, as soon as I take another breath the burden is increased again.

What can I do to be free?

"What?" She said.

"Nothing, I didn't say anything."

"Oh, I thought you did, never mind."

"What did I say?"

"Mumbo-jumbo, the sort of nonsense you usually say when you talk in your sleep."

"I wasn't sleeping."

"It must have been me then."

"You weren't sleeping either."

"Might have been."

"You were reading."

"Might have nodded off."

"Is there something on your mind?"

"Bit worried about money again. Without money you can't do anything, can't pay the bills, can't have a holiday, can't do anything. Perhaps I'll get a second job."

"Not that again, you know you come home knackered after the one you've got."

"Sometimes you've got to try a bit harder."

"Is that a dig at me again?"

"I don't know why you can't sort it out, everyone's got to do something."

"Yeah, I know, you've got to get up in the morning, and you've got to go to bed in the night, and you've got to do something in between."

"There's nothing wrong with that."
"It's not as if I don't do anything, not everything has to have a price. Some things you just need to do."
"Go to sleep."
"You started it."
"No I didn't, you were talking in your sleep."
"No I wasn't."
"Yes you were."

t h i r t e e n

"Music is easy, it's just bloody hard work."

"Explain yourself."

"Well, it's just like painting or writing or whatever, it's all in the composition. It's the composition that's the hard work."

"What about jazz?"

"What about jazz?"

"Jazz isn't composed, it's improvised."

"Is it? Yeah well, but only according to a composition of rules, otherwise it would just be a cacophony."

"What are you getting at? What's your point?"

"Music is easy – easy."

"But you just said it's hard work."

"Hard work is easy – for some. And if you're lucky enough to be one of those people who find hard work easy then you've got it made – it doesn't mean you're an artist."

"So are you saying that musicians aren't artists?"

"Not quite, though they're more practitioners, craftspeople if you like."

"John Peel played my record."

"John Peel?"

"Yes."

"Played?"

"Yes."

"Your record?"

"My record."

"John Peel played your record?"

"Yes, he did."

"Is that good then?"

"What do you mean, is that good? Of course it's good. It's John

Peel I'm talking about now."

"But he'll play any . . . ."

I should interject here dear reader before you get too confused, (fuck I'm getting confused and I'm writing it). The dialogue above is part of the transcript of the recording that accompanies the latest work of the self styled "Prophets of Performance Art" or POPA, otherwise known as Dant and Eck (otherwise known as James Davies and Alastair Francis) two middle-class boys who met at Gorseinon College in the mid-nineties and have since cut a trench through the parallel trammels of British art with their often bitingly acid creations. (I'm getting better at this bullshit. Aren't I?)

I didn't get much out of Dant and Eck in the traditional Artist/Interviewer sort of way. They each presented me with an A4 computer-printed sheet that included a complete biography starting at their births (no shame). They also sat me down in a quiet room and left me alone for the twenty-one minutes, ten seconds and two frames (that's frames in the video technology sense) that it took for the dialogue on the mini disk to end and the artwork to fade to black.

I was none the wiser but I'll describe the artwork anyway, perhaps you'll be able to work it out. It was a tapering spherical construction on a pole, like one of those disgusting pillars of meat you see in kebab shops. (Don't ask me what meat it is, I've never had it, I'm a vegetarian.) Anyway, the thing rotated as they do, but very slowly. The thing, or to give it its proper name *John Peel Played My Record*, was set on a round plinth in a pagoda-like structure with various sizes colours and types of lights, conventional and laser, placed around the room on the walls, ceiling and floor. The pagoda was constructed of what looked like balsa wood with a seemingly random array of broken sections that allowed the light to fall on the lollipop within.

According to the artists' leaflet you had to regard the art as a co-dependency between the solid object, the visual and aural experience, and your position in relation to it. There were no hidden meanings the leaflet said, the work spoke for itself and that was that. I still didn't get it but it was rather pretty.

~

Me: "Hello."
I walk into the small living room.
My Mother: "Oh, it's you."
She shuffles in the nylon-covered armchair.
Me: "All right?"
My Mother: "It's a bit late for you. I am honoured. That's twice
               in a week.
Me: "Oh, I haven't come to see you, just to pick up the
               tobacco."
My Mother: "It's on the mantelpiece. Do you want a cup of tea?
She starts to lift herself off the chair.
I walk over to the mantelpiece and pick up the tobacco.
Me: "No."
She lowers herself back into place.
My Mother: "Oh!"
Me: "When was the last time you remember me having a
               cup of tea off you?"
My Mother: "No. Don't talk soft."
Me: "It must be twenty years at least."
She sighs.
Me: "I don't drink tea here because I like milk in my tea
               and I don't drink cow's milk."
My Mother: "Don't' start."
Me: "All right."
My Mother: "Coffee then?"
Me: "Nah, it's all right, thanks."
I'm sitting down by now, in the other floral-patterned armchair.

My Mother:	"Have you got work?"
Me:	"Yeah, enough, not like I'm making a fortune or anything."
My Mother:	"Any news?"
Me:	"No, not really."
My Mother:	"What do you mean, not really?"
Me:	"It's nothing big, nothing important."
My Mother:	"Oh, go on."
Me:	"It's Phil, do you remember Phil?"
My Mother:	"Phil?"
Me:	"You know, my mate when I was younger, long hair, played a guitar."
My Mother:	"Guitar?"
Me:	"Yeah, he was really good too."
My Mother:	"Oh, Phil, yes, the one that died."
Me:	"Yes."
My Mother:	"Was it drugs? I can't remember."
Me:	"No, a car accident."
My Mother:	"Oh yes, I'm thinking of the other one."

I get up again and walk into the small galley kitchen where I know I will find an ashtray. "I think I'll have that coffee. Do you want anything? Don't get up; I'll do it myself."

"Nothing for me thanks."

I nod acknowledgement but of course she can't see me because she's still in the living room. She doesn't seem to need an acknowledgement anyway because she turns the sound up on the television – it's Emmerdale. Of all the soap operas on all the television channels Emmerdale is the only one I deliberately avoid, I even watch the odd episode of Family Affairs and sometimes up to half of Night and Day, but never Emmerdale. I don't really know why.

The cup needs a wash and the coffee is decaffeinated. I make it anyway. I'll try anything once, or sometimes more than once. I won't enjoy it but what the hell it's hot and sweet.

When I sit down again with the coffee she turns the sound down again.

"Don't do that. I don't mind. You carry on."

"I'm recording it anyway but I'll leave the sound on low. I wanted to ask you a favour. Would you mind?"

"Depends what it is."

"Don't worry, it's nothing really important. It's just some insurance papers I need to sort out, but it'll be all right."

"I hate paperwork. But let's have a look. What's the problem?"

"I'll have to get the tin."

She returns half a cup of coffee and an interminable Emmerdale scene later with a large biscuit tin and a larger cardboard box to hold the overflow.

"I think everything's in here," she says, yanking the top of the biscuit tin. "It's the older stuff in the box."

It turns out that she's trying to save a pound a month on her house and contents insurance by amalgamating them into one new policy. I help her with the sums and confirm that she is doing the right thing and in fact she can save an extra pound a month by changing the cover to exclude her grandchildren's, (and my nieces and nephews) bicycles. There's a fifty pound excess on each one anyway and they're not worth that.

I stand up to go.

"You're not going already? Sit down for a bit. There's no rush is there?"

"Need to get home, get on with it. I've got things to do, people to see."

"What were you saying about your friend Phil?"

"Oh it's nothing."

"Come on, sit down."

I sigh and sit down again.

"Do you know his mother? She's older than you though, in her eighties I think. Rita Davies."

"Rita Davies? Yes, she used to live on the estate, when we first moved in. But she wasn't here long. Moved to town somewhere. It was a long time ago, but I remember you telling me about her before, you know, after the funeral. Now her husband's sister was married to that man who worked on the bins, you know your old friend Ken's uncle, his father's brother in fact."

"Ken's uncle was a binman, I never knew that."

"They never got on, Ken's father and his brother. But Ellis was a good man, that's the one who worked on the bins, not Ken's father, can't remember his name but he always gave me the creeps. It's a wonder Kenneth turned out as well as he did with a father like that."

I got up again.

"You still haven't told me about Phil. Is it something to do with his mother? Is she dead?"

"No, not at all." I sat down again. "It's just she thinks that Phil was murdered."

"Murdered? Poor thing. It's hard losing a child, especially that young. But it's a long time ago."

"I know."

"Why is she thinking like that now? And what's it got to do with you?"

"I saw her the other day. I went round to her house. She gave me a box of papers that Phil had left."

"Oh."

"I haven't read them properly yet."

"What are you going to do? What are you going to tell her?"

"Do you think he could have been murdered?"

"Why are you asking me?"

"I don't know, you're the one who asked me to talk about it."

"Well they are a strange family, not on Rita's side but on the other side. I'd rather not know about things like that though. Any other news?"

~

I'm sitting here in the cold writing this. I don't know if I can write when I'm this cold – I've never tried it before. It's not only cold but it's late, yet I feel I have to get this down while the feelings, if that what they are, are fresh and raw. Perhaps the cold will help then; perhaps the cold will help to expose that necessary rawness. It's not just my physical attire that's cold and raw, it's my feelings (if that what they are?) that are cold and raw. In fact I would go so far to say that this is a cold and raw portion of my life to date.

It's not my fault; I've finally worked that out. I've never done anything really 'wrong' in the sense that I need to be punished for it. Sure I've made mistakes but they are usually because I'm either genuinely mistaken or because the effort of dealing with life has become so hard that I have had to take some sort of action to alleviate the pain. So survival then, and surely that's the prerogative of every living creature – to ensure its own survival. So, not 'wrong' then.

Thing is, I'm still avoiding opening the brown envelope from amongst Phil's ancient scribbles. For one thing I don't want to open it until I can do it the justice it deserves. These are precious objects; they are all that's left of a person who could have gone on to make a difference in the world. I wonder if that is what this all about? My desperate need to communicate with you; is it all a desperate need to compensate and somehow give value to young lives lost?

I was right when I started this, I can't write when I'm cold. Or is it because it's late and I'm tired. Whatever – it's time for bed.

Nos da.

~

Although it was too cold last night to write, I'm glad I made the effort, otherwise those thoughts would have been lost forever. Not that that's very important in the endless cube-continuum of existence, where countless billions of thoughts, feelings and sensations go unrecorded every infinitely small nano-second, unless you count the Akashic records, where everything that has ever been, still is, and probably where everything that will ever be, is already. But the thoughts I'm talking about are relevant to this story therefore they are important in that context. And that's what it's all about isn't it – the context, the lines we follow through the Maya so that we can experience some semblance of a coherent existence.

It's been a week now since I left Mrs Rita Davies's house with that box in my arms and I still haven't opened that envelope. I'm still working my way through the rest of the box though.

~

She's been acting very strangely lately. She's kind of distant, kind of less sharp than usual, less perceptive. Don't get me wrong I'm appreciating it, because she doesn't nag me about whether I've had a shave or not or whether I've put the bins out or whether I managed to do any work today. I've been campaigning for more of this laid-back attitude to life ever since we met and I think I've scored some little victories along the way. For example, she stopped ironing bedsheets quite early on in our relationship, it took a few more years to chuck the underwear unironed into the airing cupboard and a few more years again for T-shirts to join the club (they have to be folded though, to minimise the creases).

But lately, she's been too good, too laid back, too loving in a quiet sort of way. I can't help but feel I'm being slightly patronised. Now I can be a very jealous guy, and jealous guys are nothing if not detectives, and I take pride in my intelligence too. So, obviously, when my partner of thirty years starts acting as if my foibles don't matter any more well I've got to wonder why haven't I? And of course I've got to investigate.

It wasn't premeditated (I was just looking for my driving licence) but here I am going through her letter-rack, the one that she keeps on her desk in what she has recently taken to calling "my bedroom", with the emphasis on the "my". As usual, there's a couple of half written letters to some old college friends of hers, a post-natal appointment card for when our youngest son (who's now 21) was a few weeks old, a two-year old postcard from one of her mother's holidays in Bournemouth or Eastbourne or somewhere (hang on, I'll have a closer look, no, it's neither, it's the Canadian one. There's many other objects that can be loosely connected with correspondence and half a ripped index card with a name and telephone number scribbled on it. Neither the name nor the number are familiar to me. I'd better commit them to memory, better not write them down, don't want to leave any evidence of my snooping lying around.

But what will I do with them even if I manage to remember them? Do I ring the number and ask to speak to the name on the card or what? But what then? It's no good, it won't work, as I've said before I've watched too many soap-operas to think I'll get away with such subterfuge. Anyway, perhaps I don't want to know.

~

"But there must be someone responsible for it all."

Sam was in one of his spiritual moods. He often started conversations about such esoteric things, even though he had no education to speak of, in another life he would have been a doctor of philosophy.

"Look into this light," he said, "you can see forever."

I laughed but took the light off him anyway. This was one of those lights the council leave lying around as warnings of roadworks or obstructions or something, picked up by Sam or one of his housemates on the way home from the pub no doubt. Yes, Sam had got it together to move into a house, shared with a few other boys, a bit older than him, but then he was much more mature than you'd expect a sixteen year old to be.

"Just stare into it." Sam said.

I stared into the light. Maybe it was the drugs, or maybe it was some headfuck of Sam's but I found myself encased in amber light. Then the light stopped being a specific colour and was just light. The light oozed into every cell of my being, every nerve end, every molecule and I felt as if I was floating along a tunnel. Maybe tunnel isn't such a good word to describe it, because tunnel suggests some kind of limitation; this experience was not defined by its limitations.

"See what I mean." Sam said. "We've seen the light."

"You're not going to go all religious on me are you?"

"It's got nothing to do with religion, what I'm talking about is spiritual. It's got nothing to do with men poncing around in frocks."

"I know."

"Talking about frocks, hang on."

Sam got up from the floor and opened the wardrobe. He took out a long dress made from a dark satin material, covered in swirls of gold and silver.

"I made this." He said. "Me, I made it."

"Have you been keeping secrets?"

"It's not for me, it's for Kath."

"Kath?"

"Yes, you know we're going out now."

"No, I didn't know. You've only known her a couple of weeks."

"I know but I know that she's the one. She's the one I'm going to spend the rest of my life with."

"Oh."

"It's cool isn't it?"

"I didn't know you could sew."

"I can knit too. It's great, you should try it."

"Fucking nutter."

~

She said to me: "Are you ready?" The old woman on the bus stop, said to me: "Are you ready? I've done my bit you see, I lived through the war, lost a brother and an uncle I did. You young people better be ready, because your turn will come."

I was on my way to the Technical College. This was in the year before the big year, sometime in 1970, might even have been at the beginning of 1971.

I nod. This woman is telling me one of the most fundamental philosophical rules, I call them rules, but they're not written down or anything, they're just a natural consequence of the forces that drive human beings. I know what she means, she means that everybody has to overcome the trials of life and that's all it's about really.

"We thought we had it all right. The Great War had come and gone, I lived through that and so did most of my family, we thought we had it made, but then along it came. Men are evil. You want to remember that."

I'd thought about this sort of thing many times, but I'd come to the conclusion that the battles we, that's my generation, will fight, will be inner battles, battles of the minds, battles to change people's attitudes, to force them, if necessary, to become more tolerant and understanding of difference. That's one of the reasons

I refuse to cut my hair, or conform to normal standards of dress; I am a warrior, I have a mission.

"I know what you're thinking," she said, "but you're wrong. The world hasn't changed, it can't change, it's only the world; you have to be strong; you have to be a survivor."

She is on the ball this one, but she makes me feel uncomfortable. Am I ready? I don't know. My peace of mind she spoils.

"I know what you're thinking." She said.

I smiled at her

"You'll be all right," she said.

The bus arrived.

fourteen

The Three Bears, I just had that fucking dream about The Three Bears. After decades of freedom from it, it has returned. Except it's not exactly the same, in fact it's not at all the same, in fact it's not The Three Bears dream at all. It's got three characters in it, and me. The characters are mucking about on a dance floor. The room is empty otherwise. It's the Glen Ballroom in Llanelli at the cusp of the sixties and the seventies. There is a large disco ball turning on the ceiling, reflecting the light from the coloured spots, the only light there is. The three characters are Ken, as he is now, his daughter Lucy, when she was a girl of about ten, and Mike, my old friend Mike, who drowned before Lucy was born (as he was then, obviously).

I can't work out whether they're fighting or just playing but I'm worried for Lucy who's being knocked about a bit too roughly. I have to go and sort it out; she's a child for fuck's sake. As I approach, Ken turns to face me, he's grinning, inviting me in to the game with his arms. Mike has his back to me and Lucy gets down on the dance floor and performs a screwed up breakdance in time to the music that is playing – *"In the Midnight Hour"* by Wilson Pickett.

I push Ken out of the way and reach for the girl; I've got to help her get up and get out of here. Next to me, Mike turns and grabs my outstretched arm. With irresistible strength he pulls it towards his mouth. I look into his face, it morphs into the face of a hungry wild animal; his teeth are huge and strong. He sinks his teeth into my arm and bites.

I wake up. She's leaning over me in the bed.

"Are you all right?" She asks, with a concerned tone. (I can't see her features very well because it's dark).

"Yes, yeah, I just had a dream."

"You were tossing and turning and shouting."

"I'm sorry."

"Don't be silly, come here."

She sits up and pulls my head onto her lap. She smoothes my hair. "There, there." she says softly. "Ssh, go back to sleep."

"I'm sorry."

"Ssh."

I close my eyes but can't get Mike's face out of my mind. She sings me a song, it's an old Welsh lullaby: "Cwsg, cwsg . . .". It means "Sleep, sleep . . .".

"What's going on?" I ask. Shit, did I say it out loud, I don't want to go there, not now.

"What do you mean?"

"I'm sorry, it's nothing."

"No, come on, what's the matter?"

"Oh, I don't know, I feel like we're not on the same wavelength any more. You're so busy in a stressful job and I'm still trying to earn a proper living, I just get lonely sometimes, when you're in work."

"Ssh, you're just a little bit down that's all. It will pass. Why don't you have a lie in tomorrow?"

"Maybe."

~

Mike in Cardiff 1971, me crashing on the floor in his room. Mike got close with the cough medicine. Mike drowned.

Mike drowned. *"Adam and Eve got drown-ded and who do you think got saved?"* Pinch me, fuck me, slap me what the fuck me, anyway it's all me, I'm the one who got saved. Mike got drown-ded.

The Mike story.

Mike was a person, born on this planet sometime around the middle of the twentieth century. He talked a lot. He talked about photography even though he didn't own a camera and as far as I knew had never used one. He talked about religions, even though he was an atheist. He was an expert on everything but he'd never done anything. I think he was the forerunner of the nerdy couch potatoes of the twenty-first century who learn everything there is from dubious Internet sites or daytime telly, yet Mike's knowledge wasn't dubious, it was always spot on. We never caught him out at all.

Mike devoured libraries. He went every morning and read every newspaper and any magazine that had arrived since the day before. Then he spent a couple of hours browsing the shelves for any sign of any book of any interest that he hadn't then read. He left the television on until the dot and whether he was watching television or reading the books or both, he always had a transistor radio audible from another part of the room.

Mike was a databank and he could be fucking mind-numbingly boring; until he got stoned that was. I don't mean stoned as in smoking cannabis stoned or being drunk stoned. These days they'd probably call it getting wasted or getting fucked off his tits. But never then and never now would any self-respecting druggie talk about their experience as 'getting high'. That's much too poncey and too sixties Panorama a term to use.

Mike used to get stoned on everything and anything, and as long as he got his dose of cough medicine or travel sickness pills or valium or mogadon or pondrax or whatever, he was as happy as a pig in shit. Fuck knows how he managed it; all that knowledge and all that shit at the same time. Fuck knows how he got it together to go and live in Cardiff that time.

He moved back from Cardiff a few months after Gammy died though, as I did. He moved back into his sister's spare bedroom, even installed a television in it for fuck's sake. I visited him there a few weeks before he drowned, that's the last time I saw him, alive anyway. I'm talking late seventies now, around 78, 79. It must have been 78 rather than 79 because I just don't get the Maggie Thatcher vibe and she took power in 1979. Was it that long ago? Fucking hell, I'm living through history; history – what a farce it all is.

Anyway we were in his sister's spare bedroom watching some crap on the telly, some cop show probably, Kojak or something. I mean I was quite old by now, going on for thirty and with a couple of kids growing up quick. Mike hadn't changed much in those seven or eight years since Cardiff. He was still just as much fucked-up, still relying on drugs, but now they were more formalised, mostly dope and valium, sometimes a bit of speed, but very rare. So he had become a little slower, just as knowledgeable but a bit slow, and most of his knowledge was the old knowledge that he regurgitated in more or less a cyclical pattern.

I was ready to go, I had a life to get back to. I stood up and yawned. "It's getting on Mike," I said, "I'd better get back, I've got to get up for work in the morning."

"It's only ten o'clock, hang on for a bit."

I yawned again and hesitated before I answered. "No, I'd better not, I'm knackered anyway."

It was just enough of a hesitation to let him in, so I conceded and sat down again.

"OK then, what's so important?" I said.

"Nothing really, we all need a friend sometimes, I'm sure you're the same."

I sighed but not too noticeably. He was right, I was being selfish, I mean, what else are friends for other than to shovel all your shit into and impose on and never give a fuck about how they feel and . . . . I thought I'd better stop mentally ranting like that or I wouldn't have any friends left, they'd be long gone if they weren't already dead. But he was right, I was being selfish, he obviously needed to talk and all I had wanted to do was fill a bored hour and maybe pick up a bag of Chinese chips on the way home afterwards – that would have killed an evening nicely.

I nodded and smiled at him and waited for him to open up. He'd already made it impossible for me to get away by being so direct. I adopted my psychoanalyst's mode and leant back defeated into his sofa.

"Do you want a cup of tea?" He asked, getting up.

"Why not." Better to stop resisting and get it over with. That's another thing about Mike, he was a pedant, always did things deliberately and carefully and always had a sequence of actions planned out for the next period of time whatever that was depending on the circumstances and exactly what drug he had ingested. If a cup of tea was on the schedule then who was I to argue?

He made the tea, all the while talking loudly at me from the alcove containing a small metal-legged table and a dirty kettle; he had long since turned the room in his sister's house into a virtual bedsit. He came back with the tea, sat on the floor and leant his elbows on the coffee table. His hands were shaking as he stirred the sugar in.

"How's the missus?" He asked his voice trembling. I decided to ignore it (the tremble), I was sure he had already taken the drug that would counter whatever comedown he was on.

"Fine, fine. Everything's fine." That was all I would allow myself. I could have said "great" or "fantastic" I could have said everything was "amazing", because it was, but that was too much information to give to someone who used to be a good friend but wouldn't really qualify as a confidante. Anyway, he was the one supposed to be talking to me, he was the one who needed my psychoanalytical skills, he was the patient, I was the doctor.

"Seen anything of the gang lately?" He asked.

I wouldn't have called our group of friends a 'gang' but realised that despite all his book-gleaned knowledge Mike was really quite a simple soul. Even during that time in the house in Cardiff I'd started to see what a straight he was under the long hair and the layers of drugs.

"No, don't get out much. Young kids and all that. Besides I have to get up early for work and so on." I don't know why I bothered; he wasn't going to take the hint.

"I saw your mate Ken the other day." He said quietly through a mouthful of just-sipped, too hot tea.

"Oh aye," I said, "how was he? I haven't seen him for three or four weeks."

"Don't know, he doesn't talk to me. Grunts a bit, but doesn't talk. He's a stuck up bastard isn't he? I don't know how you and him are friends."

"Oh, he's not so bad; when you get to know him."

"You've known him a long time, haven't you?"

"Yeah, since we were kids."

"You want to watch that one."

"How do you mean?"

"There's something about him, he thinks he's so much better than everyone else."

I knew where Mike was coming from, because I knew how much Ken despised him. Ken didn't like weakness, and he saw Mike as a feeble junkie, and a boring one at that.

"You don't want to take him too seriously," I said, "he's just got some funny ideas about things that's all. It's nothing personal"

"No, I'm not talking about that. It's not that. I just don't think you should trust him. He gets between you and your, your friends and stuff."

If Mike hadn't been so fragile I'd have taken the piss out of him and called him jealous and I think that's what he must have been, I'd noticed it before. There was a time in Cardiff when Ken wanted to come and visit but I had to tell him not to bother because Mike said there wasn't enough room and there was too much going on. He was right, Mike was right, but a more accommodating person would easily have fitted Ken in. He was never any bother and he always contributed more than he should in the pub or the curry house or whatever.

Whatever drug Mike had taken took effect then because his head slumped down between his elbows on the coffee table and he fell asleep. I manhandled him on to the sofa and left him there with an LP of mellow Spanish guitar music on the stereo. I got my chips on the way home and tried to forget about my sad friend.

~

Just before the 'thing' with Ken happened (I say 'happened' and that implies that it was a natural occurrence, like an earthquake or a forest fire, or that it was something that no one had any control over, but that wouldn't be true. This was not a passive happening, this was a happening provoked by a lifetime of random occurrences followed by a conscious decision to 'put things right'.) Anyway, just before the thing with Ken happened, I happened to take a walk along the seafront in Llanelli (they call it The Millennium Coastal Park now), (I didn't actually 'happen' to take a walk. Again, it was a deliberate act designed to achieve something; probably a need to simplify the fucked-up thought processes 'happening' in my head, but I forget the specific reason.).

So, there I was taking this walk, more of a shumble really, what I mean by a shumble is the kind of slow walk you take when you're trying to simplify your fucked-up thought processes and you're not really noticing your surroundings, your environment. So, there I was shumbling along the wet sand near the quiet swell of the sea when I heard the voice of a young woman calling my name. I lifted my eyes from the view of my damp feet and looked around. There were half a dozen people within name-calling distance and I squinted at each one of them to try and identify which one it was who had called my name.

One of the figures, a slight shape situated about thirty metres behind me (in the sense of the direction I had been travelling in) waved its arms around as it walked quickly towards me. I waited until the figure drew closer to me and until I could make it out more clearly in the dimming light that signified dusk. Had I really been staring at my feet for that long?

"Lucy?"

"I thought it was you." She stopped to catch her breath.

"Hello." I said, waiting for her to explain.

"I haven't seen you for ages, that's all. Are you all right? Dad said you've been having a hard time."

"Hard time?"

"Yes. Haven't you?"

"Well, not really, not lately anyway. No."

"Typical."

"Oh."

"Are you going home?"

"I suppose I'll have to, it's getting dark, and colder. Do you want a lift?"

"Oh no. I'm with my boyfriend, he's back there somewhere, playing with a dog."

"I didn't know you had a dog."

"It's not mine, or his, it's just a stray that latched onto us just now."

"Well, I hope you have a nice time, it was good to see you."

"Please don't go."

You know how it is when an attractive girl talks to you, especially one as young as Lucy. You don't want to look at her too closely in case she thinks you're a pervert or something, so I had been avoiding direct eye contact and more or less carried on looking in a general downward direction, but I had to look at her face then in response to her plea. I noticed that she looked tired and pale, her skin had a greyness about it and she looked much older than she was.

"Are you all right?" I asked, not sure whether to offer her the hug that her demeanour demanded.

Her head slumped and she stood there passively. She seemed to be trying to speak but couldn't because of a welling up of emotion. I hugged her anyway; she was cold and bony in my arms, it felt very awkward but she didn't pull herself away, in fact she buried her head in my chest and started to sob, quietly but heavily.

"Ssh. It's all right. Listen, we can't stay here. Let's go to the café. It should still be just about open."

She nodded her head (as much as she could, considering it was buried in my chest at the time. .We started walking up the beach towards the café. She clung on to me as if she would have collapsed on the hard wet sand if she hadn't.

"What about your boyfriend?" I asked. "Won't he be worried?"

"I'm sorry," she said, "he's gone. We had an argument."

"Oh."

The beach café was empty of customers and the staff were cleaning up, but they didn't seem to mind us hugging our black coffees and nibbling at the jam doughnuts I'd bought out of guilt, thinking that coffees alone would not justify our occupation of the table. After a couple of nibbles and a couple of sips Lucy was able to speak again.

"Everything's gone wrong." She said. "My whole life is falling to bits. I don't know who else I can talk to. You've always been a nice man and I know my father's a friend of yours but I've got to tell someone."

I listened.

~

Joel Palmer likes to think of himself as an artist who is more radical than the most radical of the radical artists practising in Britain. He didn't go to art school; he's never had a good review in his life. All he has going for him is his immense self-belief. His work, if you can call it work, is to collect artefacts and found items and put them on display. He doesn't change anything, at least in any kind of permanent way. for example he might collect all the plastic soft drinks bottles, the kind you see spilling out of bins in the town centre or discarded in teams at the edge of the local rugby field after a match, and throw them haphazardly into a carrier bag he might have found stuck in a hedge on the way home from the shops. He'll then hang the carrier bag from any convenient nail or off the back of a chair, or he might even just throw it on the floor in one of his frequent self-funded exhibitions in the living-room of a half-built house or the back room of a quiet pub.

"There is complexity in the simple everyday objects that infest our consciousness," he says, "and there is simplicity in the most complex things. The trick is not to let other people affect you. You are what you are. You have value to yourself and that's the only kind of value that's got any value."

I suspect that Joel is not telling me the whole story but I might as well go along with it, you never know.

He points to one of the exhibits in the back room of the pub in Station Road, Llanelli. It's an unsmoked cigarette. "I found this outside the chemist's in the Avenue in Llwynhendy." (the Avenue is a row of shops; Llwynhendy is a suburb of Llanelli). "It was not in a packet and it wasn't wet even though it was raining."

You have to believe him – he's so earnest.

"I was going to smoke it," he says, "but I forgot, and by the time I found it again in my cutlery drawer, I'd given up smoking."

He lights a roll-up as he speaks.

"I've started again now." He said. "Do you know how many

chemicals there are in the average manufactured cigarette?"

"Lots." I say, shrugging my shoulders. As a smoker who gets nagged occasionally I have heard the statistic.

"Yeah, over two hundred I think, can't remember the exact amount now. But there's loads, loads of complex chemicals in such a small simple thing."

I sort of get his drift but I'm not sure if I would call it art. I mean if he gets famous there will inevitably be times when he can't be there to explain his work and then it will just be a discarded cigarette, won't it?

~

Sam and Kath are babes in the wood. Hippie-gothic-babes. Drug-taking-hippie-gothic babes in the wood. Naïve hippie-gothic-babes. They are confused by life, tragically confused.

~

Annie lives in a flat in Swansea. Even then, I couldn't tell her things. Things I can't talk about. And now, I can't talk about other things. Annie lives in a flat in Swansea.

~

Phil a hero? London 1969 was full of heroes. Fucked-up heroes. Fucked up-Phil. This place sits on my head like a too-heavy helmet, yet I have done the best I can. I couldn't have done it any better. But I'm still here.

fifteen

Waiting for dusk. I sit here in the middle room of the house in Llangennech waiting for dusk so that we can calibrate our new outside light complete with 110 degree Passive Infrared Sensor. Although it's only twenty past five in the afternoon dusk is definitely on its way at speed. But just when is dusk?

Day fuses into night at a speed that is both so slow it's unmeasurable by any natural human attribute and so determined that there is no human power that can decelerate its pace. What immensely powerful forces exist in nature. We, the current infestation the planet has to deal with, have no impact on its destiny, no toxin it can't survive. Sometimes you have to lift yourself out of the mundane to be able to appreciate it all the more, for in the mundane lies the true meaning of life. In the history of the planet, our sun, the galaxy, and the universe(s) the entire human story is mundane, so if there is a purpose to this life it has to be hidden in the mundane.

There is real beauty in these words even though they are as mundane as mundane gets and there is real beauty in the movement of your eyes across the page or the computer screen or the digitised audio representation or any other as yet unforeseen media that conveys these words to your consciousness.

It's thirty-one minutes past five now and I still don't reckon it's dusk yet. I reckon it will be when you can't pick out someone's features from more than four or five metres away. If that's dusk, then what's this? Pre-dusk? Or does dusk include this period and a period after the "pick out someone's features from more than four or five metres" rule? So dusk is not a discrete event, it is the blending between black and white, between light and dark.

I'm going to do some drawing now, in preparation for the

painting I'm going to do for the cover of this book – "The Three Bears". What I have in mind is a painting of the three bears along with a ten-year-old boy, i.e. me. Two of the bears will be in the background and looking relatively harmless, like well-fed brown bears perhaps. In the foreground the third bear, the biggest of course, is standing on its hind legs and towering over the boy who is dressed in yellow shorts and a blue and yellow horizontally striped T-shirt type of garment.

The bear has huge fangs and long dirty claws that are gripped around the boy's arm. It is caught as it dips its head, fangs dripping with goo, towards the gap on the arm between its paws. The boy's expression is at the moment of change from childish joy to absolute terror; somewhere in there are astonishment and shock as well.

Anyway, I'll let you know how it goes later sometime.

~

If you're still interested we cracked a few minutes early and assumed dusk to be at 6:05pm like impatient children.

~

The Booker Prize tonight. The Booker Prize 2002. Kirsty Wark loses her voice and some Canadian guy called Jan Martell (that could be Ian Martel, or even Yan Martell) wins it. He leaps about like he's going through to the final on Popstars or like he's David Beckham and he's just scored a winning goal for England or something. I think 'what a prick' or something like that.

I say: "For God's sake this is supposed to be a literary event not the 'man of the match' or 'player of the year' presentation dinner, for fuck's sake."

She says: "Shut up, I'm going to bed."

I say: "But it's early and you're not even working tomorrow."

"I'm knackered." She says, yawning and standing up as if she's going to go to bed anyway.

"Come on, I thought we were going to sort some shit out. Come on, I'll make you a cuppa and a spliff,"

"Can't we talk tomorrow? I have got the day off remember."

"But I might be busy, I've got to try and get some more work. We've done all right lately but I'm worried about next month and before you know it, it will be Christmas.

"All right. Coffee. Black."

"You don't have to. I'm sorry. Go on, you go to bed."

"It's too late now. Anyway I quite fancy a spliff and a coffee now you come to mention it."

"Are you sure?"

"Yes."

"What's going to happen next?" I ask as I sit down and start gathering the accoutrements for the spliff-making ritual.

"What do you mean, what's going to happen next?"

"You know, what are we doing, where are we going? That sort of thing."

"How should I know?"

"You must have thought about it."

"Well, I thought we'd just see how it goes for a bit. We've been doing all right lately, haven't we?"

"Hash or skunk?"

"What?"

"Hash or skunk? We've got a bit of both."

"I don't care."

"Mixture then. I'll make the coffee in a minute, when I've finished this"

"So, we've paid all the bills and we've still got enough over for shopping until the end of the month. So, what's left to sort out?"

There's still something bothering me about her. We've been

together for a long time but there's still this distance; I can't see inside her head. What am I thinking? Of course I can't see inside her head. Who could stand that anyway? How can anyone know what's going on inside anyone else's head, it's hard enough working out what's going on inside your own head. I smile at her; everything's going to be all right. I love her.

Yann Martell won the Booker Prize. I don't know anything about his book, you know how it is when you're watching television, some things you take in, some things you don't, it all depends on your state of mind and whether you're thinking about something else, like your own story, or if you're talking to somebody with only part of your attention on the telly. I suppose it must be a good book, in a Booker prize 'good' sort of way but I can never finish one of those, although I did read Ian McEwan's "Atonement" last year, for a review filmed for a TV arts programme that never got transmitted because they took it off the air due to low ratings. I read the book and it wasn't agony or anything, it was OK, a decent yarn. She read Ali Smith for the same programme and said she enjoyed it. I tried to read that as well but because I didn't have to I hardly started it.

I also read all the contenders for Welsh Book of the Year for the same programme. That did get transmitted. The book that won it was OK I suppose, but then it was only the *Welsh* book of the year, so not too much competition then. Something must be done about the Welsh Literary scene – it's bollocks. For example, a typical book from a well-known and well-respected Welsh author who publishes with a Welsh publishing house only sells a couple of hundred copies, a bit more for the winner of the book of the year I suppose. The economics of book publishing in Wales are completely dominated by handouts from the Arts Council in all its guises. Pull the rug I say, pull the rug and let the bollocks end and the real writers emerge.

~

It's a few days later and Donna Tartt is on Newsnight Review so I'm off to watch it. . . . . Well, they didn't like her very much, that's a surprise after all the hype. It took her ten years to write that mediocre (according to Newsnight Review) book. I hope it doesn't take me ten years to write this, I'd be fucking sixty before it's finished at that rate. Fuck that, you'll have to take it a bit early (about nine and a half years early, I hope) and just put up with all flaws, call them rough diamonds if you like, but diamonds all the same.

I'm going to see Malbug again tomorrow.

~

This is the third time I've been to see Malbug. Once when I interviewed her and once more on the day before the funeral, I thought she should know about it, in case she wanted to pay her respects and all that.

Consciousness is a funny thing; I don't understand it at all. I was just thinking about the funeral in Northern Ireland some years ago when some (at least one anyway) soldiers got beaten to death. I wondered what the dead person thought about it, I wondered if the dead person thought at all. Do you think he (or she?) gave a fuck? I don't, because he/she didn't have any consciousness to be able to take any notice of the events at his/her funeral.

Malbug put her index finger to her lips as I walked in that day before Annie's funeral. She motioned for me to sit down opposite her on a cheap white plastic chair plonked on the lawn outside her shed.

I waited silently.

Malbug touched me on the hand. "It's all we've got – life,

consciousness, it's all we've got. You have to be conscious of the beauty around you in this tangled world. It's all we've got."

"Annie's dead," I said. I thought it would be best to get it out of the way quickly and deal with the reaction afterwards, better than fucking it up like they do in dumb soap-operas and say things like: "I've got something to tell you." Just fucking tell, for fuck's sake.

She sighed heavily; her body heaved.

"I saw her a few weeks ago," she said.

"The police released the body early, they had everything they needed."

"She was too young. She had a lot left to do, more to give."

"She was murdered."

"I've got some of her work."

"Her work?"

Malbug got up off the other cheap white plastic chair, walked over to a cold frame at the side of her shed and opened it. She pulled out a large black plastic bin bag and set it down on the cheap white plastic table that hovered between the two chairs. It looked like a bag of bricks except it only made a quiet clatter when she put it down so it couldn't have been very heavy. Malbug rummaged in the bag and pulled out a small brightly-painted clay bust of a man.

"It's you," she said. "Here, have a look at it."

The bust was about three inches tall and represented the head and part of the neck of a human body. I didn't recognise it as a likeness of me at first, but I studied it for a bit and was astonished to realise that it was a representation of what I would have looked like, if everything in my life had worked out for the best. For example, that time in London, when I was seventeen and working both as a roadie's assistant and as a photographer's assistant, you remember? Well, the bust of me looked like what I would have looked like if I'd developed my contacts then and become a successful photographer who specialised in album covers or portraits of rock stars or something. That's only an example mind; it's impossible to be specific because the effect of Annie's work was to add a new sense to your repertoire that the human race has not yet developed a language to describe – there are no points of reference.

"It's weird." Were the only words I could say.

"There's more," Malbug said, "bagfuls, there's one for every significant person she ever met." She tipped the contents of the bag onto the table as she spoke. Dozens of heads tumbled out and settled in awkward angles on the plastic.

I picked one or two up and studied them carefully.

"They're very well done," I said, glad that the strangers' heads hadn't invoked the same weirdness that had tongue-tied me when I saw the one of me.

"She was a great crafter as well as an artist. She had a way of distilling the essence of someone in a handful of clay. There's a few more bagfuls stashed in her sister's flat in Swansea."

"I didn't know she had a sister. I didn't know she was an artist. I can't have known her very well at all. Who was she?"

"She liked to unfold slowly. You would have known most of her secrets eventually." Malbug picked a head up from the table. "This is me." She said.

The weirdness returned as I handled Malbug's bust. She must have seen it in my expression.

"The effect is different when you know the subject," she explained.

Suddenly I felt sick. Sick and guilty. Why hadn't I recognised this in my friend, one of the few people I thought I was close to?

"The funeral is tomorrow," I said, "don't know if you can come. Listen, I'd better go. I've got things to do."

Malbug didn't come to the funeral. A woman I took to be Annie's sister was there, she was a little taller and thinner than Annie but had the same round features. I kept myself in the background, still feeling sick and guilty from the day before.

So, the third time is today. This is the third time I've come to see Malbug.

"I've got all of Annie's busts." Malbug points to a small black mountain of bin bags stacked up next to the cold frame.

"I wanted to ask you more about Annie." I ask. "She was so good to me, so important in my life."

"You know everything I know."

"There must be more."

"Annie's sister dropped these off, soon after the funeral. She didn't know what to do with them. She's been here a few times when Annie cadged a lift off her. But I don't think she understood her sister at all."

"Did anybody?"

"You can have them if you like. They're no good to me. They'll only slowly disintegrate. I've got no space here. I'll keep the one of me though."

"I only came to find out more about Annie." I say.

"Well, these will be a good start then."

~

God, I'm getting quite excited now, as I'm reading over the story so far. I want to know about these characters who appear before me with their grand entrances and their tragic exits. I want to know where they come from, what they feel. But I can't know everything and you can know even less than me. Do you know how complex the human being is? Just one human being, one character. If I tell you everything I know about every character then I'll never finish writing this and you'll never finish reading it. So you'll have to make do with small bits of information, small bits of information like photographs taken from a particular angle and with a particular light and at a particular moment.

But you too are a character, a human being, and you too are just as complex; so I'm sure you can use your intelligence, your experience and your imagination to fill in some if not most of the details yourself. Your version most certainly will not be exactly the same as mine but what the fuck, it's just as valid.

Take Sam and Kath, now there's two characters about as complicated as you can get – complex, fucked-up, tragic, but good characters. Two of the good guys – Sam and Kath. You won't find me slagging them off. Anyway, they're dead, and you're not supposed to speak ill of the dead (unless they're Hitler or cunting Ken of course.) If I had to say something bad about them it would be that they were too good, good in the sense of naïve and stupid, so maybe not good but innocent. But it isn't hard to say that they were too good for the world they normally inhabited – the world of scummy, scrounging cheats and rapists, bent police and shit-head parents. The world where just because someone is open and honest and trusting and probably too soft and thick to say no, No, NO, the blood-sucking fuckers think they can move in and gorge themselves on their gullibility.

Sam and Kath got married in Llanelli Registry Office. After the ceremony we went to a pub in Station Road.

This was 1970 or 1971. The landlord kept the pub open for the afternoon, laid on a few sandwiches and gave everyone except Sam and Kath just one free drink each. They, Sam and Kath, were allowed to drink as much as they wanted for free, which was a relief to the rest of us because we were all practically skint anyway, as we always were.

After about an hour Sam was truly pissed and stumbling around the pub kissing everyone he bumped into. He slobbered his lips over my cheek. I wasn't drunk.

"Fuck off Sam." I said, pushing him away, only half jokingly.

"You know what." He said. "You're a fucking good friend you are, a real friend."

He staggered away looking for his next victim. I noticed Kath sitting on her own in a dark corner with her head down.

"Hey," I said, "drunk too much already?"

She looked up at me and smiled but her eyes were wet with crying. I sat down and put my arm around her, reckoning that the stress and the alcohol had got to her; she was never good with her drugs.

"Silly me." She said, patting her eyes dry with the flared sleeve of her black dress.

"Hey, you're not silly."

"But I am, I am." She started to cry again.

I hugged her more tightly.

"See, silly me." this time she laughed.

"What is it?" I asked.

She looked up at me with her dark tear-stained eyes and started to open her mouth but instead of speaking she seemed to see something over my shoulder and her expression froze. I looked backwards puzzled. Ken had just arrived and was standing behind me looking at Kath with an expression that was almost as miserable as hers. I felt an instinctive need to protect her. I stood up and faced Ken, using my body to hide her from his view.

"I thought you weren't coming." I said.

"I know, I'm sorry, I just wanted to come and wish the happy couple the best of luck for the future."

"But I thought you couldn't handle it."

"No, I'm all right. You were right; it's time to move on. Time to grow up a bit."

I felt sorry for Ken then, one of the rare times I've seen him show any real emotion. I knew where he was coming from. I was a recovering victim of unrequited love myself; I knew how hard it could be. As we spoke he kept twisting his neck to try and get a view of Kath. I looked back at Kath and she shrugged as if to say, 'Go on, it's all right.' I stepped aside and went to stand in the doorway of the small back room where we were.

Ken approached Kath slowly and sat down. She took his hand and leant towards him. Their faces were only inches apart. I couldn't hear what they were saying from where I was but it looked as if Kath was doing her best to be nice to him. I assumed she was being kind because she knew just how big a crush he had on her, not that he called it a crush; from what he'd told me in one of his drunken off-guard moments he was completely obsessed with her. He'd told me he wouldn't be coming to the wedding because he didn't think he could handle it.

After two or three minutes Ken stood up and walked slowly, with a defeated slump of the shoulders, towards the door. He paused at the door and looked at me, I'd never seen him look so disappointed, so tired, and his eyes were wet with crying now as well. I smiled at him and he nodded before pushing past me. Just then Sam staggered back into the small back room. I felt myself tense at the possible consequences but didn't need to. Sam grabbed Ken and gave him the same wet kiss he'd given me.

Ken's posture immediately changed. His back straightened and he stood at his full height, which happened to be a good few inches taller than either Sam or me. He pushed Sam away firmly and gave one last glance back at Kath before he left. I noticed then that the despair had gone and his face was once again set in that implacable expression I'd come to recognise him by.

s i x t e e n

"I'm a polymath."

"Don't you mean a Jack of all trades?"

"Well, I know I'm not a polymath but I could have been."

"Hmm."

"Yeah, under different circumstances. You know how good I am at everything."

"Well, let me think now. How about earning a living? Not to mention swimming and sailing and let me think, decorating and gardening. In fact there's not much you are good at is there?"

"Oh come on, play fair."

"Play fair? Play fair? OK then, what about bringing up normal kids and . . ."

"I'm not talking about those sort of things. They're not important. I don't mean they're not important, they're just don't amount to much in the scheme of things. What I'm talking about is, and this is going to sound naff now, stupid, but it isn't really, there are just not the words to describe what I'm thinking about because it's beyond words. It was there before words were invented, so to speak, and it will still be there when all the words in the world have died out."

"What do you fancy for tea?"

"I mean, if my parents had been more well off, or if I hadn't met the wrong types on the estate, or if I hadn't argued with the gym teacher in school and got thrown off the rugby team, things would have been different wouldn't they?"

"Pasta? Tagliatelli or something like that with a simple tomato sauce?"

"It's not my fault is it? No, I'm asking, is it my fault? I mean loads of people have overcome obstacles in their life, fucked-up childhoods, traumas, illnesses, that sort of thing, and still done great things."

"Perhaps we'll have some green beans to go with it."

"Green beans?"

"I'll do it."

"Um, never mind eh."

"Pasta all right then?"

"Do you love me?"

"Pasta and green beans."

~

After Her there was a year of misery. You remember Her don't you? The Her with a capital H. The Her that fucked me up when I was seventeen. It wasn't her fault of course; in fact she had almost nothing to do with it. I only went out with her for two weeks for fuck's sake, it was all in my head, some kind of madness. That was a bad brain time. That was the second of two significant periods in my adolescence, one marking the beginning and one the end. In the beginning there was a before and an after. Before was mostly cuddly, with the odd greasy moment, the occasional fright; and after, in the in between there was confusion and pain and being all over the place. Then there was Her; then very soon there was after Her. That was the time when all the bollocks came screaming out of my teenage head and turned me into a person – it was a terrible time but worth it, because I am that person.

Now there is an After Him as well; not that I fell in love with a Him or anything. It's Ken I'm talking about, perhaps it should be After Ken, AK instead of AH, one of the advantages is that it couldn't be confused with the other AH, After Her, anyway calling it After Him would only give the bastard more kudos than he deserves, not that he deserves any kudos at all, that would imply that he personified 'The Him' when in fact he was just a fucking pathetic insignificant wanker. So, now it is AK. AK AK AK AK AK AK AK AK. And that's what it feels like AK AK AK AK . . . ., a long harsh choking of confusion and relief, guilt and redemption. Don't do it. Don't kill your demons, they are part of you and you will feel the pain too.

She turns the key in the door and I'm still sitting at the kitchen table, the contents of Phil's box in scruffy piles on the softwood surface. What the fuck, there's nothing to hide any more.

"Hello." she shouts from the hall. "You got up eventually then."

I was still in bed when she went to work, pretending to sleep off a hangover that I pretended to have after I lied to her about where I went last night. She came into the kitchen.

"You haven't even bothered to get changed." She looked around the room as her buoyant expression started to sink, her eyes settling on the piles of papers on the table. "Been writing have you. Well I hope it's fucking worth it." She left the room before I had time to react and clumped upstairs.

I found her in the bedroom going through her letter rack.

"It's about time I sorted this out," she said, "there's things in here I should have thrown out years ago."

"I know." I said. "What's the matter?"

"It's just work that's all, and then I come home and you look like an alcoholic tramp in your own kitchen."

"It's not what it looks like," I said, "I'm all right really, very good in fact. I'm starting to sort my life out once and for all."

"I don't like seeing you like that." She said.

"Nor me, that's why I don't look in the mirror very often." I laughed but she didn't.

"Tell you what," I said, "forget about cooking food tonight. I'll go and have a shower and stuff and then we'll go out for a curry. We haven't been for a while."

"Can we afford it?"

"We're celebrating."

"What?"

"I don't know. A new start perhaps. I promise I'll make more of an effort from now on, you'll soon see a difference."

"Why, what's changed?" I noticed she had been crying.

"What's the matter?"

"I'm fine, honest. Yes that's a good idea, let's go out and have a curry. You go and have your shower, I'll tidy the kitchen up."

The shower finally got rid of the intense emotions I'd felt the night before. The curry afterwards was not so good, but the wine did the trick. The last thing I thought about before I fell asleep was Ken's face, something I'd never see again, thank fuck.

~

A couple of weeks after visiting Malbug in Tenby and bringing Annie's bin bag home with me I was languishing at home on my own watching a stupid programme on daytime television about a couple who wanted to move from their basement flat in Earl's Court, London, to a property in the country. They had something ridiculous to spend, nearly half a million quid and to be honest it made me feel a bit sick. I mean half a million pounds is more than most of the people I know will earn in their lifetimes and this couple weren't anything special, just some kind of admin worker and some kind of 'consultant', whatever that's supposed to mean. I suppose it means that they hang around in London and take big salaries to tell other people who hang around in London how to milk more money out of the system. Or maybe it just made me feel sick with jealousy, either way I couldn't watch it all the way through and being at a loose end and because the bin bag had been on my mind anyway seeing as I kept passing it in the hall where I had dropped it after returning home from Tenby that day.

So I took the bag into the living room and dumped the contents on the large pine coffee table that was a remnant from the office of one of my failed business ventures. There were a lot of heads in there, and some other objects that I had difficulty identifying at first. I took them to be ashtrays, or finger bowls or saucers or at least receptacles of some sort. I put them aside and concentrated on the heads.

Of course I examined the bust of me first. As soon as I picked it up, the feeling I'd had when I first handled it in Tenby returned and it freaked me out a bit because I'd assumed the thing in Tenby was just an aberration, a reaction to the grief I felt after Annie's death. Funny thing though, I found that I was compelled to examine every scratch, every bump, every nuance of the article and after a few minutes I came to accept the feelings it evoked; feelings of endless possibilities, feelings of the limitless potential involved in being human, feelings that needed to have their way before they released you in a more enlightened state. Putting it down carefully I started rummaging through the other heads.

Although the other heads I picked up didn't affect me in anything like the same way, they were beautiful objects, in a rough diamond sort of way and I believe would have been just the sort of artefact that middle-aged middle-class Welsh media or political types would be comfortable displaying on their raffia tables in their heavy Italian-tiled vestibules. I picked a head up, selected randomly from the pile on the table, and immediately dropped it because it caused a sharp tingle that travelled up my arm and did something creepy with the contents of my stomach.

The head landed on its face and afraid to touch it with my bare hands again, I found a pencil on the mantelpiece and poked it until it flipped over and lay there staring at me with the face of Ken. I suppose it must have been some sort of voodoo.

~

I think it's accelerating, the pace at which this world is going mad.

When I say this world, I mean the world that is presented to us for an increasingly longer period each day through the media, particularly through the medium of television. For example, I just watched Neil and Christine Hamilton performing a comedy sketch with Stuart Cable who used to be (or still is?) a member of the Stereophonics pop/rock band, on the aforementioned Stuart's chat show on BBC 1 Wales, appropriately titled 'Cable TV', although it's not just on cable TV, it's on terrestrial television as well. And that's where the madness lies; I could understand it if it was on cable TV because you expect that sort of thing on those sort of television channels, but BBC 1 (even if it is only BBC 1 Wales) – now that's mad.

The above is only one small example (have you ever heard of a big example?), and I accept that it doesn't help when it's late and you're tired and you've got a roomful of plastic doors and self-assembly kitchen cabinets (as yet not self-assembled) and you're sitting at a computer screen, typing on a plastic device that transmits letters, words and paragraphs to a metal device that displays them on a glass device. (Now that's mad as well).

It's time to pause and meditate, time to allow the multifarious strands of madness rewind and come to rest, time to regroup, to re-evaluate, to allow the healing to take place, like in Lord of the Rings, when the company of travellers that constitute the Fellowship of the Ring stop off in some Elfish paradise and stuff themselves with the fruits of the earth (even if in the book, which I read a few times a long time ago (ha, ha – so there!), Tolkien doesn't exactly restrict his characters to a strict fruitarian diet), even if it is Middle Earth. Can I make a plan for that, I wonder? Can I heal myself?

Evidence? Evidence? You need more evidence of the madness of the world? OK then, you asked for it. First, put this book down and put the television on. (That's assuming you have a television and that you're reading this book in a place where there is access to a television, and that you can be bothered. In other words, it is not compulsory, or even necessary, for you to put the book down. Just close your eyes, lie back (or sit back, or lean back, or just stay still and relax), and remember. Bring to your consciousness those memories of the things you've seen and the places you've been over the last twenty-four hours. Good. Now select a one-minute sequence of events and try to replay it over and over again in your mind.) Actually, thinking about it, it would be better if you recorded a one minute sequence of Eastenders or something and then play, rewind and replay that as many times as you can bear.

It's mad isn't it? That sequence of events, whether real or lived vicariously through a serial drama on the television makes absolutely less sense the more you get to know the nooks and crannies of its true nature. We couldn't have thought like this before the advent of video players. I'm telling you, the world is mad and the mad technology we keep inventing is both a product of and the instigator of that madness.

At the time Phil wrote that stuff of his, the madness of today's world was the stuff of science fiction writers and they got it all wrong, and even though the world was mad then as well, it wasn't anything like as mad as it is now. (And I should know, because I was there then and I'm here now.)

~

"I suppose I am."

Linda steps out of the watermelon.

"Compensation for being a little person. Yes. That's what I do."

She sits on the hazelnut.

"It's just another way of looking."

She kicks the pea across the room. It knocks over the person-sized sculpture of a carrot. This is what she does; she creates huge vegetables.

"It's to do with looking at things from a kind of sideways perspective."

"Do you mean like lateral thinking?"

"Well, I don't really know what that is." She says.

"Well, it's like you said, you look at things sideways or whatever and that might lead you into discovering something different about something, or a new way to achieve something that doesn't follow the normal, for us Westerners at least, logical, step by step way of doing things. There's a lot of businesses use the techniques now, it's not only for creative people."

"They'll be categorising turds next."

I laughed There is something engaging about Linda, Linda the plant as she likes to call herself. Her papier-mâché giant vegetables are brightly coloured and appealing enough to be left hanging about in children's nurseries alongside the Tellytubby toys and sensual enough to grace the boudoir of the highest class Parisian prostitute. She is a nice person. I give her a good write-up.

~

I still haven't sorted out Phil's stuff properly. I'm beginning to feel guilty knowing that Rita Davies and her son Paul are probably very pissed off with me by now, but there's nothing I can do about it. I've never been like this before, I've always been totally reliable, I mean when I say I'll do something by a certain date or time, I do do it 99.9% of the time, and on those occasions when I feel as if I'm not going to meet the deadline I get in touch and let whoever it is that's involved know that I'm going to be late or whatever, but this time I just can't do even that.

So it's been a while now and I still haven't got back to the Davies's and I still haven't given Phil's writing the going over I should have. I've got a spare couple of hours, I'm home on my own, I've just finished watching Neighbours and Doctors and can't find any more excuses not to do something. Let's have a quick look.

As I'm retrieving the box, the phone rings. I go to pick it up, leaving the box on the floor in the middle room, it's such a mess in there that no one will notice an extra box of papers.

I see from the caller display unit that's it's a number withheld. In the second or so it takes me to pick the phone up and say 'Hello.', I think of all the possibilities of who it could be. It could be her, phoning from work, or it could be the BBC saying they love the script I sent them and they're going to make a 26 part series out of it and they desperately want to give me a hundred thousand pounds advance and nominate me for a BAFTA, or it could be one of the myriad of telephone salespeople who plague innocent couch potatoes with no regard for the time of day, or it could be the tax office, or the Electrical Wholesalers asking me to go ahead with the £10,000 software development quote I gave them last year. More than likely it's somebody after money.

"Hello."

"Hello, sorry about this, but can you come and pick me up early."

"Why, what's the matter?"

"I'm just feeling like shit, and I've got a few hours owing to me, so I thought . . ."

"How do you mean 'felling like shit'? No, hang on, I'll be there as soon as I can."

I'm bombing down the coast road when an unmarked black police car pulls me over. I see their uniforms in the rear view mirror. They're half my age but they make me feel very nervous and guilty. I wind the window down.

"Is this your vehicle sir?"

"Yes."

"Would you mind getting out?"

I get out – of course.

One cop is talking to me and the other walks around the car scrutinizing every bit of glass, metal and plastic.

"May I ask where you're going?"

"I'm going to pick my wife up from work, she's not well."

"Do you know you have a defective brake light?"

"No, I didn't."

"Well, we won't take any further action this time, but get it fixed as soon as you can, if we have to stop you again we'll have to make it official."

"Thanks."

Bastards. Smarmy young bastards. Everything is so black and white to them isn't it? Either a thing is right or a thing is wrong. Society has deemed it so, so there it is. Haven't they got any fucking imagination of their own?

She's waiting outside.

"Sorry I took so long, I got pulled by the cops."

"Oh." She looks pained.

"It's all right though, it was only the brake light, and they only gave me a warning."

"How's the other car?"

"All right, it'll be ready tomorrow."

"That's good."

"How are you? What's the matter anyway?"

"It's like I said on the phone, but it's not too bad, it's probably a touch of flu or something, there's a lot of it about."

"Why didn't you take the time off sick? You kept that time for a proper holiday."

"Holiday? When was the last time we went on a holiday?"

"You know I don't mean that sort of holiday. I mean a holiday from work."

"So you think it's a holiday to spend time at home, with you, do you?"

"Not all that again – please?"

"No, you're right. It's best to leave it now. Just get me home now."

"OK."

Touché.

seventeen

I'm going on a pilgrimage, a pilgrimage to visit all the graves of my lost friends, all the people I've known who have left this life before me. There's something about going bankrupt that forces you to re-evaluate your life, something that makes you look back at the store of sensations and experiences that you have accumulated on this planet. How can that all end? It doesn't seem possible that God would create all this, our common world and all the incredible stories that exist only in every individual's memory and then it just goes, vanishes, as if it never happened.

So, I've decided to go and spend some time at their respective last resting places. In all the years since they started dying off I've never been to visit any of their graves once. I must have been avoiding it to avoid the question of my own mortality. But I'm ready now; I'm in the right mood at last. Perhaps by facing up to their deaths I'll be able to come to terms with my own. At least it should put the bankruptcy thing into perspective.

First I've got to decide an order of visiting. Should I work chronologically? Should I visit the grave of the person who died first? Or should I work backwards starting with the latest? Perhaps I should do it in order of age of death? Perhaps I should pay my respects in some sort of order of importance? Who was first anyway? Who was the oldest, and who was the youngest? Who was the most important, or most significant?

Hang on, I can't do this, I'm not a pedant, I don't work like this. What do I think I'm doing? Planning everything out as if I'm ever going to be able to follow a plan; plans are for pedants. Ok, I admit that there's some value in planning, but not if you actually try to follow the plan as if it's a plan or something. A plan is only good for planning, after that it's redundant, like a shopping list; if you write a shopping list before you go to the supermarket and then forget it, it doesn't matter, the act of writing the shopping list is enough to fix the important things in your memory, the things that matter.

So, OK, I won't go and visit all the graves of my lost friends then, at least not in any kind of planned way. (Phew, I'm glad about that, I nearly committed myself to something I've been avoiding all my life and that wouldn't do, because then I'd be someone else; I'd have to change for fuck's sake.)

What I will do, if only to help me come to terms with where I've been and where I'm going, and what I'm doing now come to that, is to metaphorically visit all those graves and make a list of the circumstances and the time of each death, thus eventually freeing me from any guilt I may still feel by analysing them in an objective way.

First. Now who was first? I suppose it must have been my paternal grandfather, but he died before I was born, so he doesn't count. No, the first one I can remember is my maternal grandfather, but he's irrelevant as well, at least in terms of this story, so I won't bother with him, or other people like him who are not relevant to this story. God, that's scary, I've never thought of it like that before, it's not really a thought, more of a feeling really. There is/was a man without whom I would not exist and I know almost nothing about him. I suppose that's what drives all the family tree nerds, the need to know. But even if I got to know my grandfather, or my great grandfather or even my great great grandfather etc, there's bound to come a time when there will be an impassable barrier of unknowingness, so what's the point? You are what you are; I am what I am and that's that. Like my father used to say: 'The only reason for life is to procreate.' It sounds simple but think about it for a minute.

So, the first significant one then? But why bother going in chronological order? I don't think like that and neither do you, so why should I force us two amazing human beings to get bound up in some kind of artificial structure thus stifling any spontaneity and creativity we have?

OK, the first one that comes to mind then, or the second, or the one that comes to mind immediately after I hear the next mention of the word 'man' on Chris Needs' programme on Radio Wales, which is what I've got on on the desk next to me as I write. Here we go . . . . waiting . . . . . . still waiting . . . . . ah fuck, he's playing a song now, never mind perhaps there'll be a 'man' in that. The song's finished, good, come on Chris, say 'man' there's a good boy.

Fucking hell, it's the next night and he still hasn't said 'man', that's what happens when you make stupid rules for yourself, but I'm not one to constrain myself with silly rules if they fuck things up, so I'll change the word, let's think, how about 'garden', OK, I'll wait for that. Here we go, Chris said: *'and don't forget Sam the dog either, they'll be going in the garden this week.'* (Note the use of the word 'garden', and I know it's cheating because of course, Chris Needs has a radio show which is based on a garden, it's a special kind of garden but I won't go into it here, if you want to know more about Chris Needs' garden you'll have to listen to his show on Radio Wales. The show is on normal FM radio if you live in Wales and on digital satellite or on the Internet if you don't. Do a search on Google or something if you really want to know.)

Oh fuck it, I'm going to bed, long day tomorrow. Have to face that fucking copper.

~

It's another day and I've lost the desire to go over all that bollocks. The copper came around to talk to me like she said she would. I got the feeling she didn't like me as soon as I answered the door;

there was a negative chemistry between us, a distinct awkwardness. I decided straight away that if anyone was going to see through my bullshit it was her, so I decided to play stupid, I certainly looked the part – unshaven and dressed in a scruffy grey T-shirt and an open fronted lumberjack shirt, and I was wearing slippers – the smelly ones with the loose heels. I didn't do it deliberately, it's just that she came earlier than I expected and I hadn't sorted myself out by then.

I made a pot of tea and mumbled something about working all night. She didn't seem interested. I suppose she was knocking forty, a shortish, stoutish, woman with straight blonde hair. She didn't say much as I made tea and dug half a packet of limp bourbons from the back of the fridge.

I sat down opposite her at the kitchen and tried to smile. She looked at me the way Columbo eyes the chief suspect, weighing me up and freaking me out. The smile dropped.

"I'm sorry to disturb you." She said.

There was a pause.

I felt I had to respond. "No problem," I said. "Do you want a biscuit?"

She shook her head from side to side, all the time keeping my eyes in her gaze.

There was another pause.

"Well," I said, "how can I help?" I winced as I said it, it reminded me of the way the murderers in Columbo behave. Now I really felt guilty.

"I just wanted to clear up a few details about the night Annie died. Where you were, what you were doing, that sort of thing."

"As I told the others, that was one of my teaching nights, I teach a computer class in a community centre. It's easy to check, there's a register."

"I know that, and the class finished at nine o'clock."

"That's right."

"We have a report of a car, just like yours, in the area, not long after Annie died."

"Oh."

"That would be about ten o'clock. Did you go straight home afterwards?"

"No, I went to see my mother but she was out so I went to the pub to talk to my brother."

"That would be the Joiner's Arms?"

"Yes, but he wasn't there either, so I went to look for him in town."

"And then?"

"I caught up with him eventually, in the Verandah Tandoori restaurant."

"And why was it so important to catch up with your brother?"

I'd already prepared the answer to this one. I didn't want to tell the police that my brother knew a bloke who knew a bloke who lived with a bloke who reputedly could sort me out for some weed, but I couldn't say that. Could I? So, instead I said: "He owed me money, and I needed it to buy petrol for the next day because I had to go and meet someone in Bridgend – about some work."

"So what time did you arrive home then?"

"Just before eleven I think."

"Thank you sir. We probably will not be bothering you again. I'm sorry we had to ask you these questions but we have to cover everything, make sure everything is closed off and explainable. Elimination and all that. Thanks again."

She stood up to leave and I followed her to the door.

~

I got really freaked out earlier. Thing is I'm still not sure if it was a dream or not. I don't remember it as a dream; it's as real as this keyboard I'm hammering, but it can't be real so it must have been a dream. I was having a dream; I know that one was a dream because I did the trick of trying to wake up from it and I succeeded, but I ended up in an even more unreal situation. I did then try and get out of that 'dream' in the usual way, you know, by concentrating very hard and trying to shout (it's hard (if not impossible) to talk in a dream, have you noticed?), but it didn't work and she was still there, like Princess Leah from Star Wars, she appeared before me in three-dimensional actuality.

"There will come a time," she said, and her voice was quivering and distant. She continued, as I stood dumbstruck. "There will come a time when the life energy that is me will finally fade and the planet will forget I ever existed. But that time will not come until those that carry their memories of me are cleansed of their guilt and of their association with the darkness."

She sounded so formal that I didn't recognise her at first; so formal and yet so peaceful, I don't mean blissfully peaceful, but kind of resigned peaceful if you know what I mean. She had a look that was chillingly flat and yet there was no pain in that expression.

"Annie?" I said.

She looked at me then and I found I couldn't move or speak.

"There are things that I know that you cannot know, things that are outside your experience, but there are things you must know if you're ever going to make any sense of your existence."

I nodded, petrified. The first time you see a ghost you will nod speechlessly too. It's not an experience that anyone or anything can prepare you for.

"Life is not to be understood, just experienced and accepted, but there are certain things that get in the way of that acceptance. The acceptance I am talking about has nothing to do with weakness, it is the meek, not the weak that will inherit the earth.

"There are parts of you that hold mysteries, mysteries that can provide the key to happiness, true happiness. For in the end there is no prize on that scratch card until you rub the latex off. Until you do that you will never know if you have won or not. That potentiality is only that, it is only potentiality, it is not actuality. Yet there are actual actualities – truths.

"Take my hand."

She reached out her hand and I took it meekly. As I touched her, or the illusion of her, whatever it was, I felt a surge of energy burning through every capillary in my body, every cell lit up with an intense fire that scorched and inflicted intense pain. The pain was so great that I passed out, or maybe I fell back asleep, or maybe I was never awake in the first place.

I felt myself dissolving and reforming into a thing without form. I became the wind, the heat from the sun, the sound of a river, the cry of a baby. I became not I. I became everyone. I became everyone at all times. I became everyone at all times at all places. I became not I. I became no-one, nothing, nothing and everything at the same time. I felt nothing but pure bliss. I disappeared.

I woke up.

I was still me.

~

"I have a feeling of a life. The feeling that whatever goes on in a person's life, whether it be physical, emotional, mental, in the sense of mental processes, or spiritual, there is always that consciousness that sits at the back of everything and lives in a state of bliss. It's not like schizophrenia or voices in the head or any of that, because this consciousness is not part of anything we can, or will ever define. Take this piece for example."

I let him hand me the cricket ball sized object. It's outer surface, at least, is made of hammered brass-coloured metal. The light bounces off it and around it as I turn it in my hand. It has a satisfying weight and feels like it enjoys being handled.

"You can open it if you like." He says.

I try. I look for some sort of catch, but I'm afraid to treat it too roughly.

"Twist it," he says, "it's hard to spot but the join between the two halves is just there."

He points with his claw-like finger, he's a tall man, skinny and big-boned.

I twist it; it needs quite a wrench. It opens like a chocolate Easter egg, except round.

"Put one half in each hand, hollow end up and lift them up and down, as you do when you're trying to compare the weight of two objects."

I comply. This is a very satisfying experience. With the two halves of the ball in my hands I feel completely balanced.

"What's it all about? I ask.

He smiles and shrugs his shoulders. "Essentially, all I do is to play with materials and I'll keep on and on at them until one day something will click and it will be complete. I don't ever know exactly when the click will occur, but it will, as long as I keep working it on long enough. Sometimes the click doesn't come for weeks, months even, and sometimes the click comes so fast I have to put the object down very gently at that moment otherwise it would change and then I'd have to scrap it or keep playing with it for god knows how long."

"How does this relate to what you were saying just now about that feeling of life you have?"

"It demonstrates, to me, and I hope to many other people, that merely by being, simply by walking and talking and breathing and going with the flow, is what it's all about, it's not about where you're going, but where you are now. I mean, it's all about honesty, no, it's all about truth, truth I mean. The truth is that we live, we exist and it's beautiful."

I leave the studio in a pensive mood, but I was starving, so I stop off for some chips in Pontarddulais on the way home. The man in the chip shop reminds me of someone. He looks at me as if he knows me and yet I'm sure that I've never met him before. I pay him the money and leave.

When I get home a few minutes later, I retrieve the chips from the passenger seat of the car, they're still warm but if I'm going to enjoy them I'll have to get in the house quickly. My neighbour is coming out of her front door.

"Hello." I say.

"Oh, hello. How are you?"

"Fine, busy"

"Don't let me keep you."

"No, I didn't mean that, it's all right, honestly."

"I've got a parcel for you," she says.

"A parcel?"

"The postman dropped it off earlier, I'll just go and get it."

She goes back in the house and comes out with a padded envelope the size of a London telephone directory, bulging, but not as heavy. I take it off her.

"Thanks."

In the kitchen, I eat the chips before they get cold and stare at the parcel. It's got a local postmark. It feels as if it contains paper, I can't imagine who would send me something of that size, I mean it can't be junk mail, not even junk mailers would waste such resources on a vague prospect.

I don't know why but I can't open it. Even after I finish the chips and wash my hands and make a cup of tea and tidy the kitchen up, I can't open it. I feel sure that it's got something to do with Annie.

I carry the parcel into the middle room and drop it on the edge of the desk while I check my e-mail, all I get is a pile of rubbish about remortgages and something from Tanya, a supposedly Russian girl looking for a nice American man to marry. American my arse. All the world's American, the new world anyway, I suppose we've just got to live with it. I need a piss so I get up after disconnecting from the Internet.

Unfortunately, or fortunately, or sub-consciously deliberately, I knock the bulging parcel off the edge of the desk. It falls to the floor and splits open. It is paper, or papers. I half expect them to be more stuff from Phil's mother and brother and I feel guilty because it's been a while now and I haven't got around to taking his papers back and reassuring them about his death. Not that I've even read them yet, other things just keep getting in the way.

No, these papers are of another kind. I gather them together tentatively, and gradually get engrossed. At first all I can see is pages of information, numbers mostly, columns of numbers with headings at top of the columns. Then I recognise them. They are the pages of accounts information printed on a laser printer from the computer program, Sage Accounts.

I look more closely; this is the Audit Trail from a set of accounts, there are hundreds of pages of transactions. I look even more closely. They are the accounts of a company, which, according to this computer printout, is called Lucy Holdings. Then I realise – these are the accounts of my old friend (bastard) Ken.

By fuck.

eighteen

I can tell you how to replace the ceiling of your kitchen, if you have an old lath and plaster ceiling that is, an old lath and plaster ceiling where the plaster is cracking and crumbling and falling down in big black chunks. The other proviso is that you intend to replace the old lath and plaster ceiling with thin tongue and groove boards made from spruce from sustainably managed forests. I can tell you that because I've done it.

I can tell you about the nails that we used (two different kinds, or three if you count the ones we bought that were too small for one job and too big for the other), I can tell you about the tools I borrowed from my brother and the fine black dust that coated every surface in the house for days afterwards and I can tell you that wearing a mask and goggles doesn't work because of the condensation, you can wear a mask or you can wear goggles but you can't wear both, not if you buy the cheapest mask and goggles in the do-it-yourself superstore like we did.

What I can't really tell you is the other things. Things like the feeling that by putting that work energy into bringing that filthy old plaster down, you are destroying all that old negative energy that it has absorbed and bringing a light from your soul into the world. I can't tell you about the flip side of that, which is that the old negative energy has a habit of inflicting pain as it escapes. How it gets into the relationships that have developed under that ceiling, the misery, the family talks, the bulb of resentment that bursts under the hammer of renewal.

It's joyous and it's painful, sometimes too painful, but if you don't do it the bloody thing will fall down on your head one day and knock you so senseless that you'll never recover awareness again. Even houses have to be detoxed occasionally.

I know that there are people who live in the same house all their lives. There are those that get born in a house and grow up there; then they stay on in their adulthood, they may even give birth there; then they grow old there and eventually die there. There are others who leave a house when they become young adults and do not return. These people sometimes make pilgrimages in their later years, pilgrimages back to the place they were young in, and write wistful reminiscences as if there is some magical far-away quality to be had from such journeys.

But, the place is the same and the ones who stay behind continue to live ordinary lives without ever knowing the magic of returning. Take me, for example. Despite making efforts over the years to leave the village where I have lived for the past two decades or so, I have not been able to. There are forces out there (or in here) that must be stopping me. (To be honest, thinking about it, I have not really made much effort, perhaps I secretly want to stay here, (when I say secretly I mean there are unexplained motivations (or forces if you like) that will not allow me to move away yet), perhaps there are things that I still have to do here)

Like replacing the stinking ceiling.

~

It's done now – the ceiling, all but done anyway. It still needs a coat or two of varnish and maybe a bit of wood filler here and there – where the knots have fallen out, but otherwise it's done. The rest of the kitchen's the same; it's all just about done. That's me all over, just about done, I can never seem to finish a job, perhaps I'm afraid that if I ever do then I'll be done too. There's always some unresolved business, unrealised potential, I always hold something back, something substantial. Why can't I give? I ask her.

"Why can't some people change?"

"Change?"

"Why is it that some, most, people don't like dramatic change in their lives? What are they afraid of?"

"You're not going on about that again are you?"

"No, no, I'm just being philosophical, just theorising, you know, imagining."

"Yeah well, I'm tired of it all."

"But things have to change, everything changes, nothing lasts forever."

"What about diamonds?"

"I don't know. I suppose even diamonds get crushed to atoms, even atoms get crushed to sub-atomic particles, if they go into a Black Hole that is."

"There's only one thing for it then."

"Oh yeah. What's that?"

"I thought you knew everything."

"Oh well, if you can't be bothered. If all you want to do is take the piss . . ."

"You're so precious, you know that. So bloody precious. Why can't you just get on with it like everyone else has to?"

"Hang on, this isn't meant to be an argument, I was just thinking that's all."

"That's all you ever do. It's no good for you, thinking too much, why can't you just enjoy life? Why can't you just be happy? What's the point of all this doom and gloom?"

"It's not doom and gloom, I'm not freaked out or depressed or anything. I just like to look behind things, work out what's going on, that sort of thing."

"Start a religious bloody cult or something then. Yes, go on, start a cult and then you can go and live with your followers in some American desert or something and then you can talk bollocks all you like, but I'm just tired of it all. All I want is to do my job and have a good time now and again."

"What's up with you?"

"What do you mean?"

"What's really up with you? What's going on?"

"Oh, I don't know. I'm sorry. I didn't mean to snap."

"Come here."

We hug, but I'm not sure if she really wants to or she just wants to shut me up. I get the feeling that she's making a face over my shoulder, like they do in soap operas, so that the audience get to know something the characters don't. I'm getting to feel more like a character in a soap opera all the time lately, what with cheap video cameras and infestations of CCTV everywhere you go. Maybe I'm watching too much telly?

After a decent interval where we just make a meal together and discuss only banal things like how many carrots to chop up for the aduki bean pie, or whether to use olive oil or sunflower oil to sauté the onions and garlic in, I tell her about the woman copper who came around to see me yesterday.

"Why?" She asks. "Why are they still bothering you?"

~

There was one painter that I interviewed who really freaked me out. Come to think of it it was her who first inspired me to start writing this book, she was my muse if you like. I call her her, because it sounds right because that is what she wants to be called. Her name was Mandy and she was a pre-op transsexual, come to think of it, she's probably a post-op transsexual by now because it was a couple of years ago, but I've lost touch with her, I think she moved to Australia or somewhere I bet she's a famous Antipodean Artist by now.

The things that freaked me out most of all were her paintings of The Three Bears. In fact, she only ever painted variations on the theme of the Three Bears. Come to think of it it was probably one of her paintings that subconsciously inspired me to think of the design on the front of this book (I don't know, did the Three Bears design make the front cover? Anyway, even if it didn't I still thought of it and wrote the description down.)

Mandy worried me. She was a beautiful woman, with eyes that challenged and warned you at the same time. She was in her late forties I guess, with a converted barn full of her work, which, as I've already said, was paintings on the theme of the Three Bears – and Goldilocks of course. As I said, at first, she freaked me out but as I spent more time in her company and in the company of her work I felt that I had to give in to the feelings they invoked and when I did, I felt a deep peace flow through my being – it was like I became a hollow vessel filled with the tingle of warmth and light.

"Ever since I was a little girl," she said, "I've had a thing about Goldilocks; I suppose I identified with her, still do. I'm not sure but I think it's because I feel alone and threatened in this world, just like every other living creature. I guess I see the world through the eyes of a vulnerable being, but a vulnerability that is mitigated by her precocious spirit. I want to show that in my work – the strength and unpredictably of this scary planet represented by the teeth and fur of the wild bears and the innocent courage of the little people, represented by the girl with golden hair. To me, this is the ultimate dichotomy of existence; we are all sliding along the edge of the knife, hovering in that thin territory between life and death. In that sliver of existence there is everything; love, beauty, light and the essence of humanity itself."

And there is a certain light in her work that does invoke those feelings of insecurity and yet uplifts your spirit. Her paintings are full of blood and pain and porridge and the compositions are awesome. Or perhaps it is my particular viewpoint that makes them so. In any case, they are very well executed, with the right balance of colour and texture. It's well worth keeping a look out for any exhibitions of her work.

~

Back.
Back.
Back.
No, don't stop until I tell you to stop, just keep rewinding, don't worry, I'll stop you when it's time. Go on, faster, rewind faster. That's better.
Back.
Back.
Back.
OK, stop. What's this? Cardiff, 1971 again. What's that all about? I thought all that was finished with. Obviously not. Let's see.

Hang on, it's not 1971, it's a year later, 1972, 1971 – the year when everything happened. 1972 – the year when everything changed. Back in Cardiff with her and a baby. Who else is here? What's the point of being here?

On a bus, leaving Cardiff. On a bus with them, going back to Llanelli to visit parents and so on. There's an old tramp. He's talking to us.

"It's cold." He said.

"Oh." I said, trying to avoid any more contact, but damn it, we were stuck on a bus somewhere between Bridgend and Port Talbot. He's old and he's cold and he's got to me. Before he got off in Port Talbot I gave him a beautiful Welsh woollen blanket, almost new, a wedding present probably. I don't know why. She didn't mind too much although it pissed her off a bit.

I'm so arrogant.

~

Before Her and before her I must have been alive, because I have memories of that time. I lived in a long summer and worked on a farm for the holidays. I was thirteen years old and I was a good boy. It was 1965 and I got paid four shillings a week for seven days of 12 hour working. It sounds like shit doesn't it? But it wasn't, in fact, at the end of that summer I had gained a Post Office savings account because I never spent a penny of my wages. As well as the money, we were provided with bucket loads of food and drink, including bottles of cider at haymaking time, and cigarettes, endless supplies of woodbines. Thing is, I didn't drink or smoke, I suppose I should have been paid more but the Boss was a tight old bastard and the Missus didn't even tell him I was getting the four bob.

Here I am on the farm.

It's seven in the morning and I've just walked the two or three miles from my house on the council estate to the farm on the marshland overlooking the Burry Estuary. The Missus calls me into the farmhouse – breakfast is ready. A fisherman is just leaving and there is a large fresh flatfish frying on the hob. Later on we'll have sackfuls of chips, bread and butter, and tinned peaches in heavy syrup. The Missus grabs my arm and pushes two two-shilling pieces into my hand.

"Don't tell the Boss."

I nod and smile.

"Sit down. There's plenty more."

I sit down on the heavy oak bench. She slides the fish onto a plate and puts it down on the table in front of me, next to the stack of bread and butter and the large teapot.

I tuck in.

Two other boys of the same age arrive, they've come from the opposite direction, I think they actually live across the Loughor river, which is really the territory of the next town – Swansea. I'm not impressed with them, nor them with me. Luckily, there is usually so much to do we don't have time to kill each other.

Mikey, the fat one, who is about a year older than me, shoves me along the bench and grabs my plate of fish.

The Missus smiles at him: "Mikey, be patient will you. There's plenty more, and I've kept a nice fat one for you, you're a big boy."

He smiles with spoilt pleasure and shoves the plate back towards me. I'm not hungry any more but I have to eat it to avoid offending the Missus.

The Boss comes in from the yard.

"Come on boys," he says in his gruff voice, "there's cows to be milked, they're waiting in the cowshed, come on boys, time is money."

I get up straight away, leaving only a few bones on my plate and follow him outside, at least it's better than sitting with those horrible Swansea Jacks.

After the milking and after the cows have been herded back into the field we have time for a short break. I choose to sit on a bale of old hay near the entrance to the old barn where the chickens that run wild in the farmyard lay their eggs.

I forgot to say that my friend Ken is here as well, well I didn't exactly forget, thing is, I'm pretty pissed off with him at the moment. We had an argument you see, a pretty bad argument. and I don't want to talk to him or talk about him for a while, so I'm hoping he won't show up.

He shows up.

I ignore him.

"Come on mun," he says, "be a sport. There's no need for that.."

"You shouldn't have done it. It wasn't right."

"You're being soft now. He deserved it and you know it."

"But he's the boss's son. Anyway, it doesn't matter who he is, you still shouldn't have done it."

"But he threatened us with a shotgun."

"No he didn't, he was only joking, it wasn't even loaded. There was no need to steal that money out of his pocket."

"Halvers," said Ken, "we'll go halvers, a fiver each."

"You keep it."

"You're a stupid bugger."

~

Funny isn't it. If my kids were that age now and if they wanted to go and work on a farm for seven days a week, twelve hours a day for whatever today's equivalent of four bob is, I wouldn't know whether to think they were incredibly brave or incredibly stupid, but I do know one thing – it would never have happened.

You know when you're young and your older relatives keep reminding you about how tough it was when they were young? Well, when you get older you realise they were right and not only that, but your own children are having it even easier then you did. So, you can imagine that by the time your grandchildren have grandchildren, their children will be so soft and spoilt that they'll turn into squashy blobs.

~

Time is a triangle. Past, present, future. The three sides of the triangle and not one of them is a hypotenuse, not one of them is more real than the others.

~

When you're a parent you want to protect your family. You have a purpose, a duty (not a duty that you feel any reluctance to do, well most of the time anyway), but when they grow up you realise you can't protect them forever. I mean, we went to Tesco earlier on tonight, mainly to get petrol, but we popped into the shop to get a few bananas, tomatoes and stuff as well and to be honest, we went as a way of breaking up a boring evening in front of the telly.

While we were there we went to the small baskets queue and bloody hell, we queued behind a pair of old codgers with a proper wheeled trolley, and it was full to the top with cheap, reduced food (it was about half nine). The woman was obviously in her eighties and the man in his sixties – mother and son I guessed, still together after all that time. Don't get me wrong, they looked happy, in their own way, happy, but eccentric, in today's world at least.

The cashiers didn't know whether to be amused or annoyed at their behaviour, and to be honest, neither did I. In the end I came down on the side of mild amusement, but then, thinking about it now, that was a bit patronising of me. Just because they choose to eke out their limited income by spending a couple of hours scouring Tesco for cheap, but perfectly eatable food and they looked like something out of the early fifties when post-war rationing was still in force, doesn't mean I have the right to judge them or snigger at them in any way.

That poor old woman couldn't have known that when she gave birth all those decades ago she'd still be caring for her son in the twenty-first century. I don't know if I'm that strong, it's difficult to accept that much responsibility, but then what do you do? You give them a good education and you school them in the ways of the world, at least as you see them and you then have to let them go. Then what have you got left?

What is left?

n i n e t e e n

"The world is getting more spiritual. When I say spiritual I don't mean religious, I mean that there is now more discussion in the media about the nature of reality. The media is often blamed for the disintegration of society but I believe that the media will be our saviour. The new incarnation of God on this planet is not in the form of an avatar as in the past. There is no single person who embodies the essence of all that is holy. The new messiah is a global being that is made of electronic signals transmitted miraculously through the essence of physical life itself, i.e. the air that we breathe. Reality Television in particular is contributing to the new spirituality because it challenges the myths that we have constructed to represent 'real life'. We know that what we are watching is real, but we also know that it is not real. This leads to thought processes that question the reality of our 'actual' real lives. There is a danger associated with this phenomenon, a danger of mass madness and consequently mass medication by prescribed or recreational drugs, which would obviously lead to the weakening and eventual demise of the human being."

So writes John Messenger in part of the justification for his exhibition at a disused television studio in Cardiff. Messenger's work consists of a melee of video screens of various sizes and specifications, from multiple video walls to hand-held televisions. Some of the screens are hooked up to CCTV cameras located in the area around the studio, others are linked to webcams positioned in busy shopping streets and private homes around the city, the country and the world and others play DVDs compiled by the artist. Because of the random nature of the material, every visitor will have a unique experience of the work, just as every individual has a unique experience of life itself. I won't spoil it by describing it in any more detail, just go and see it; it's an enlightening experience.

Thing is, you can't actually go and see John Messenger's exhibition, at least not in the disused television studios in Cardiff, because that exhibition ended a long time ago, but you get my drift. It's a complicated life. There are so many variables; it's impossible to guarantee that things will go according to your plan, whatever that is. Take me for instance, there I was going along, quite happily, thinking that although, granted, I, we, had had a hard time, we still had each other. That's her, and me. But I'm not so sure any more, she's been acting very odd lately. I know she works hard, and she's a woman and all that but there's something different about her lately. It could be me I suppose; it could be my perception of her that's changed.

"Do you think there's such a thing as a male menopause?" I ask.

"You'll be wanting to have babies next." She says.

"No, I mean, I read something about the bone structure changing or something. Changes happen, physical, physiological changes."

"I'm sure they do. Just keep taking the tablets."

"I mean, when things happen in your life, things change don't they? Not just things, but the way you see things changes as well."

She looked disinterested.

"How's things in work anyway?" I ask.

"All right, usual bollocks, staff problems, admin problems, but nothing I can't handle."

"How about you? How are you feeling now?"

"All right."

"The other day you were in a right state, aches and pains everywhere, tired, nasty."

"Nasty?" She says.

"Yes, you were very nasty to me. If I'd taken any notice of what you said I'd be long gone by now."

"Oh shut up, you know how it is."

"But you told me you hated me. Called me a pratt."

"You are a pratt."

"Am I?"

"You can be – sometimes."

"When?"

"Like now, for instance."

"Oh."

"Yes, shut up. I've had a hard day and I've got ordering to do tomorrow."

"Poor you."

~

"It's my mother." Lucy said, and it was obviously something very traumatic for her because she could hardly talk with the emotion.

I waited.

"It's my father."

"Your father, Ken? Why? What's wrong Lucy?"

"I found things out."

"Things?"

"He's a bastard."

I, of course, agreed with that sentiment, but there was no way I was going to tell her that, so I said: "Well, he's always been brilliant with you. I thought you were happy. What's he done?"

"It's what he is."

"How do you mean?"

The emotion came again but before she could speak the lights went out behind the counter of the beach café.

"I think we'd better get out of here." I said. "I'll give you a lift home, we can talk on the way."

"I don't want to go home. I can't, not now."

"Well we'd better get out of here anyway. We can talk on the way to the car. It's parked about half a mile away, in a side street. The things I do to avoid paying for parking, I don't know."

She nodded, still too choked to speak properly. We left the café and walked in the dark away from the beach to the quiet street where I had left my car. We sat in the car silently for five minutes while Lucy composed herself. I put the radio on and rolled myself a cigarette.

"Don't suppose you've got anything stronger?" She asked. "I could do with a smoke now."

At last she was coming back to life. "If only." I said. "How are you feeling now?"

"Better," she said, "it's good to talk."

I nodded, still waiting for her to open up. To be honest, I wasn't being truly altruistic; sure, I did care about her, as much as you can care about an old friend's daughter, a girl I had observed growing up without a mother. A girl I thought had a secure and loving relationship with her father, even if I did now think of him as a manifestation of evil. In a way I was glad, perhaps Lucy would give me information that I could use to finally put paid to the fucker.

~

My uncle's funeral today. He was 75. I meant to go although I didn't want to, I felt I had to go and say goodbye to the old bugger. So, I dressed up in my finest and drove to Llanelli Town Centre. I parked in the Asda car park (50p for two hours and a full refund if you spend more than a fiver in the shop) and walked through town towards the Catholic church. Uncle Ronald had converted to Catholicism a couple of decades or more ago and all he wanted when he was told he was going to die before Christmas was a Catholic mass and then internment in the town's Box Cemetery. I assume he got his wish because I didn't actually go to the funeral. What it was, was that I arrived in town too early and killed some time (I wonder if killed time ever has a funeral?) by going to a bank to pay in some cheques for my daughter, anyway, there was a queue in the bank, so by the time I'd paid the cheques in it was too late to go to the church.

That's a feeble excuse I know but as I shuffled in the queue in the bank, I thought about it and decided that I couldn't face the funeral after all. I wouldn't have been able to go to the cemetery afterwards or to the 'do' in the New Dock Stars rugby club after that because I've got to go and do some teaching early this afternoon. Instead I sat in silence for one minute on a bench outside the entrance to the shopping centre and contemplated his existence. I chose that particular spot to sit in silence because that's the epicentre of where he used to hover and harangue innocent family members, acquaintances and strangers with his nonsense babbling. I lost patience with him eventually (he'd been doing that sort of thing ever since I was a boy) and learnt how to dodge him or to cut his psychobabble short by being rude.

I don't feel particularly guilty about the way I treated him because he was a bit of an emotional leech and a time-stealer but a hell of a character and a nice man all the same. Anyway, he's gone now; they're putting his leftovers in the ground as I write this, at least he had his faith.

There is a part of me that wants to make everything perfect, but thank fuck it's only a small part. It has a quiet nagging voice that can make life a bit of a pain in the arse, but it's not me. The only thing that keeps it going, the thing that feeds it, is failure. Every fresh failure (and I get plenty of those) extends its life, gives it more energy (that's a funny word to use for something so negative, energy is always a good thing, isn't it?), and so the nagging continues. I'm hoping that some day, the failures will be over and then I can sit back and watch as the light of success obliterates the

quiet nag.
   Not yet.
   Not yet though.
   Soon.
   I promise.
   Soon, I promise.
   Death or success.
   Death or success?
   Success then.
   That year, that year 1971, the year when everything happened, that was the end and the beginning, the beginning and the end. All the seeds of the rest of my life were sown then and the sower became the reaper, as sowers do. The sower sows life, the sower sustains life, and the sower reaps life. The sower is the reaper, don't you see? I didn't, not then, but I do now.

~

There are certain rules to living; choose to ignore them and you'd better be sure you're a good swimmer. For example, it is essential that you get up early every day and oblute thoroughly; then you're ready for anything and it's not even 8 am. Next, don't panic; the best way to achieve this is to keep everything orderly, and finally do not spend money you haven't got, or else that's all you'll think about is money – how to get it, how to pay it back.
   Trouble is, unless you're my mother-in-law, the rules are anathema to the essence of all that is human.
   Talking about being human, you remember that artist? That John Messenger? That artist, John Messenger and all that shit he spouted about the media being the saviour because it exposes the illusion that is reality, (Or the reality that is illusion? You decide.) Well, I forgot to add that I met him again and he went on to say that that isn't reality at all. He said that the only thing that mattered

in the end was love, and he wasn't talking about the love between two people as in a loving partnership, although that's part of it. No, he was talking just about love, which is the same as respect, the same as harmony, the same as tolerance, and that the media construction he had constructed was nothing more than a construction. Quite obvious really isn't it?

~

Me and her are sitting in the kitchen. We've just come back from Tesco shopping, you know, the kind of shopping where you prowl the aisles of Tesco or Sainsburys or Asda or wherever and scowl through the comestibles and consumables, avoiding eye contact in case you have to recognise the opposition's humanity and concede some love and respect to them, while resenting every mass-produced piece of shit you put in your trolley. So, we've just come back from shopping and we've put the tins and packets in the cupboards of the new Japanese Maple kitchen units and the fruit and veg and such like in the fridge, and we're having a cup of coffee and reading the Saturday Guardian as our reward when she turns to me and says:

"There's a piece in here about you."

"Me? Where?"

"It says . . . . oh, you'd better read it yourself." She hands me the paper.

"Where? What?"

"That little piece there, about grumpy miserable men, about how they suddenly realise they're not immortal and go off on one getting obsessed about something."

"What do you mean? I'm not obsessed about anything."

"Hmm"

"Let's see, what does it say? Right, so, mmm, no, it doesn't say that at all, and anyway I'm not grumpy and miserable, or selfish, like it says here."

"You're self-obsessed."

"Why are you starting this now? Do you want an argument?"

"Well, you have to admit that you've been very introverted for the last couple of years."

"Introverted? Me?"

"Introspective I mean, very inward-looking, as if that's all that matters is what's going on inside your head."

"I think I've done all right, more than all right, considering . . ."

"Yeah, yeah, this is what I mean."

"You don't understand. I just think in a particular way that's all; I can't help it. I mean, some people are Buddhist monks, others are popcorn sellers in Venezuela, some people wander around India with hardly anything on and scrounge off everyone else. It doesn't mean they're bad, just that they've got a different take on life, that's all."

"Why don't you just go and be a Sadhu then, or a fucking monk."

"Hey, hey, what's going on?"

"You think you're special, a special kind of person with a special kind of outlook on life and you have to go and shove it down everyone's throat, as if you're the only one who's ever thought about these things."

"It's not that. I just don't care about the things most people care about, I'm different that's all."

"Arrogant bastard, you mean better don't you? Not different, but better."

"No, I don't think that. I mean in the scale of things, on a universal level I mean, we're hardly different, or better, whatever that's supposed to mean, than chimpanzees, or even fish. I just like to look at the wider picture."

"You sanctimonious bastard."

"Whoa, whoa."

"I'm not a fucking horse."

"What is it?"

"Just read the fucking article. You're having a mid-life crisis, the male menopause. You've just realised that you're mortal, that you're a creature of blood and guts, something you've never had to deal with."

"What? Only woman bleed? Is that what this is all about?"

"I don't know."

"Maybe you're right. I'll read the article, I'll look into it." Fancy another cup of coffee?"

~

Remember The Relevant Artist? Do you remember him? He was the pompous old git whose wife was having an affair with Ken, and I stitched them all up in a review on the Internet. Anyway, if you don't remember, it doesn't matter. This is the story so far.

Ken was screwing this woman who was married to this old-guy artist. This artist was very famous and talked of in the same sentences as Kyffin Williams (who is a big artist type of cheese in Wales). At the time, I wanted to hurt Ken, having gradually come to the realisation that he was a completely amoral bastard, but he didn't get touched at all by it. Well, that wasn't the exact truth; truth is, Ken did get affected by it, but not in the way I thought.

"Hey," he called after me as I was coming out of the bank in Stepney Street. "hold on."

I stopped.

"You clever bastard, what the fuck have you gone and done now?"

"What do you mean?"

"That fucking artist I put you on to. He's fucking dead."

"I know."

"Yes, well, I didn't realise before that he knew about me and his wife."

"Oh yes."

"Aye, she told me last night, she'd just buried the old bastard. Came looking for me, in the club. Haven't seen her for months."

"I know. She went to live with her sister in Scotland."

"Oh, you knew?"

"Well, it's my job."

"He made her go, said he'd not give her a penny if she didn't go."

"I know. He didn't give her much choice."

"How do you know?"

"As I said, it's my job, I hear things. If he hadn't paid her off there would have been a huge fuss and he was up for chairman of the Arts Council or something. His mates in Cardiff wouldn't have liked a fuss."

"She said it was something to do with you."

"Oh."

"Yes, something you wrote. I didn't get all the details."

"It's funny how things, especially words, can be misinterpreted. I didn't mean anything by it."

"Whatever. Anyway, you did me a favour. She was getting on my tits to tell the truth, getting a bit long in the tooth for me. After she disappeared I hooked up with Tanya, now her old man's a big cheese in the building trade. One of the best contacts I ever made."

"That's good." I said.

~

I am a child. I am less than ten years old. I go to school every weekday, except in the holidays. Yesterday I saw a boy being cruel to a cat. He tied a banger to a cat's tail and lit it. The cat ran away and the banger fell off and rolled under a car. The banger exploded with a little pop.

The next morning, in school assembly, the headmaster made a speech about how it is very bad to be cruel to animals. He said that some boys on the estate had been torturing cats and that the police knew who they were and all they were waiting for was for them to do it again and then they would be arrested.

Last night, after seeing the cat and the banger, I had a dream. The dream wasn't about cats. It was about me playing touch with three bears. One of them bit me and I woke up. Luckily, my mother had left a sausage meat sandwich and a glass of water by my bed, and even more luckily, my brother was fast asleep next to me and hadn't eaten it.

I told my mother about the dream but she just laughed.

So I told her about some of the other thoughts I got, about lying in bed and sort of staring through the ceiling into space and past the stars and on and on forever, except that's where my mind said stop and I got scared.

She got angry then, and told me to shut up.

"What's the point of thinking like that?" She said.

twenty

This is 'The Three Bears'. I was going to call this book 'This is my Reality' but I heard David Icke use the same phrase on 'Diners' the other night so I changed the title. You know David Icke? Well, he's that nutter who used to be a sports presenter on the BBC or somewhere. He seemed like any other sports presenter at the time but suddenly we heard, about ten years ago I suppose, (through the media of course) that he'd packed it all in and become some sort of new age prophet or something. 'Diners' is a programme on BBC Choice (and sometimes on BBC2) where pairs (it's usually pairs) have a free dinner in a restaurant and the BBC record their conversations with hidden cameras, (the participants know the cameras are there somewhere, but can't see them).

Anyway David Icke reckons, according to the conversation he had on Diners, that the world is controlled by a group of aliens or something, I can't remember the details, so I thought, fuck that, I don't want to be associated with a nutter like that. I mean, come on, aliens? But then I thought that it doesn't matter a fuck anyway. I mean, why should it bother me who controls the world? It could well be aliens, whoever it is, it's not me, and in the end even aliens must be mortal, so it will all end anyway, everything ends; everything ends because it begins. But by then, I'd changed the title anyway and now I can't be bothered to change it back, anyway I quite like the image of the Three Bears. (I suppose I could still call it 'This is my Reality' and still have a picture of the Three Bears on the cover. Anyway, time will tell.)

~

Lucy. Lucy. Lucy. What am I going to do? Here you are, suffering, wondering. What's happening to you? This shouldn't be happening to you, but it is. It's so unnecessary, so much wasted time, suffering unnecessarily. Unnecessary suffering, if only reality didn't get in the way. I'm sorry Lucy, I have to go and deal with reality. I'll get back to you as soon as I can. Just hold in there, and remember – this too must pass.

~

Let's get the fucking paper the right way round. Let's get the correct pen. Let's get the fag rolled, the ashtray emptied, the fag lit and then let us begin. This is an exercise in creative writing, no, that's Creative Writing, with two great big fucking capital letters, one at the beginning of each word to signify they represent more than the expression they convey. This is an exercise in Creative Writing.

The first rule of Creative Writing, they say, is to write about what you know, your own reality (ies?). So then it's not exactly Fiction (another word with a capital first letter, watch out for these, and *italics,* and underlined, and bold – they mean that you're not being creative enough), but it's not exactly fact either (should Fact be capitalised?). You've heard of poetic (or artistic) license? Well that's the third rule. (I forgot the second rule is not to use words with Initial Capital Letters unless they're proper ones and not to use things like *italics,* underlining, bold etc. (or things like etc. come to that) Are there any more rules? Not really. In fact, the first three rules aren't that important, in fact, fuck the rules, all of them.

There are no rules in this game boy.

That's when I usually wake up, but get this, sometimes when I wake up it's only into another dream, but it takes a few seconds to realise that, sometimes longer, and then, after squeezing my eyes tight shut before opening them again and finding myself in another place that could be a dream, and it is, and I'm getting suspicious by now and wondering if I'll ever get back to fully conscious reality, so I settle for this.

But it's been a long time now, in this reality, so I guess it must be the real one, at least it will have to do for the time being because I'm too tired to fight it any more and here I am, here is where I've made my home.

So, in this reality, there are things I have to deal with, things besides the essentials, like sleeping and eating and earning a living. Things like Ken and Lucy and Her (capital allowed), because that's all that's left now. These are the only things I have to deal with now, so what's stopping me? Maybe I've just run out of steam, maybe there's no oomph left in me, I'll just have to accept all these unresolved things that are bugging me.

But then again, maybe not.

OK, Ken. Here I come.

I'm going to sort you out at last.

Ken will be in the club, he's bound to be, it's like his domain, his kingdom, and he likes to sit on his throne in the bar, his fat gut pressed against the dark wood table, the cheeks of his fat arse hanging out the sides of the chair. He'll be drinking as usual, smoking dope, nipping off to the toilet or his office now and again to stick some cocaine up his ugly nose (although he pretends to have a weak bladder), that's the one thing he seems to be ashamed of – his weakness.

Problem is, I can't be seen in the club, can't be seen by anyone tonight, got to avoid the CCTV cameras and the nosy cops – got to get through the network of Ken spies like Gollum – got to kill the bastard. That's the only way it will end unless I just disappear, vanish into that land of bumness where nobody knows and nobody cares. But I'm not going to do that, because I've got pride, and besides I wouldn't leave the rest of them in the shit like that, because there's bound to be some repercussions (not all of them bad I'm sure but I can't take the risk).

So it's got to be Ken.

He's got to have it.

He's got to go.

I've got to kill the cunt.

And it's got to be tonight.

Why?

Why has it got to be tonight?

Well, it's got to be some time, and if I leave it any longer it'll just go on and on, and it can't because it's got to stop.

So, I'll wait. I'll wait in the shadows behind the club. I'll wait in the derelict site where Ken parks his Jag, and I'll wait until he leaves, and I'll approach him in the shadows, and there'll be no one else there, and there'll be no CCTV. And he'll give me a lift, even though he's been drinking his stinking whisky all night, because he knows he'll get away with it; he know the cops won't touch him in his Jag, because . . . .

Sorry, I've got to interrupt, there's a hundred thousand bits of shit floating about in space, a hundred thousand bits that have fallen off space rockets, and scientists have discovered that orang-utans have culture – wow, for fuck's sake, I could have told them that. They'll be telling us next that animals don't like being slaughtered for food.

Sorry, car radio on – World Service News – 2am. Still waiting for Ken in the shadows. Where is the bastard?

The back door of the club opens and Ken spills out with the light; he's obviously pissed. I turn the radio off in my car and make sure the interior light is set to permanently off; I open the door and close it carefully. I wait in the darker shadows. Fuck, someone else comes out after Ken and they walk to his car together, it's a woman, one of the bar staff if I remember, a skinny, greasy woman called Cynthia, late thirties I guess, though she could be younger and just have had a hard life being a slave to bastards like Ken. She's not his type.

They get to the car and he gets in and drives away. She puts her head down and shuffles up an alley to the main street – perhaps she lives in a flat around the corner or something. I get back in my car and sit there for a minute wondering what to do. Then I decide, fuck it, I'll follow him, perhaps I'll get a chance if he stops for a piss or something, he does live a few miles out of town.

He's well away by now and it takes me over five minutes to get his taillights in sight. He's driving quite slowly. I wonder what's on his mind. What do evil bastards think about? He probably gets off just by thinking about all the innocent fucks he's screwed today. He probably counts his money in his head. He probably bathes in smugness and animal satisfaction like a dirty dog that's just fucked the neighbourhood bitch.

Wait, he's pulling in to a bus stop, I'll just cruise past nonchalantly and turn right as soon as I can. I turn right about a hundred yards further along the road and immediately do a three-point turn and end up parked in the mouth of the junction with my lights off. I can just see the bus stop from where I am and Ken's car, glistening and lit up as if he doesn't have to worry about flattening the battery. He takes his time. I get impatient. I drive past him slowly. He's talking on a mobile phone. I carry on back the way we originally came and turn right at the next junction – a gravelly lane beside a closed petrol station. I do the three-point turn thing and get out of the car. I'm not happy with the position, I can't quite see his car from here, unless I get out of my car and lean out into the road. I'll have to risk it and get back in front of him.

As I pass the bus stop again, he tries to pull out in front of me. We nearly crash. He sees me and his anger turns to amusement. I wave at him as if it's the most natural thing in the world that he should almost bump into me at something past two on a deserted road, miles away from where I live. I'll have to check the tide times out, maybe I can blag a fishing trip? But that wouldn't work because he knows I'm a vegan. I carry on driving away from the town and towards Ken's house. There's no turning offs for the next mile and a half, I hope he doesn't catch up with me before that.

But it doesn't work, a minute later he's behind me flashing like a kid with a new torch. I have to pull over. There is a dark layby on this barely lit stretch of road, the sort of place where bacon butty vans park up during the day and councils dump their surplus chippings. Tonight it's deserted and quiet – too quiet.

Ken jumps out of his car seconds after me and yells at me immediately.

"Hey you old git, what's going on, have you got some bint on the go up here then?" The volume of his voice decreases the closer he gets to me.

I laugh. "Ken." I say.

"How you doing?" He asks.

"Well, I was just . . . . "

He interrupts me before I need to search for the excuse in my brain. "Guess what? Go on, guess what?"

I shrug.

"I've had a bit of luck my boy. Uncle Ken has finally hit the big time. I'll see you all right now. If anyone deserves it you do, after all you've been through. I told you I wouldn't forget what you did didn't I? Well now your luck's in at last."

I shrugged again.

"Tell you what," he said, putting his drunken arm around my shoulders – patronising twat. "Come back to mine for a drink and I'll tell you all about it. There's nobody else in, Lucy is out with some friends in Swansea or something. You can leave that old banger here, let the gippos pick it up, you won't be needing that any more. Come on, jump in. Come on."

Might as well, I think. This could be my chance.

When we get to Ken's house, and I've not been near any of his houses for a few years, I'm shocked by the tacky opulence he lives in. The place smells of expensive, sickly-smelling aftershave and what I can only describe as stale cum. It's furnished with ornate chairs and gold-framed mirrors with a very expensive but horribly patterned deep wool carpet. The rooms are crammed with shiny and shitty objects, as if he'd visited the department store of the rich but stupid and bought the most expensive stuff there without regard for the style.

The first thing he did was to spill some cocaine on the shiny top of a dining table and snort a huge noseful. I declined, never done it, never want to do it.

"Come on, we're celebrating, don't be up your own arse so much for fuck's sake. Don't you want to share in this special occasion with your bestest, oldest mate?"

There was a look about him that said: sniff or be damned and since I was here to kill him I thought I might as well play along.

"OK. OK, " I laughed and took the rolled up fifty off him and leant down towards the coke. As it happened he lost interest then because he was so into his own reflection in one of the mirrors, so I rearranged the powder to make it look as if I'd taken some and made the appropriate noises.

"Good, isn't it? Only the best from your old pal."

"Yeah, cool," I smiled as wide as I could. Perhaps if I encouraged him, the drugs would do the deed for me. I wondered if you could do a fatal overdose of cocaine.

Ken got some nice lead-crystal tumblers and tipped some Jack Daniels into them. That I could handle. We sat down and he pressed a button on a remote control. Music came from every corner of the room, it was only cheesy eighties music but it was OK and it sounded good through the expensive system.

"What's it all about?" I asked.

"Sex, drugs and rock and roll." He laughed.

I forced a chuckle.

"You and me," he said, "you and me, we've always been mates

as long as I remember, we go a long way back, in fact, you're the only person I call a friend in this fucking world of fucking sharks and scorpions – treacherous bastards."

"I suppose so." I said.

"There's no suppose so about it," he said, "I know we've had our ups and downs but at the end of the day, we're the same, you and me."

"Are we?"

"We both think the same way about life. The world is full of wankers, piss-artists, bastards trying to rip you off. Tossers."

He got a fit of the giggles then and dropped his glass on the glass-topped coffee table. It smashed.

"Never mind," he said, still giggling, "it doesn't matter any more, none of it matters, you can say goodbye to this stinking little corner of the world. Hang on, I need a piss."

Ken grabbed the bottle of Jack Daniels on his way to the toilet and took huge swigs out of it as he stumbled across the carpet. As he staggered into the downstairs loo I got up and followed him in.

~

Remember I told you that I was telling this story live? That I was just letting it all flow and that there was hardly any editing or going back and rewriting as I went along. Well that's all gone to fucking pieces now. It all fell apart about halfway through. Thing is, I don't think like that, and I can't behave like that no matter how much I try, it just doesn't work for me.

I am a grasshopper.

I live in the garden.

When I compress my muscles to jump I lose control and close my eyes, that way you never know where you're going to end up. I just leap into the dark.

~

Mike the loser eventually drowned. What the silly bastard was doing near water I'll never know; he could never swim. I remember once when we were dossing in Tenby, we all wanted to go for a boat trip to Caldey Island to see the monks. When I say 'we all', I mean the group of freaks we had hooked up with that year. There was a guy with long, wavy blond hair with a big nose – he was kinda cool. Then there was this ginger guy from Gorseinon, he was a fucking lunatic, he used to drop a whole tube of travel sickness pills in one go, the ones with some anaesthetic drug in them that induced what was called a 'twilight sleep', whatever the fuck that means. I think his name was Jake or something, anyway it sounds about right for a redhead. The tall blond one was Mark, I think. As well as Mark and Jake there was me, of course, Mike, and a couple of local boys who used to hang around with us freaks for some kudos or something.

We got on the boat but Mike wouldn't come within fifty feet of the water, it was all we could do to get him to sit at the top of the beach when the tide was out. So we left him there, jammy bastard. He ended up getting off with a sweet English girl who was on holidays with her parents. The boat trip turned into a fiasco after Jake started hallucinating and thought there was a squad of heavily armed frogmen circling the boat.

The point is that Mike was shit scared of water, so what the fuck was he doing boating in Blackpill in Swansea. They fished him out of the water one day, they said he had taken a boat out on his own and not come back, at the end of the day they went looking and found his body semi submerged in some water weeds.

I'd lost touch with just about everybody by then, apart from the ubiquitous Ken of course, in fact it was him that told me what had happened to Mike. Come to think of it, it wasn't long after that time I went to visit Mike in his house. I didn't even know that him

and Ken still had links.
Anyway.

twenty one

Thank God for failure. Too easy success makes you smug. Smugness is bad. Smugness leads to failure. Failure is good. Smugness is good. Success is good. Everything is right. Everything is wrong. Wrong is right. Life is the bit that changes in time. Culture is the way we deal with change – with life. Society is a collaboration with inevitably. Make it work for you. That's all you have to do. Unless you're a bum, and you can't. But you're not, are you. Are you? Imagine no bums, no criminals, not that bums are criminals. Successful criminals are not bums. They have made it work for them. Imagine no crime . . . . . . No Locks. No Police. No Courts. No Lawyers. No Government. No Profit. No Loss. No Bums. Unless you're a happy bum. Are you?

It's not far away, one redundancy, one broken marriage, a couple of months of losing it, and you're a bum. How desperately we cling on to our little bits of security – our jobs, most of us that is, all of us who have any sense. But not me. Oh no, I can't cling on to anything; it's all falling away from me. Where is she? She's the only one who can help me when I get like this. She doesn't know it, but just her being there, in the same space as me, she doesn't have to be in the same room even, just within earshot say. It's like, without her, and I know it's a cliché, but without her I'd be nothing, a bum perhaps.

On the other hand I know that's not true, because I'm a normal human being and as such am very adaptable, we have to be to survive don't we? Anyway, I'd survive, I suppose. What if she doesn't come home? What if today's the day? It's got to happen some day, it's inevitable. Where the fuck is she?

There was a time, and it was a long time ago, in human life terms that is, about thirty years I suppose, when I used to have the same feelings that I'm having now. Well, they're kind of the same, but not exactly of course. And then again a long time before that, a longer time, perhaps ten years before the thirty years. I heard someone say the other day that time shrinks as you get older so for example the ten years between the ages of ten and twenty are actually longer than the thirty years between the ages of twenty and fifty. I don't know if I agree with that, in fact I do know, I don't agree with it, in fact, I think it's bollocks, it's just a way for some bitter old git to freak all the beautiful young things out.

It's so easy to forget all those feelings you get that mean you're alive. The fear and the unknowing, the feeling of an endless stretch of time in front of you, but when you look ahead you can only see a fuzziness. In time the fuzziness resolves but it's never the same as you imagined, still, we're all creatures of blood and bones and fur and feathers, and we all have to live in this gross world, except it's not supposed to be like that is it? It's supposed to be all light and love and success and fulfilment. Is it better to work hard and earn your comforts? Or is it better to go for it and only chase the things that make you feel good? Or can you work hard and feel good at the same time?

Why is life shit?

How can I answer questions like that? How can anyone answer? Why does she, Lucy I mean, expect me to know these things?

"I don't know," I say, but I feel I have to say more. The young are very demanding. So what do I do? Do I tell her the truth? Yes Lucy, life is shit and I don't know why, or do I pretend that she's just going through a bad patch and that it'll be all right in the end?

"This too must pass." I say, and smile at her with the most benevolent older, wiser expression I can get together considering that I'm probably feeling more shit than she is.

"What do you mean?" She asks, already coming out of her black hole, there's nothing like a bit of cod wisdom to distract the unnecessarily introvert.

"It's just something an old friend of mine said to me once. When I was younger than you. I was going through something at the time. You know, I can't remember what it was now, something to do with drugs I suppose. Anyway, I remember when and where – approximately. I was sitting with him, Sam his name was, on a bench in People's Park in town. He was a good friend, the best."

"Where is he now?"

"He died."

"Was it drugs?"

"No, not directly."

"Did my father know him as well?"

"I suppose so. Yes, he did. But anyway, this isn't about me."

"But I'd like to know what he was like."

"Who, Sam?"

"No, my father. What was he like when he was young? Were you and him always friends? Was he always such a bad person?"

"He had his good points. Listen, I've got to nip up the shop for some potatoes. Do you want to come for a walk? You can wait here if you want. At least it's nice and warm."

"And safe. I've always felt safe with you, even when I was a little girl."

I smile, but wonder what I've let myself in for. Ken was the only parent she knew and even though he was a complete evil bastard, he always doted on his daughter. Now that he's gone she's got no one else. Still at least some good came from Ken's life, she's a lovely girl.

On my way up the road to the shop all I think abut is Lucy. How am I going to tell her that her father was what he was? I know she hates him at the moment and perhaps she'll tell me the details when I get back but how can I tell her what I know? Perhaps I won't say anything, perhaps she'll get used to not having him around. I'll do my best, within the constraints of my own life but I can't promise her too much.

I'm getting to the top of the road, it's a cold day but the old boys are out in force along the street. I stop and talk to one of them, he's one of the younger old boys, still in his sixties I suppose, still active, he might still even be working. I heard that he found his wife dead in the bath last year but we don't talk about that, I haven't got that kind of relationship with him, it's more like this:

Him: All right, how you doing boy? Still messing about with computers?
Me: Yes. Bit of this, bit of that, you know.
Him: Bit of the other.
Me: *(laughs)*
Him: Bloody cold today.
Me: Bloody cold. Um, how's the club?
Him: All right, could do with a few more members. How about you?
Me: Me? Bowls? I don't think so. It's not my cup of tea.
Him: You'd be surprised, there's a lot of younger people getting involved nowadays.
Me: It's not that. I've never been interested in sport. Never been any good at it I suppose, and I was put off by a bastard of a gym teacher in school.
Him: Bloody cold isn't it?
Me: *(fake shiver)* Yes, better get on.
Him: Tara.
Me: Tara.

I buy a scratchcard in the shop, one of those where you can win a car. I scratch it surreptitiously as I walk back to the house. I win two pounds. I hide it in the inside pocket of my big black coat. I'll get two cards to replace it the next time I'm in the shop, if I remember.

My world disintegrates when I get back in the house. Lucy is naked. I think 'how old is she?' She's well into her twenties. She's lovely, like something out of a Greek legend.

"How do you like it?" She asks. Her face is kind of blank but smiling. She's not lovely at all, in fact if I were the same age as her I wouldn't fancy her a bit. Just because I'm older doesn't mean that I fancy every younger woman. Who does she think she is for fuck's sake, I mean.

I stop in my tracks and take a step back.

"What's the matter?" She tries pouting and makes a step towards me.

I hold out my hand like a traffic policeman. "Stop!"

Her blank expression screws up, her smile drops down, she starts to sob. I nearly go over and put my arm around her, she looks so pathetic and vulnerable, instead I turn to face away from her and say: "Go and get dressed and then we'll talk." I hear her sobbing as she leaves the room.

Five minutes later and the kettle's just come to the boil. Lucy is sitting with her head bowed, at the kitchen table and I'm spooning fair trade coffee into two chipped mugs.

I give her one.

~

The other day, I thought I was going to die, I mean I thought I was actually dying. I had this pain in my left shoulder and a kind of throbbing in my left arm, then, to top it all the little finger in my left hand went numb. I thought, that's it, the game's up, no more me. I will admit that despite all the spiritual bullshit I've spouted and all that philosophical crap I've banged on about, about not being afraid of death etc., I got very scared. Not scared that I thought my life was in immediate danger as in a few seconds away, but scared in the sense that this was the beginning of a short journey through examinations and hospitals and drugs and operations, that would last a few months at most and would be signposted by pain and humiliation.

I've been in hospital before you see, for what was supposed to be a simple hernia operation – but that's another story, anyway, when I was there, I was in the same ward as old men dying, proud old men disintegrating rapidly, and it wasn't a pretty sight. Anyway, I thought I was prepared for all that and I thought that all I had to do was to put something in the world, you know, leave something behind as a legacy, even if it was only a novel or a painting or a book of poems. I'd go so far as to say that in fact I was desperate to leave something behind me, some gem of genius that shone a light on the human condition for hundreds of generations to come. That's all I wanted.

I was sitting on a chair in the living room, she was sitting on the settee; we were drinking tea and arguing, the usual bollocks about me not liking the place we live and her not wanting to move, in fact she was telling me to go and move away on my own if it was so important and I was trying to get her to see the bigger picture. It was Friday afternoon about five o'clock.

"I feel funny," I said. Not very imaginative is it? But it's an effective way to get the ball rolling. It would lead to questions and then to my responses and I'd have flagged my impending demise to her so that she wouldn't be too shocked if I keeled over there and then like in Abigail's Party.

Obviously she sensed that this could be something serious. Hostilities were immediately suspended. "What do you mean?"

"I've got a pain in my shoulder and my little finger's gone numb."

She paused, we both knew what that could mean.

"Shall I call the doctor?" She asked.

"I don't know. Let's leave it a few minutes and see."

"You've gone white." She said.

I wasn't surprised, I could feel the life draining away, my body was beginning to withdraw from the world. Funny thing was that instead of worrying about all the things I'd left undone, all the stories I'd not told, all the heritage I hadn't left in the world, I worried instead that I'd leave a mess. Finally I understood the obsessions that old women have about keeping their affairs in order and having enough money tucked away to pay for a decent funereal. All I wanted was to have a couple of weeks grace so that I could burn or bury all my bits and pieces. I had a desperate urge to leave the world untouched by my presence; I wanted a clean slate.

Anyway, we went to the hospital eventually and we had to put up with the usual palaver of dealing with the NHS, but for once I didn't mind. The doctors didn't really know what it was all about but I sussed it out myself. What it was, was that the pain in my shoulder was caused by bad posture in front of the computer and the numbness in my finger was caused by leaning on my left elbow while endlessly clicking the mouse with my right hand as I played stupid card games, and the throbbing in my arm was some sort of muscle spasm probably emanating from the same cause.

So there, the symptoms subsided during the evening and we never got to finish our argument and once again our marriage resumed its bumpy trundle towards death do us part.

~

After the hospital we went home and talked for a bit. We talked about what we were going to do about our future(s). We didn't come to any conclusion, because every time we got to a point where there was imminent danger of some sort of consensus about what we were going to do with our life(lives), she backed off. It's hard to explain so I'll give you a snippet of part of that conversation.

Her: "Has that made you feel any different?"

Me: "I suppose so. It does make you appreciate what you've got, I know it's an old cliché but it does, it really does."

Her: "So, does that mean you won't be nagging on about moving away."

Me: "I don't think so. There's nothing wrong with wanting to move on in life, experience different places, different people."

Her: "You still want to move then?"

Me: "Well yes, but maybe I can be happier with what I've got while waiting for the right time."

Her: "What about a holiday this year?"

Me: "That's a good idea, yes."

Her: "Good, good. We can start planning and saving."

Me: "I hope so."

Her: "So, you'll be happier from now on then? No more miserable faces around the house."

Me: "We should still plan to move, like we discussed."

Her: "We've got to wait for the right time. Maybe in the summer."

Me: "Maybe in the summer? I suppose so, if that's the way it's got to be, but I can't help feeling that you're stalling, you know, playing for time again."

Her: "We never go anywhere. We've got to have a holiday."

Me: "That's what I don't get. All these people go to work nine to five and shopping on Saturdays and visiting relatives or going for a spin on Sundays and washing cars and cutting lawns, just so that they can spend two weeks on the Costa Del Sol every year. Why don't people just live that life anyway? Why torture yourself with a job that ties you down like that?"

Her: "I'm not talking about that kind of holiday. Something more relaxing, somewhere where we can pause and think. Commune with nature, that sort of thing."

Me: "You still don't get it do you. I don't want to go on holiday because I want to always be in that state of holidaying."

Her: "Wherever you are and whatever you're doing, you want to be somewhere else and you want to be doing something else. That's you all over."

Me: "What do you want then? What do you want me to want? What am I doing wrong?"

Her: "Listen, sorry, this is a mistake. Talking like this now, after your scare. You should be relaxing, at least for tonight. Please can we stop having this conversation? I promise we'll talk about it soon, OK? Please?"

I smile at her, partly in amusement because she's avoided the issues I really want to talk about, with her usual deftness and partly because I genuinely do feel happier and more satisfied with what I've got, where I am, what I'm doing.

Touché.

~

I did look at Phil's stuff, I opened every last envelope and prised apart every last bit of paper, I even read some of the stuff very carefully. I've got to say that I was a bit nonplussed by most of it, despite my earlier enthusiasm, and that might have been part of the reason why I avoided taking it back to Rita and Paul. The real reason was that I didn't want them to know about Phil's screwed-up life; I wanted them to keep on thinking about him as that lively son and brother that they remembered. There was no evidence to suggest that he was murdered except perhaps the little book of poems that went on and on about his unrequited love for some anonymous female and how his life was nothing without her, and how he could never ever get what he wanted for her while there was this huge, un-passable object in the way.

Not long before he died in that car accident, I remember he was acting a bit odd and he tried to confide in me. This is how I remember it, but you've got to understand that it's a long time ago and we all have our different versions of events don't we? Phil might tell a different story, if he was alive, but he's not, is he?

I am.

Phil and me, we'd gone to score some hash in a pub in Gorseinon, I can't remember the exact place now, but it was quite scary, we were quite young.

"Hey, there they are." Phil says, nodding in the direction of the front door.

Two guys, a bit older than us come towards our table in the darkest corner of the pub and sit down.

"Get them a drink." Phil says.

Of course I complied. "What you having?" I ask.

"Pint of bitter for me," says the one with long hair and a beard.

"Pint of cider for me," says the one with only long hair.

"I'll have a coke." Phil says.

I don't have any trouble getting served despite being obviously underage. I watch Phil and the other two from the bar. The bearded one hands Phil a cigarette packet. Phil puts it in the inside pocket of his leather jacket. I take the drinks over.

They pretend to be interested in us long enough to finish their pints and then leave. Phil looks pleased.

"Come on," he says, "let's get out of here and go and try some of this, it's Red Leb, very nice."

We find a corner of the park where there's no one else and make a couple of joints. Now I don't know why Phil bothers to smoke because it makes him very paranoid. I don't mean paranoid in the sense of thinking that everyone's against you or there's aliens tuned into your brainwaves or anything like that. I mean paranoid in the sense that you can only see the dark side of everything, it's like what we know as physical reality is only a very thin veneer over what is essentially a tragic, black life.

Fair play, in between joints, I forget that this happens to him, even if the gaps are only a day or so wide, but the funny thing is, he does too, he forgets as well. You'd think someone would remember something as important as that. It's the dope I suppose.

He turns to me and looks up at me at an angle where he's exposing as little of his face as he can.

"I forgot again." He says.

"Fuck." I say.

"It's just that, sometimes, I feel so alone. I know there's more to it, but I just can't get hold of it. I'm not allowed to. I'll never find happiness."

"Don't be silly."

"No, but then, you'll never understand. You'll always be all right. I know you will, you're the sort."

"Sorry," he says, as he walks away quickly towards the bus station.

"Hey," I shout after him, "what about the hash?"

He stops and rummages in his coat before turning and throwing the rest of the Red Leb towards me.

I pick it up and laugh – more for me.

twenty two

"Well, why didn't you tell me earlier?"

"You weren't around, then I forgot."

"How can you . . . oh – fuck it."

"Anyway, he never said it was urgent. He didn't ask me to ask you to phone him back. Anyway I thought you'd fallen out."

"Oh fuck it."

"Fancy a cuppa?"

"No thanks, oh all right then, coffee."

This had to be the day. This had to end. Never mind the consequences, whatever they'd be they wouldn't be as bad as the consequences of being born in Afghanistan or Iraq in the latter part of the twentieth century.

~

Paper, pen, alphabet, words, sentences, paragraphs, chapters, books. Every novel starts with a stroke. It's so fucking obvious, as obvious as Newtonian physics, as obvious as breathing. But, enough of that now. What we really want to know is what happens next. The truth is, I don't know, because next hasn't happened yet. I'm writing this live, this is about as close to a live performance you're going to get. I mean, if you want real live then stop reading and get down to the theatre, or go and torture yourself with a male voice choir – if that's your bag. Better still, just get out there and interact – meet "real", "live" people. Ah! What would we do without people, eh? What would we do?

Bugger all, that's what.

But it's not as simple as that; there's lots more going on. The sun shines, the rivers run, the world turns – and things change.

Time is a triangle, the past, the present, the future – a triangle held together by equal forces. But if we can have three sides it's just a little leap to four, then five, six, seven, eight, nine – that's the myth, the more sides, the extra ideas, the bollocks.

It's all bollocks.

But then, in the end, move we must, and move we will, because we are moving already, we are always moving.

~

Lucy is a little darling and in another life who knows, but no, I've already covered that, even in another life and even if we were the same age and with similar tastes I wouldn't fancy her, even though she is sexy and beautiful and fit. I mean, I don't think I even like her very much, I hardly feel anything, but here I am and here she is and she's pouring her heart out to me opening up her chest and pointing at her pulsating red heart and she's saying – go on then – come on then – please – please – love – hate – damage – mental cruelty – my father – hurt – pain – pain – pain – help – Help – HElp – HELp – HELP!!!! And all I can feel is – so what, so what. But I've got to make an effort because somewhere along the way I assumed some responsibility for her and if I turn away now and if she fucks up big time or something then I'll feel guilt and I'll never know if I could have done something to save her life.

So I say: "Tell me about it."

And she says: "Why can't my own father be as cool as you."

And she lays her head on my shoulder and dries her tears in my manky T-shirt. And I make some sort of patting gesture on her head because I'm too afraid to pull her closer and comfort her like I feel I'm supposed to.

And now she's trying to kiss me.

Fuck.

~

Pasty yellows, pastel blues, creamy whites, weak reds, like deckchairs – deckchair colours. This is what Walter Nankerville presents to the world as his art. He paints in thick acrylics on cheap cork notice boards, of the sort you can pick up in Woolworth's or Wilkinson's for three or four quid. He paints abstract surreal dreamscapes composed of ugly polygonal shapes, like a simplified representation of the geography of countries. Imagine the leg of Italy turned 90 degrees and coloured in a sickly yellow on a sea of lime green. Sounds horrible doesn't it? But somehow it's not. Everything falls together like a canvas deckchair in a rain shower – everything falls together and lies flat and functional, yet there is also something of the childish idyll in his work – with sunshine and lollipops and kind adults in funny hats.

The man himself looks like an Asda trolley boy, young and nerdy with unhealthy hair. He doesn't have much to say about his work, which has been acknowledged as significant by the great Melvyn himself, though not in print or in front of a television camera.

Still, it takes all sorts.

~

Let me tell you something about love.

I wasn't sure whether to put this bit in or not, but then I thought, fuck it, every book in the literature sense, like a novel or a book of poems or whatever has to tell you something about love; otherwise where's the value, eh? Where's the value?

See, the thing about love is, is that there's a lot of it about, not too much, but a lot. Love is about sharing; it's about caring and it's about daring – daring to be brave and sometimes giving up things that you really want so that the other person, or persons, you know, the one or ones you love, get happier, or stay happy or at least don't get hurt, physically, emotionally or mentally (spiritually is beyond your powers).

You can feel lots of emotions about another human being. some of them hurt and some of them make you smile and feel safe.

~

Even in a small country like Wales (and Wales is the definitive small country), there are many tribes and factions. Even in the smaller virtual country of Welsh-speaking Wales, there are many. Take Pobol y Cwm for example. Pobol y Cwm is a Welsh language soap opera, filmed mostly in Cardiff and set in the Gwendraeth Valley between Llanelli and Carmarthen. (Pobol y Cwm is Welsh for People of the Valley.)

The programme is made at the BBC studios in Llandaff, Cardiff, on behalf of the Welsh TV channel S4C. If you were to pronounce S4C phonetically in Welsh it would sound like *S ped war EK*. It's known by some (cynics that they are) as *S ped war Cheque* because of the generous dollops of cash it splashes over its actors and programme makers, especially those associated with Pobol y Cwm.

So, there I was on the set of the Deri Arms – the local pub in Pobol-y-Cwm-Land, pretending to be a pub owner from Llanelli who had come to buy a few kegs of beer from the local brewery.

I arrived in the Green Room at about a quarter to nine, not even knowing I was playing an actual part; up until then I'd only done work as a background extra. So this director came to see me at about five past nine and gave me about five lines to say in a scene with one of the brewery's owners, something to do with complaining about the beer being too expensive.

Anyway, my Welsh is crap, and the director was a Gog (a Welsh speaking Welshman from the Gogledd (North)), so, by the time I went on set at half nine I was in bits.

The thing about Welsh is that apart from the differences in language that occur even between neighbouring villages, there is a distinct North/south divide, so the lines the director gave me would not have been spoken by a geezer from the South, especially Llanelli. But my Welsh language skills were not good enough to make the dialogue sound right. I was away from there by ten anyway, but because it was a 'walk-on' part, I got paid about £170, not bad for an hour or so's work.

Anyway when the episode was screened they cut three of my five lines because they were so crap. Needless to say, they never asked me back after that, not surprising since I couldn't speak Welsh and couldn't act.

Before that episode, I'd visited the Pobol y Cwm studios a few times, sometimes with my cool younger son (who can speak Welsh and can act, by the way), who himself did a couple of 'walk-ons', and I'd got by all right, mostly by grunting and nodding at the director and the other actors. I only did it at first because my son started when he was young enough to need a chaperone. Thing is, I like to think of myself as an intelligent sort of guy. (Did I tell you I joined Mensa once? I won't tell you what I thought of them in case I get sued).

But what I realised after that was that, in Welsh at least, I'm as thick as two short planks. The memory that the Pobol-y-Cwmers have of me is of a slow stupid, idle, middle-aged man who couldn't understand simple directions and could hardly construct a sentence. In fact, I don't suppose they remember me at all, that one hour between 9 and 10 on a normal weekday workday was, to them, just a tiny part of their whole experience during all their years on that job. To me it was a massively traumatic hour that I still churn over in my mind years later – it's all about perspective isn't it? Our characters are made by moments like that; change and trauma are the raw materials of life.

I mean, like now, I'm sitting in a computer training room in a car components factory. This is the shithole I use to work in a couple of decades ago, before I packed it in to start my own computer business (but that's another story). I've come back now, on a temporary, part-time, freelance basis to teach under-educated shop floor workers how to use a word-processor. Why they just don't grab hold of a mouse and suss it out for themselves is beyond me – but there you go – there's a pot of money allocated by the government for this sort of thing and there's thousands of people like me all over the country sucking cash out of the pot, a bit like the Pobol-y-Cwmers and their ilk getting their Tuscan holidays and their Gites paid for by grants and subsidies.

I come here twice a week for a few hours and when I'm here I often meet people I used to work with twenty years ago. There's a lot of them still here, and bugger it, they're still the same, still dreaming about their Post Offices in the Shetlands or fantasising about packing it all in and buying a beach bar in Benidorm.

But they won't. They'll just keep on coming here day after day, keep on paying their phone bills on time and patronising the shit-food joints and the same poxy pubs on the weekends until they retire or keel over from cars or cancer. What's the fucking point of all that eh?

I'm telling you – change is life. Right?

~

There was a woman who lived in the same street as me when I was growing up. She was a kind woman who lived alone in a nice private house on the edge of the estate. I bet she didn't dream about the three bears. She wasn't that old. She'd been a refugee from Liverpool during the Second World War and had stayed with a family from the Seaside area of the town. After the war finished she stayed on and married a local boy who had been sent home from North Africa early because of an injury. His name was Dai Wire, because he laid cables for the signal operators.

Anyway, Dai Wire died in 1955 when his remaining kidney packed in after some mystery illness. I'm sorry the details are a bit sketchy, that's because it was a long time ago when she told me, and I wasn't paying that much attention at the time because I was only interested in the free apples she was giving to me. The reason I'm telling you this by the way is that Dai Wire had a son, he was only about 3 years old when Dai died; but because his mother became totally obsessed with the memory of her husband and never made any progress in her life afterwards and then the son, also called David, or Dai, but whose nickname was Skin, later changed to skinny on account of his lack of hair rather than his weight, became an artist; a screwed-up artist whose early work, to be honest was a load of old crap. Skinny Wire as he now officially calls himself started with watercolours but they were mediocre to say the least. It was only when he changed his medium that his true talent showed itself; he made military models like airfix or action man but he made them out of coloured glass (later plastic) and carefully worked them with kitchen cutlery and tools.

I met Skinny Wire in People's Park, on a bench near the pond where the swans and the coots (or were they moorhens, I can never tell?) hung around. This was a place I used to know well, having spent many a summer Saturday getting stoned or tripping on acid around the pond's perimeter, in the long grass where hardly anyone ventured. These days it's much busier down there, ever since they developed the old steelworks site into a park and built new paths and roads. Anyway, we sat on a bench overlooking the pond and talked. As we talked, he pulled his pieces one by one out of a large cardboard box that he'd wheeled in on an Asda shopping trolley.

So, while we were talking and he was showing me his sculptures (if that's what they were?), he stood up suddenly and threw one far into the pond almost killing a coot (or a moorhen) in the process. It was a particularly fine piece, and I'd told him that just before he did it.

"One day," he said, "when some future regeneration scheme fucks with the landscape again, some worker will find that soldier, and she or he will wonder why it's there. That's all I want," he said, "that's all I want, is to affect someone's life at some point in the future, it doesn't matter who, it doesn't really matter when, preferably after I'm dead, but I can live with someone finding it while I'm still alive as long as they don't know where it came from and as long as I never know who finds it. It's not so much my mark in the sand as my sand in the world. They're like my children, random genes thrown forward in time to let the fuckers know that there is more than working in some stinking office to make some rich cunt's life a little more comfortable. Perhaps the person who finds it will put it on his (or her) mantelpiece and his grandchildren will take it to some future version of Antiques Roadshow where the expert in obscure artists of the early twenty-first century will put a stupidly high value on it because by then I'll be a dead artist whose genius has finally been recognised. And that's what it's all about really," he said, "I'll never have children, but my genes will continue to have influence and therefore I will live forever but without the pain."

"Fair enough," I said.

"I like you," he said.

"Thanks"

God, there's some complicated fuckers in this town.

~

Done this already? Have I done this bit already? Have I told you about London '69 and why it's relevant to this story? I suppose I could go back and check, but then I can't be bothered. To be honest it's not that I can't be bothered, it's just that if I interrupt myself then I'll never get going again, not at this particular moment, and then it would never be the same, it might be better, but it'll never be the same. Besides, even if I told you before, this time I'll tell you different and more than likely new facts will emerge, facts that can only help with the story, otherwise they wouldn't be in it, would they?

A year since the black cats in the kitchen, near enough. A year is a long time when you're thirsty (or if you're a black cat I suppose), but in the multi-dimensional endless loop of universal existence, a year isn't even fly puke – one fly's puke on one occasion. The scale of difference between that one puke of that one fly, and a year in the life of every living creature on this planet is still infinitesimally smaller than the scale of difference between all human life and the endlessness of all that is, was, or ever will be. So, what's the fucking point in fretting about it?

What's the fucking point?

Here I am, and this is what I have to deal with – two long-gone black cats, animals, which, according to the vet, who delivered a lethal injection to an earlier black cat, are obligate carnivores and therefore susceptible to kidney failure. Why aren't things perfect? Why don't black cats live forever? Why do we aspire to perfection? It's an unreachable goal but it's the only thing we do.

The cats. Two black cats with yellow eyes. If they'd been bigger, browner, and if there was one more of them, they'd be the three bears. But they are small and black and even though they've got claws and teeth and eat disgusting food, they're no match for us humans.

And now it's time to tell the truth, because there's no point in lying any more. The act is over and the acting and the masks must be put away.

My love is a big white-faced clown with a bulbous red nose and it's not funny. It comes to me when it wants, in the form of a long wet pavement stained with vinegar, and eats pizza with a passion as deep as a ferret's hunger for rabbit.

Have you ever handled a ferret? I have, and a shotgun (for shooting rabbits, although it was my mate's and I didn't like it) and a grass-snake, and endless lizards and frogs, and even more toads and slowworms.

And in the year that's just clicked, I left something behind. I left behind a wet footprint on the bathroom floor and now I'm tired and I want to tell you the truth.

Thing is, I would tell you the truth, honest, if I knew it, but I don't, not THE truth, not even the TRUTH. Hang on, perhaps that bloke hanging about outside the toilets in the pub will know. I'll ask him.

"Piss off – you're pissed."

But I'm not, but I piss off anyway.

I told you it was a flow so I'm sorry if you're disappointed or at least a little pissed-off, that I didn't tell you about London '69 after all, but what else can I do? The story is going in this particular direction because it has to. It wouldn't be doing it otherwise, would it? Anyway, I can't help it – so there.

~

Funny thing, over all the years we've been together, that's me and her, and over all the same years that me and Ken have been friends, they, that's her and Ken have hardly ever met each other. In fact, I can't remember any one time that they've been in the same room together. The other day, though, there was an afternoon when we, that's me, and Ken, and her, and Lucy as well, ended up sharing a table at a hotel together for a few hours. The occasion was the launch of a new initiative by the council to create a network of local businesses. Because of my years of starting up and then of course, running down, various businesses, I got an invitation. Not that I usually accept that sort of invitation, but at the time, I was in one of my more optimistic moods regarding entrepreneurship, and this one was a little different in that there was a free buffet lunch, not that there'd be anything there that I, as a vegan could eat, but it's the thought that counts.

Anyway, she came with me, gods knows why, she never usually took any interest in my efforts to earn money, except perhaps, to find out how much they were worth; she must have been having a good day as well.

When we got there, we looked around for a spare table, preferably a two-seater, but the tables had been arranged so that either six or eight people could and obviously, should, gather around each one.

Ken and Lucy were already there; it goes without saying that if I'd known he was going to be there I wouldn't have even thought of going, but there he was and I just had to put up with it. Of course, he saw us and invited us to sit down with him and his daughter, so we did. Happily, or unhappily, depending on which way you look at it, no one else bothered us all afternoon, apart from the waiters, who kept wafting past with thoroughly unsuitable foodstuffs arranged prettily on stainless steel trays.

So, there we were, listening to a very boring talk by one of the council officers, something about how wonderful and altruistic they were towards local businesses, and letting our eyes wander around the room and across our own table, continuously assessing the other players in the game. This part of the afternoon went on too long, although in some ways that was a blessing, I didn't have to make pretend small talk with Ken, for example. You must know by now that this was in that period between starting to suss the bastard out and deciding to kill him, a period that lasted a good few months.

Anyway, the first half hour or so after the speeches ended was

OK, because Ken wandered off to circulate the room and remind all his victims that he was still around and still wanted blood. Then he came back and sat down with a smile.

"Good this," he said, looking at me, "you want to get out there and lick a few arses," looking at her, "if you'll pardon the expression. It'll do your business a lot of good."

Normally, I wouldn't have bothered to play their stupid fucking games, but then, after seeing the look on her face, as if Ken was the most charming man she'd ever met, though I don't suppose it was her fault, she didn't know what I knew, and being as it would give me an excuse to get out of his company for a while, because to be honest, I was beginning to feel sick – physically sick, I decided it would be a good idea to go and mingle, so to speak.

I mingled for as long as I could, but then the MC came back, (yes, the council had hired a cheesy MC) and started prattling. Everybody else went back to their seats , so I had to as well. As I approached our table, the sick feeling started to creep back, especially when I saw Ken and her sharing some sort of joke and laughing, a little too closely, together.

"How did it go?" He asked, still laughing.

"All right." I said.

"Hey," he said, as I sat down, "you want to bring her out more often, she's a great asset to you."

"Smarmy cunt," was what I wanted to say, but I just grunted and pretended to smile.

The MC was still prattling on in the background but nobody was listening to him, I think everyone had drunk a little too much of the free wine, disgusting as it was. I'd had a couple myself, seeing as she was driving.

Lucy looked miserable. Selfishly, in an effort to distract attention from any conversation that Ken and me or Ken and her might have I turned to Lucy.

"Everything all right Lucy?" I asked. "I suppose it is a bit boring, isn't it?"

Lucy rolled her eyes upwards. "I'm used to it," she said, "the number of times my father has made me suffer for his business is nobody's business."

"Rightly or wrongly," Ken said, "this is the sort of place where real business takes place, if you know the right people to start with that is."

"Oh yeah." I said.

"That's a good point." She said.

"Yes," Ken said, "but how do you get to know the right people in the first place?"

"In the golf club?" I said.

Lucy laughed.

"Maybe," Ken said, "but all you've got to do is to find out where they drink. Birds of a feather flock together."

"How long does this go on for?" Lucy asked.

"Lighten up," her father said, "it's not as if you've got anywhere else to go."

"Nice place." She said.

Everyone turned to face her, glad of the relief.

"I only said that this was a nice place," she said.

"Oh yes" Ken said, "always did have a touch of class old Frederick."

"Frederick?" She said.

"Frederick Tarr," Lucy said, "the owner of this establishment. Frederick bloody Tarr."

"Aye, me and Fred go back a long way," Ken said, "he's a good old boy, and a good businessman."

"I know him." I said. " . . . ."

Suddenly the MC stopped prattling and some loud dance music drowned out the rest of what I was going to say, it didn't matter anyway, because I didn't really have any more to say, nothing I wanted to say out loud anyway, about the relationship between

Ken and the infamous Frederick Fagin Tarr.

When I say 'loud dance music', I don't mean dance music of the sort today's DJs play in clubs or in fields, sending their audience of E'd up munters into paroxysms of ecstasy. No, I mean 'loud dance music' of the sort that has infested mainstream discos for the last three decades or so, music that should never be played loud because listening to it at volume is like being overrun with red biting ants.

I wanted to go there and then, this wasn't my scene at all. God help us, they'd be having Karaoke next.

Ken stands up and shouts something to me as if he's asking a question. I shrug. He grabs her arm and leans into her face saying something. She nods. They go to the dance floor together, where a dozen or so pairs of dancers are already getting down to the music man. Moronic fuckers.

Now it's just me and Lucy at the table. Her looking more miserable than she had earlier and me pretending to be happy that the biggest bastard in the world was dancing with her.

Bastards.

twenty three

I'm sitting alone in the house looking around and remembering. I'm not sure if I like this at all – this remembering, this being in a too familiar place and remembering things that went on here over two decades ago. I'd rather have the memories without the stimulus of the place. These things, these objects, these artefacts, these bits of matter are like scars, always there to remind me of my past injuries. I would rather remember my past in the abstract where the place and the events are only memories, but there you go, you can't always have the things you'd rather have, and have to settle for what is. Many people, I'm sure, judging by the way they like to stay in the same place all their lives, want, need, the same familiar places and objects to keep them anchored, and that's fine – for them.

I like things to begin and I like things to end but I'm not too good on the sustaining stuff, perhaps that's why I fail so much – I'm not a sticker you see. One thing though, one thing I always wanted to continue was my love for her. Now it seems even that is ending, not my love, because that can not end, but the relationship at least is ending, I'm not sure of course but the way she'd been behaving should have given even my dull slow mind a clue.

Now, there's a new kitchen and no more black cats. They came and they went and afterwards we did up the kitchen; I think they came for a reason – these two black cats. We went to the RSPCA in Swansea to get a cat because we had mice. We caught the mice in a humane trap and let them go on the beach road. One was a small skinny animal with a long tail, the other was fatter with big eyes that looked at me for a moment before it sunk into the coarse grass that grows along the coast. We went to the RSPCA and it ended up costing seventy or eighty quid because of the adoption costs and the litter and the food and the little tinkly balls we bought them.

They were both females, neutered of course and they were both completely nuts – an incarnation perhaps of our own insecurities and a manifestation of the negativity that had built up between us. We went a few times before finally deciding to take them. We didn't want two cats and we didn't want black cats and we didn't want lunatic cats – but that's what we got – two black lunatic cats. It's a long story but they took a while to settle in and there was a lot of drama with deep scratches and smells and loads of shit and disgusting tins of cat food.

After a few weeks we had to get rid of them – don't worry, we took them back to the RSPCA, and it was all to do with her catching a terrible lung infection and having to pump steroids around her system and nearly dying for lack of oxygen – but really it was about the fact that their purpose was done, their time with us was over. They had absorbed what they had to absorb and then gone on their way to continue with their divine duty. We had a call from a vet in Preston a few months after the cats went back to say that our cat had been found wandering around the area (they had little microchips in their necks or somewhere that can be read by a scanner of some sort), but by then of course they weren't our cats any longer. That was weird, because at the time I was avoiding phone calls from Preston (by screening them using Caller Display – the code for Preston is 01772) because some debt collector was nagging us from there on account of some unpaid mobile phone bill (get a pay as you go and you don't have to put up with that shit). That morning I answered and I was going to tell the fucks to fuck off, good thing I held off until after the intros.

So, the cats came and went (we've had cats before so I know what I'm talking about) and we carried on, for a bit, but now it's all coming to a head and I don't know if it's sustainable any longer. Here's an example:

HER: You're a bum.

ME: *(after a pause and a shake of the head)* How can you say that about me?

HER: Easy. What do you do?

ME: Loads of stuff. I'm into painting and writing and I'm pretty good with computers even if I do hate the fucking things. And I cook and I clean up – sometimes. And I write and . . .

HER: You already said that, and anyway that's not what I asked. What do you do to earn money?

ME: I, we, get by.

HER: Exactly, get by, and only just, and only because you keep finding new ways to borrow.

ME: Play fair. It's not as bad as that. I do bring in a bit. I earn a bit here and there.

HER: I'm fed up of being poor. When was the last time we had a proper holiday?

ME: It's not about that. A relationship can't be built on how much money we bring in. That's not that important. You can be stinking rich and still be miserable.

HER: Well, it's important.

ME: You make me feel like a failure.

HER: You don't need my help for that.

ME: What about love? Don't you love me?

See what I mean?

~

Anyway, let me tell you something else about love.

~

Now it's really now. This is the point in the story at which there is no more going forward, because it is really now and as we all know you can't go forward from now. Well, the truth is that you can look forward, you can plan ahead, you can hope and you can try to predict, but you can't actually tell a story that hasn't happened yet. So, this is as far as it goes, everything must now come to an end, albeit a temporary end, because as sure as flowers wilt (except perhaps everlasting flowers, although that's obviously cheating because they're not really active, live flowers, just dried pieces of matter arranged in a flower shape), yes, as sure as flowers wilt, everything ends, but everything continues as well.

So, because it's really now, this story must now come to an end and all the multifarious strands must somehow tie together to allow that feeling of completion that we all crave. The point is that she's gone. Yes, she, the most important person in all this, has finally fucked off and left me. Can't say I'm surprised, after all she's had to put up with, what with my obsessions and my mini-madnesses.

The thing that sparked off her decision to leave was my relationship with Annie and the fact that she found some of the early drafts of this story, the bits where I spilt a little bit too much of my guts onto the page, bits that have now been firmly edited out of this story. Bits that no-one else will ever get to read, the untold stories. But she found them, and she read them, even though she doesn't normally like to read what I've written, she's more into Hardy and Dickens and Atwood and Austen and Bronte and Joyce and Morrison and McEwan, if her bookshelf is anything to go by. So, I never expected her to rifle through my files and my printouts and so I got caught out. And I tried to convince her that it was all made up but she said that there was too much truth in there, and that meant that even if what I'd written about my relationship with Annie didn't actually happen then I must have wanted it to happen and that was just as bad as if it really did happen. So I broke down and told her the truth, the actual truth and that done it and she left me.

When I say she left me, she didn't really leave me, truth is, I left the house and moved into this stinking little flat, the one with the mice and the prostitutes living upstairs and the drunken, foul-breathed madmen that bang on the front door at one o'clock in the morning demanding service.

And then there's Lucy.

This is how the Lucy thing ended:

"So?" She said.

It was the next day. It was the day after Ken finally died.

I mean really died.

There was me and there was Lucy, and we were sitting on a bench in the Sunken Gardens outside the Magistrates Court, after walking into town after visiting the Registry Office to register her father's death. She didn't want to go straight home, so I thought it would be a good idea if we walked – just walked, well, walked and talked maybe. I left my car outside the Registry Office and we walked. We skirted around the town, avoiding the busy streets and found our way to the bench in the Sunken Gardens, outside the Magistrates Court. It was quite quiet; it was late afternoon and the light coloured everything like a Noddy Book.

"Well?" She said.

"Are you all right?" I asked.

"Yes. Why wouldn't I be?"

"I don't know, you know."

"I'm a grown woman. I am in my twenties you know. You don't get much more grown-up than that."

"I know." I said. And I thought, you don't ever grow up at all really, you just add layers, and eventually the layers get so thick that it's too hard to unpeel them and find that beautiful, naïve child and so you just tend to accept the mundane more and more. I suppose it's only natural.

"What do we do now?" She asked.

"I don't know." I said.

"You're not married any more, and my dad's not around to hassle me any more."

"You're younger than my daughter." I said.

"So?" She said.

Fuck.

Fuck.

Fuck.

I hadn't even fucked her yet and already I felt as if I was responsible for her. I didn't even fancy her for fuck's sake.

"He abused me."

I sighed; this was not unexpected.

"My dad."

I sighed again, put my arm around her and pulled her close. This is not what I wanted to do.

"You get used to it."

I pulled her closer. This was another kind of demon. Ken would always be a part of my life.

"You need time." I said.

"What do you mean?"

"You need time by yourself; time to think about your future. You're young. Ken must have left a bit of a stash. You need time."

"What about you and me?"

"Your father's dead," I said. "He's dead and you've got to start moving on."

Lucy pulled herself away from me and stood up. Her eyes were wet.

"Right then, I'm off."

She walked away and I haven't seen her since except at the funeral where she kept her head down and attached herself to some old aunties.

~

Isn't it funny how some people explode into your life and totally change everything, so that no matter what certain path you've been following for however long it suddenly turns into jelly and once again you find yourself struggling to make a coherent picture of your reality. Annie was like that; although it took me a while to recognise the massive dent she made in the life I had constructed for myself. I suppose it has some similarities to an epiphany but only in a limited way. It's more like a different light illuminating things in a different way, showing you bits you haven't noticed before. It's so easy to get into thinking that the choices you have made and the people you are close to are the pillars of your reality, but then the glass shatters and all the time you didn't know it was cracked and fuzzy before.

So, I don't know if it's my fault; I mean my fault as in I chose to (or at least I didn't resist) get to know Annie. I mean if I wanted to I could easily have waved her on her merry way that day, couldn't I? Or would it have happened anyway? Every relationship has a life cycle even if it's only until death do us part. Whatever, it's happening, it's happened, it's over, she's gone from my life and she's blaming Annie for it (even though Annie's dead). I think it's just an excuse because she doesn't want to take the responsibility herself.

Anyway, she's gone, or to be more precise, I've gone, and now I'm here. Finally, I'm here, alone, really alone, for the first time in my life (unless you count the night I spent on my own in a beach hut in Tenby in 1970 or 1971, when I argued with Bill and wouldn't go back to the tent we shared). I'm alone and I now have to face those monsters in my head, the ones that have chased me and bitten chunks out of my arms and driven me to behave in ways that I have tried to forget. But now, alone, I have to face them.

Let's see. Here I am in this poxy room; I'm surrounded by the accoutrements of my trade, the bits I have already rescued from the home I shared with her for over two decades. – bits of paper mostly, bits of A4 sized laser-printer paper containing the output of my word processing adventures over that time. There are boxes and bin bags everywhere; journals, half-formed ideas, ten drafts of the same story, television scripts, film treatments, finished novels printed in different ways with different fonts and my paintings scrunched up behind the manky settee. There are other people's bits here too, dead people's, Annie's heads and Phil's box. I'm surprised that Mrs Rita Davies and her grown-up son Paul haven't tracked me down and demanded the return of Phil's scribbles – but I expect they've given up and sunk back into their morosity.

Alone and it was all my fault – it was me all along – I did it, I killed them all. Gammy, Phil, Sam, Kath, Mike, Annie and the one I don't regret, that cunt Ken. All those lives, all that responsibility.

But no, it's time to come clean, time to face my weaknesses. I'm too useless even to sort my life out like that. I did not kill Ken. Ken is still alive and strutting this earth like he always has. The other stuff is true, well most of it. For example, Phil really did die in a car accident way back whenever and Gammy died too, from too many drugs. There are other truths and other lies but does it really matter if you know which ones are which? Does it? Oh, all right then. It's time to tell you the truth.

I've lived a very ordinary life, the usual fuck-ups, the usual frustrations, the usual failures (perhaps a few too many of them) and the usual niggles and struggles. I'm still not convinced that the events are unrelated but if I can't pin everything on Ken then who is really to blame?

She comes in to the room and interrupts me in my flow of confession.

She sits down next to me at the word-processor.

"What are you writing?" She asks, good thing she's too far away from the screen to read it properly, besides I click quickly on the minimise window button and this text-infested white page of my soul shrinks to a few pixels revealing the bright green of the card game.

"Ah," she says, "so, are you writing or are you playing cards?"

"Bit of both," I say. "Why?"

"What do you mean why? Can't I just come and have a chat with my husband without an interrogation?"

"Depends what it's about."

""Nothing special, I was just wondering what you were doing tomorrow. I might have to work late."

"This and that, little bit of both, I suppose."

"Both what?"

"Bit of writing, bit of playing cards."

"Haven't you got any work to do?"

I look at her and wonder what it is that has kept us together all this time. I wonder whether she thinks the same way.

"Is everything all right?" I ask.

"How do you mean?"

"You know, we haven't had much chance to talk lately, what with your work taking it out of you, and most nights you're too tired to talk and the television is on all the bloody time, and on the weekends I'm pretty useless."

"Well, I'm here now, I'm talking now. What do you want to say?"

"I thought you said you wanted to talk to me?"

"OK then, tell me about Annie."

"Annie's dead," I say.

"Yeah, but what about when she was alive? You haven't been the same since she died. Was there more to your relationship?"

"What?"

"You and Annie, was there more to it?" There is a distant chill in her voice

"Well no, not really, not at all." I feel myself flushing red. I look at her and I think: Who is this woman?

She looks determined, as passive as a statue yet as unchallengeable as an angry gorilla. I stand up, it's a natural reaction to threat I suppose, I'm bigger than her, taller and fatter and heavier and I'm a man for fuck's sake.

"Sit." She says.

I sit.

"It's obvious there was something going on – obvious."

"She was just a friend, just another fucked-up human being who I met along the way, someone to share a coffee with now and again, that's all."

"I don't believe you."

"I never did anything, we were just friends."

"You've always been the same, looking for someone else; I've never been enough for you."

"What's going on? Are you all right?"

"Never been better. All these years I've looked after us; looked after you, and now I realise you're not worth it. You've never been worth it. I've given up my life for you. The things I've done for you, don't you see? Can't you see?"

"I don't know what you're talking about."

"It's too late anyway. Too late."

She's got a knife, a fucking knife, I've never seen it before, it's long and new and sharp.

"What's that?" I ask.

She lifts her arm and I realise she's going to stab me; I stand up again and keep a distance. I notice she's holding the knife above her head in a classic *'I'm going to stab you'* pose. I manage a chuckle – how often have I seen this in a film – this is silly – what she should be doing is holding the knife below her waist and then pushing her arm upwards in a quick strong stab so that the knife hits some soft tissue in my torso – much more chance of striking a lethal blow – this way I can easily deflect it – I might cut my arm or something, but so what – I can survive that. She brings her arm down and I lift mine to defend myself. The knife is deflected and I get a millisecond of triumph before I feel a bruising thump on my chest and hear a clink as the knife penetrates my ribcage – fuck that knife must be sharp; I crumple to my knees; I am aware of a massive ache in my chest; I look her in the eyes – they are fixed and calm – beautiful. Suddenly I realise. The killings, the screw-ups, the way my friends disintegrated one by one. Now she is all I have and . . . and . . . . .

It was her all along, the murderous bitch.

I'm finding it hard to breathe. I crawl past her, out of the room and into the kitchen.

She follows me, saying: "What do you think I was? Who do you think I am? Do you think I've been happy all my life following after you like some sycophantic puppy? It's always you isn't it. Everything revolves around you. Your ambitions, your potential, what you have to give to the world, how it's so important for you to leave your pathetic fucking scratches in the fucking sand. Arsehole! Bastard! You're a fucking monster. You're the cause of it all. It's your fucking fault. Yours."

I make a noise like a cat that's just been sat on.

She's still holding the knife.

She says: "Now you've completely fucked it up. You killed him. You did it."

I try to stand up but stagger backwards and clutch onto the worktop, the one in the colour of black granite, stuck onto the fake Japanese Maple covered cupboard units, part of the kitchen that I'd spent a week and a half installing on my hands and knees because we couldn't afford a professional. I thought it was a labour of love.

I say: "But I didn't kill him. I didn't."

She stabs me again. I slide to the floor. I'm losing consciousness. There's a blackness there but I'm not afraid, at last I'll find out what's next. I don't mind death any more. I've done what I set out to do. I've completed my work here on this planet. I've left my pathetic scratches in the sand.

I look up at her from the cold tiles. I realise I don't know who she is. I never knew her. In the end, I realise, we don't know anybody, anything; we don't even know ourselves. It's not important to me any more, but, and I don't know if she can hear me through the rage, but I say it anyway:

"I didn't kill him. He's not dead."

It's over. Her face sinks slowly into the black pool. It's the end.

But where did it all begin?

It's about
Life . . . .
You twit.

Derec Jones
March 2008.

Printed in the United Kingdom
by Lightning Source UK Ltd.
128629UK00001B/286-315/P